SHAMELESS

ELIZABETH KELLY

EK PUBLISHING INC.

SHAMELESS

A man haunted by his past. A woman determined to save him.

Maddie

I'm a good girl. Always have been and always will be. Born on the right side of the tracks, I've spent my entire life doing the right thing, being the good girl I'm supposed to be. Until the night I discovered my fiancé's deepest secret and the lies he'd been keeping from me. Now I'm in the wrong place at the wrong time, and my only hope of survival is a dangerous man who claims I belong to him.

Riley

I'm not a good man. Never have been and never will be. But I swear I only meant to protect the luscious, curvy goddess who stumbled into the bar at the exact wrong moment. Until I tasted her. Now, my blood burns for her, and I'll stop at nothing to take what's mine – even if it destroys us both.

* * *

CHAPTER 1

Maddie

My car dying was the final straw. As the engine sputtered, choked, and coughed, I steered it to the side of the dark, silent road, shut it off, and rested my forehead on the steering wheel. The hot tears slid down my cheeks, tears I had desperately held back for hours. I let loose with a primal scream of fury and despair that echoed in the quiet interior of my car.

I screamed until my voice was hoarse. Until the rage and sorrow and utter disbelief that had been crowding my chest finally dissipated enough for me to take my first deep breath in hours. Panting harshly, I banged my fist against the dead car's dashboard before reaching for my purse.

I didn't have my cell phone. Of course, I didn't have it. I'd left it at home, determined not to have anyone interrupt my night of seduction. I planned on making Jordan turn his off as well. I wanted the night to be perfect, and hearing his damn phone chirping every five minutes wasn't a part of the perfect night.

I sighed and wiped at the tears still flowing down my face. Crying wasn't going to help. I needed to get my fat ass out of this car and back to that bar I had passed a few miles back. I hadn't given it much thought at the time, just a quick glance at the garish neon sign blinking in the darkness as I drove past it. Now, it was my only chance.

If I had been thinking clearly, I might have decided to wait in my car. I might have taken my chance with the next person who drove down that deserted country road. But my mind was still reeling, and my heart was still breaking, and I wanted nothing more than to be back in my tiny, lonely house. I used to hate that house. I dreamed nightly that Jordan would invite me to live with him in his perfectly acceptable townhouse. But now I wanted my home with a desperation born of panic and a desire to pretend my entire world hadn't been blown apart around me.

I grabbed my purse and my keys and climbed out of the car. I slammed the door harder than I needed to before trudging down the road. It was cold, and I pulled my thin wrap tightly around my curvy body. I glanced at my shoes, cursing myself in my head. I'd be lucky if I could even walk back to the bar in the damn things. They were stilettos and excruciatingly uncomfortable to walk in. Of course, I had worn them tonight intending to be fucked in them, not walking in them.

I put my head down and walked faster, teetering a little on the damn heels before catching my balance. The cold wind knifed across my body. I wasn't dressed for the weather. I tugged at my too-short dress and tried to use the wrap to cover my bare arms completely.

It was pointless. The wrap was poor protection against the wind. I wished bitterly that I was wearing my usual yoga pants and cardigan. At least then, I'd be warmer.

Of course, one didn't seduce their fiancé in yoga pants

and a cardigan, did they? No, they seduced them with six-inch stilettos, stockings, barely-there underwear, and the quintessential little black dress.

At least, I had assumed one did. After walking in on what I did, obviously I was mistaken. Or maybe it wouldn't have even mattered. Jordan might have been alone, taken one look at my chubby body poured into this ridiculous dress, and rejected me like he had so often in the last six months. And why wouldn't he? He was handsome, with a perfect body and a metabolism that allowed him to eat whatever the fuck he wanted. My overly curvy body and my constant struggle to lose weight had often been an annoyance to him.

It has nothing to do with you, Maddie. You know that, right? He lied to you. He hid his true self and strung you along for four fucking years. You're better off without him.

A sob escaped my throat, and I wiped savagely at the fresh tears. I needed to forget Jordan and his lies and concentrate on getting home.

* * *

IF I HADN'T BEEN SO COLD, IF MY FEET WEREN'T BLISTERED AND bleeding, I would have kept right on walking past the bar. Bikes and nothing but bikes filled the parking lot, and the building appeared on its last legs. It looked rough and dangerous and everything I had avoided my entire life but if I didn't get out of the wind soon, I really was going to freeze to death.

My entire body trembling from the cold, I climbed the splintered wooden steps and stared at the giant of a man blocking the front door. He was bald with tattoos scattered across his skull, and he looked me up and down as I cleared my throat.

"Um, can I go in?" I asked.

The man grunted, and I squeaked in surprise when he reached out and touched my dark hair. He gave me another once-over before stepping aside and opening the door.

"Entertainment's here, boys!" he shouted. I stepped back when I heard the roars of approval coming from within the bar.

"Go on, girl. Ain't no point in being shy now." The man leered at me before grabbing my arm and nearly shoving me into the bar.

I stumbled in my heels, reaching out and grabbing onto the nearest table in a desperate attempt to keep from falling flat on my face. I breathed a sigh of relief at the warmth of the bar. I was anxious to find the ladies' room to remove my shoes and rub some warmth back into my frozen toes. If I were lucky, maybe they'd have some Band-Aids I could slap on my bleeding blisters.

I glanced up, my face paling at the sight before me. The place didn't look like a typical bar. It had a long, curved bar with a mirror behind it and rows and rows of liquor bottles, and there were a few pool tables scattered about, but there were only a few tables, and most of the seats were torn, sagging couches and dirty overstuffed armchairs. But it wasn't the décor that made my blood run cold. Besides the bartender, the entire place was filled with men and only men. They were all big, tattooed, and absolutely dangerous looking, and every single one of them was staring at me like I was a glass of water and they were dying of thirst. I took a lurching step backward.

"I'm sorry. I – I think I'm in the wrong place."

I turned to flee. I didn't care how cold I was or how much further I had to walk. I had made a terrible mistake coming to this place.

"Where do you think you're going, pretty little bitch?" A man snagged my arm, pulling me to a stop.

4

He squeezed my arm as I stared up at him. He had long blond hair tied back in a ponytail and was built like a truck. He studied me briefly before his face broke out into a wide grin.

"Only one tonight, boys, but I reckon she's got enough meat on her bones to handle us. Don't you?" he shouted.

The men in the room laughed, and I pulled against his grip. "I'm sorry. This was a mistake, I don't -"

"Shut up," the man said. "We ain't paying you to talk."

He yanked my wrap away before reaching for my large breasts. Without stopping to consider the consequences, I slapped him as hard as I could across his face.

His head rocked back, and he stared at me in surprise before touching the blood on his lip. "You'll pay for that, you stupid bitch."

He raised his arm, and I cringed back. Before he could slap me, a hand caught his arm and yanked him away.

"Back the fuck off, Jenkins. She belongs to me."

"The fuck she does, Riley," Jenkins said.

"The fuck she doesn't," Riley said.

I stared numbly at the man standing next to Jenkins. He was a mountain of a man, and even though I was over six feet in my heels, I still felt short next to him. He wore jeans and a tight blue T-shirt. A black leather vest clung to his broad shoulders, and tattoos covered his thick neck. His dark hair was cut short, and my eyes lingered on the scar that was visible on his left temple. His nose had obviously been broken a few times. He pushed Jenkins back before taking my arm and yanking me into his embrace.

I had a quick, fleeting glance at his dark blue eyes before his mouth claimed mine. He shoved his tongue into my mouth as his hands gripped my ass, and he pressed my pelvis into his.

He was incredibly warm, and my frozen body instinc-

5

tively pressed into him, seeking out his heat like a bee to a flower. As his tongue licked and stroked mine, I was shocked to hear my soft moan and even more surprised at the flicker of lust that lit in my belly. In all of my twenty-eight years, I had never once been kissed like this. I had never been so utterly and completely owned by a man's mouth, and my hands clutched at his broad shoulders as I returned his kiss shamelessly.

He curved his tongue under my upper lip and sucked hard on it, eliciting another soft moan before he tore his mouth from mine. I stared dazedly at him, not entirely willing to believe that it was his erection I was feeling against the curve of my belly. He gave me a warning look before sighing loudly.

"I told you not to drop by tonight, Kitten." There was an edge to his voice as he squeezed my waist, his fingers digging into my flesh. I knew instinctively that this man and his claim that I belonged to him was the only thing that would save me tonight.

"I'm sorry, baby," I said. "My car broke down, and I didn't know where else to go."

He sighed again, a *Can you believe the shit I have to deal with?* sigh, before turning to face the others. He kept his arm around me, pressing me tight against him as he waved his hand at the men in the bar. "Boys, this is Kitten. Kitten, these are the boys."

The men stared silently at me, and I licked my wind-chapped lips. "It's nice to meet you."

One of the older men with a long dark beard shot through with streaks of grey bellowed laughter. "There ain't no way in hell this pretty little filly would ever be seen with your ugly mug, Rye."

Riley scowled at him. "What the fuck is that supposed to mean?"

"He's sayin' you're ugly, boy." Jenkins clapped him on the back before giving me a once-over. "And this bitch ain't your type."

"How the fuck would you know what my type is?" Riley raised his eyebrows at him. "And stop looking at her like that, or I'll rip your fucking eyeballs out of your head. Got it?"

"Jaysus, boy." Jenkins gave him an exaggerated look of hurt. "Cool your jets. I didn't know she was your woman. Fuck, you never talk about her."

"Maybe because I didn't want you fucking leering at her like the goddamn pervert you are." Riley took my hand and led me toward the door. "C'mon, Kitten."

"Where do you think you're going?" A short man with a large beer belly and long white hair stood from one of the couches.

"I'm gonna take my woman home, and then I'll be back," Riley said.

"We got business to take care of," the man said.

"Yeah, I know. I won't be long."

The man shook his head. "She can stay."

"Frank, she doesn't need to -"

"I said she can stay. Unless," Frank cocked his head at Riley, "she don't know how to keep her mouth shut. Do you trust your little *kitten*, Riley?"

I started to tremble. Riley had stiffened against me, and there was something in how Frank looked at him that made my stomach churn.

"I trust her," Riley replied.

"Then there ain't a problem with her staying," Frank said.

Without speaking, Riley led me toward one of the dirty, worn armchairs. He sat down and pulled me roughly into his lap, pressing me back against his chest. My dress had ridden up until the tops of my stockings were showing. He rested his hand on my thigh, his fingers stroking the thin band of flesh that was peeking out from above the stocking.

I pulled on the bottom of my dress, trying to tug it down, and he grunted with disapproval before pushing my hand away. "Don't, Kitten."

The rest of the men were ignoring us now. A few of them had returned to playing pool while the others were conversing in small groups. Only Frank was still staring at us. I gave him a nervous look as Riley slipped his other hand under my long, dark hair and held the back of my neck in a firm grip.

He continued to stroke my smooth thigh, and I pushed down the new bite of lust. I was in deep trouble, and now was not the time for my libido to rear its ugly head.

"I have to use the bathroom," I whispered.

He pushed me to my feet and led me toward the back of the bar. I followed him meekly, my hand gripping his. I staggered a little when he led me down a dark hallway. He glanced back at me, his eyes unreadable in the dim light, before opening a door on the left.

"You have two minutes."

I hurried into the bathroom. I realized with surprise that I really did have to pee, and I eyed the dirty toilet with distaste before layering the top with toilet paper. I peed quickly, sighing with relief as my bladder emptied, then flushed the toilet and lurched my way to the mirror. I gripped the sink and stared at my reflection. My face, always pale to begin with, was deathly white, and my bright red lipstick was smeared.

I turned on the tap and used the water to wash my hands and scrub the remains of my lipstick from my lips and face. My hands were shaking badly, and my feet were screaming at me.

There was a small stool in the corner of the room, and I

limped my way to it before sitting down and slipping off my shoes. My feet practically shrieked *hallelujah,* and with a small groan, I massaged them gently. I was just inspecting the blood-soaked blister on the back of my right heel when the bathroom door banged open, and Riley walked in.

I shrank back as he slammed the door shut and squatted before me. He held my chin in a firm grip. "Who are you?"

"N-no one," I whispered.

"What are you doing at this bar?"

"I told you – my car broke down, and I just wanted to use a phone to call a tow truck, that's all. Please, let me go. You can slip me out the back or something, okay?" I pleaded.

"There isn't another place around for miles. You'll freeze to death."

"I'll walk back to my car and stay there until morning. Someone will come by, and I'll use their phone," I said.

He gave me a grim look. "The only people who will drive by are the men out there. Do you want them stopping to help you?"

I shook my head and blinked back the tears as Riley rubbed at his forehead. "Fuck. What's your name?"

"Maddie."

"Listen up, Maddie. The only way you'll survive this night is by doing everything I tell you to. Understand?"

I was so scared my throat had gone bone dry, and I couldn't squeak out a reply. He squeezed my chin. "The men out there are brutal and dangerous. If they think you're not who I say you are, they'll rape you, beat you, and leave you for dead. Do you understand?"

"Y-yes," I said.

"I can't let you leave out the back. If I do that, they'll beat the shit out of me and then find you and hurt you. Your only chance - *our* only chance - is to keep pretending that you belong to me."

"Why are you doing this?" I asked.

He hesitated before glancing at the bathroom floor. "You remind me of someone. Someone sweet and innocent who I failed to protect. And I'll be damned if it happens again."

"Who?" I said.

He frowned at me. "What?"

"Who do I remind you of?"

"It doesn't matter. Just keep your mouth shut and do whatever I tell you. Do you understand?"

"Yes."

He studied me carefully, and alarm flooded my nervous system when his eyes dropped to my large breasts. My dress was ridiculously low cut, and he got more than an eyeful of my cleavage.

"Christ," he suddenly muttered. He forced his gaze to my face, and my thighs trembled at the look of pure need on his face. I stared at his mouth, those full lips that had touched my own and made me forget that I was in a room full of dangerous, terrifying men.

Don't be ridiculous, Maddie. Someone like him would not find someone like you attractive.

No, he definitely wouldn't. Even though he wasn't conventionally attractive, something about him called to me. I had no trouble believing he could easily have whatever woman he wanted. His body was pure muscle, and the scar on his face only made him more mysterious and attractive.

It was absolutely the wrong moment for my lust to come roaring back to life, but apparently, I had zero control over it. I wanted him to kiss me again. I wanted to feel his hands on my breasts and his cock in my pussy while he whispered dirty things in my ear and –

"Fuck, Kitten. You've got your need written all over that pretty little face of yours," he groaned.

I jerked in surprise when he dropped to his knees in front

of me and yanked me forward. His crotch pressed against me, and my eyes widened when I felt the hard evidence of his arousal.

"Wha- what are you doing?" I squeaked.

"Giving you what you want," he growled.

His hands cupped my head, and he dropped his mouth onto mine. I tried to wiggle out of his grip, tried to squirm away, but the wall was against my back, and there was no place to go. He threaded his fingers in my hair and yanked my head back before licking and sucking at the sensitive skin on my neck.

"Hey," I moaned. "Just wait a minute…"

He ignored me and licked a searing path to my breasts. I moaned again, my hips pushing against him even as my mind realized how insane I was acting. He groped behind me, grabbing the zipper of my dress and tugging it down before pulling the dress down to my waist. I made no protest when he unhooked the front clasp of my bra and peeled it away from my large breasts.

Maddie, what are you doing? You don't even know him! This is so bad!

His hands closed around my throbbing breasts, and I moaned again when his rough thumbs brushed my hardened nipples. Bad or not, it felt good – felt fucking amazing, actually – and I clutched at his head when he sucked one nipple into his hot mouth.

"Oh!" I cried out with surprise when he bit my nipple. He growled in reply before cupping the back of my neck and kissing me hard on the mouth. His tongue pushed insistently at my lips, and I parted them and returned his kiss frantically as he kneaded my breasts with his large, rough hand.

"Please." I stared at him with a dazed look of hunger.

He stood and pulled me to my feet, turning me around and pushing me up against the sink. I gripped the sink and stared wide-eyed at the woman in the mirror. Her face was flushed, her mouth swollen and red, and the look of raw hunger in her eyes was frightening in its ferocity.

Riley dragged my dress up around my waist and pulled my ridiculously skimpy underwear down my legs. I shimmied out of them, feeling like I was in a dream, as Riley stroked my ass and pushed my thighs wide. He reached between my legs, and I bit back my shriek of pleasure when I felt his fingers against my swollen clit.

"Jesus, Kitten. You're so fucking wet."

I whimpered in disappointment and stared at his reflection in the mirror when the warmth of his hand disappeared. He gave me a hard grin and reached into his pocket.

"Patience, Kitten. I have what you need."

There was the crinkle of a foil wrapper. Nearly paralyzed with need and want, I watched in the mirror as Riley dropped his jeans. He tore the package open, and I stared down at my hands, still gripping the sink as he slid the condom over his cock.

Riley's hands gripped my thighs, and he pulled my legs apart until I could feel the strain in my muscles. He lifted me to my tiptoes, and I bit my lip when his gravel-rough voice said, "Ready, Kitten?"

I didn't – couldn't – reply, and his hands tightened on my hips for a moment before I felt his cock nudging at my pussy.

Maddie! Are you fucking crazy? What are you doing? This guy is dangerous, very dangerous. Do not fuck him! Do you hear me? Push him away and –

I squeezed my eyes shut. After what I had walked in on tonight with Jordan, I needed this. I needed to feel wanted, to know I was attractive and desired.

I shut my inner voice down with a viciousness that surprised me.

"Do it." I barely recognized the voice as my own.

Riley groaned under his breath, and then his cock thrust into me. I bit down on the moan of pain that wanted to escape. He was huge, and while I knew I wouldn't actually be split in half, I certainly felt like I was.

"Jesus Christ, Kitten, you're so fucking tight. Tell me you've been fucked before."

His hand threaded through my hair, pulling my head up until we stared at each other in the mirror. "Have you been fucked before?"

I nodded and thought I saw a brief flash of relief in his eyes.

"Just never with someone as big as you," I groaned, and a tight grin crossed his face before he thrust back and forth.

I cried out, not caring who would hear me, and dropped my head to stare at the sink again.

"No, Kitten." His hand tightened in my hair again, and he made me raise my head as his other hand swept around me and cupped one large breast. He pulled on the nipple as he stared at me in the mirror.

"You'll watch as I fuck you. Do you understand, Maddie? I want to see the look on your face as I fuck your tight little pussy."

Another shudder of desire went through me, and he grinned before cupping my throat. He rested his other hand between my shoulder blades, and I gripped the sink and held on for dear life as he plunged roughly in and out, his gaze never leaving mine.

I studied the way his hand cupped my throat, refusing to admit how turned on it made me to be trapped in his large grip as he fucked me hard and rough.

"You're so fucking hot, Maddie." He leaned forward and nuzzled my cheek. "I can barely stop from blowing my load."

I moaned in reply, and he moved his hand down my back and squeezed my ass. "Bend over, Kitten."

His hand moved from the front of my throat to the back of my neck, and he pushed me down over the sink. I made a loud cry of pleasure as he leaned over me and kissed the small daisy tattoo on the back of my left shoulder.

"You feel so fucking good around my cock," he breathed into my ear before nipping at my earlobe. The smooth material of his leather vest rubbed against my back, and I moaned when he reached down and gripped one dangling breast. He pinched the nipple, and another loud cry of pleasure escaped my mouth.

His hand moved from my breast to between my legs, his rough fingers finding my clit easily. He rubbed it, and I stiffened against him, his fingers digging into my neck when I tried to wiggle away.

"Oh God, oh no," I cried as my entire body began to shake. "Please!"

"Say my name, Kitten." He eased up on the pressure against my clit, and I whined in protest. "Say it."

"Riley!" I gasped. "Please!"

"That's my good girl."

He increased the pressure, and I writhed and squirmed against his hand and around his thick cock.

I was close to an orgasm, my entire body vibrating, and I shrieked in surprise when a voice behind us drawled lazily, "Well, ain't that a sight to see."

"Get the fuck out, Jenkins," Riley snarled without stopping his rough rhythm in my wet and oh-so-willing pussy.

I tried to squirm away, embarrassment eclipsing my pleasure. Riley slapped me on the ass before making another harsh noise of frustration. "I said get out, Jenkins, before I kick your fucking ass."

"Okay, okay." Jenkins held up his hands and slowly backed out of the bathroom. "The boss just sent me to check on you. I'll tell him you're dick deep in your little bitch."

My face flamed as the bathroom door slammed shut. I reached behind me and pushed at Riley. "We have to stop!"

"No fucking way, Kitten," he said through gritted teeth.

"Riley, I'm not going to -"

My breath caught in my throat as Riley reached between my legs and pinched my clit. The desire that disappeared when Jenkins walked in on us returned with a roaring, shrieking rush that made me tremble. Riley thrust harder, his breath coming in harsh gasps as he pulled and tugged on my swollen clit.

"OH! Oh God! Riley!" I muttered his name in a harsh groan as my entire body stiffened and my climax roared through me. It was so intense the pleasure bordered on pain. I arched my back as Riley's hand tightened on my neck, and he thrust so hard that I was nearly knocked off my feet. I fell against the sink, the cold porcelain digging into my belly. Riley made a low roar of ecstasy, and his entire body shuddered against mine.

I waited beneath him as he dropped his forehead against my smooth back, and his body twitched. His breath was hot against my skin, and I squirmed restlessly before trying to straighten. Riley pulled out of me, and, my face red, I gathered my bra that was twisted beneath my arms and tried to straighten it. My skin was sweaty, and the thin material stuck to it as I cursed under my breath.

Riley had already dropped the condom into the garbage and buttoned his jeans. He watched me struggle without speaking. Embarrassment coursing through me, I spun around and yanked the bottom of my dress down before pulling viciously at my bra. It refused to untwist, and I could feel the hot tears leaking down my face. What the fuck had I just done? I was a damn whore, and I –

I tried to jerk away when I felt Riley's breath on my back.

He gripped me by my shoulders and pulled me against his hard body.

"Shh, you're okay, Kitten." He cupped my bare breasts and squeezed them gently before rubbing his hand along the curve of my belly. "Let me help."

I stood mutely with my body trembling as he patiently untwisted my bra and tucked my breasts into the cups before hooking the front clasp. He stared over my shoulder, and I shivered lightly when he ran the tip of his finger between my breasts.

"Christ, your tits are fucking amazing."

He helped me pull up my dress and zipped it, pushing my hair to the side so it wouldn't get caught in the zipper. He handed me my shoes and purse, and I started toward the door. I needed to get out of this room. It smelled like sex and my perfume and Riley's ridiculously enticing scent. If I stayed much longer, I'd be tempted to beg him to fuck me again.

"Wait, Kitten."

I reached for the door. "No, I -"

"Your panties," he said.

I flushed and turned around. He held the flimsy material in one large hand and grinned at me. "Normally, I'd be all for you going without them, but I don't want anyone else seeing that pretty little pussy. I'm not good at sharing what's mine."

I stalked toward him, ripping the panties from his hand. "It's not yours."

Quick as a striking snake, he pushed me up against the wall and shoved his hand between my thighs. He cupped my bare pussy, his thumb rubbing against my still-swollen clit. I made a soft moan of submission as he grinned fiercely at me.

"Tonight, this belongs to me. Say it, Kitten."

I shook my head defiantly. His smile widened, and he bent his head and took my mouth in a rough, demanding kiss. He kissed me until I was breathless and squirming against his hand. He slid one finger deep inside my pussy, and I cried out into his mouth.

"Say it, Kitten," he repeated against my mouth before nipping my bottom lip.

"It's yours," I whispered.

"That's right, all mine." He nipped my bottom lip again and slid his hand out from between my thighs.

I flushed bright red when he slipped his finger into his mouth and sucked away the moisture. "You taste fucking delicious, Maddie."

The desire in his voice brought another flood of wetness between my legs. He grinned at the look on my face. "I wish I had enough time to taste you properly."

I moaned as a vision of his dark head between my thighs popped into my head. He kissed me a final time, thrusting his tongue into my mouth before licking my upper lip. "Another time, maybe."

I pulled up my panties, sliding them awkwardly under my dress. I washed my hands and splashed water on my face, smoothing my hair down as best I could.

He snorted with impatience. "Come on."

He held out his hand, and I took it gingerly as he led me to the bathroom door. "Remember what I said, Maddie. If you want to leave here tonight, do exactly what I tell you to and keep your mouth shut. Understand?"

I nodded, and he searched my face briefly before leading me out of the bathroom.

CHAPTER 2

Riley

I had lost my goddamn mind. I should have kept my mouth shut, but the woman standing in the bar's doorway reminded me so strongly of Andrea that I was on my feet and shoving my way toward her before my brain could tell me to stop.

She didn't favour her in looks. Andrea had been the spitting image of our mother, small and blonde with light blue eyes and tanned skin. The woman standing in the bar was tall and curvy with dark hair, dark eyes, and pale skin. Her tits were fucking amazing, wrapped up like a Christmas present in that tight-as-hell black dress. She had wobbled in on those ridiculous *fuck me* shoes, and half the dicks in the room had sprung to attention, mine included.

But it wasn't her pale skin or her large tits that had me rushing to claim her as mine and save her from the gang like I was some goddamn Prince Charming wannabe. No, the obvious fragility that surrounded her like a thin shield and the wounded look in her eyes – the same one that had been in Andrea's and I had ignored – made me do it.

And I swear on the fucking grave of my mother – God rest her soul – that I meant only to pretend she was mine. That I was going to hustle her out of the bar and take her somewhere safe, but then I tasted her, and my good intentions flew out the fucking window.

And Jesus, the way she looked at me in the bathroom – a man only had so much willpower. She wanted me to fuck her, and I never turned down an offer to stick my dick in a warm pussy. Now that it knew exactly how wet and tight she was, my dick was crying out for more. I wiped a trembling hand across my forehead as the woman stumbled behind me. I gripped her hand and threw her a scowl before hurrying her down the hallway.

It didn't matter how wet her pussy was or how fucking hot she had looked bent over that sink while I fucked her. I had made a huge mistake. I needed to get her out of here before Frank asked too many questions. There was no way a woman like her would ever be with a man like me. Of course, Jenkins wouldn't have been shy about spreading the news that I was fucking Maddie in the bathroom.

It was a mistake to fuck her, and I had no one to blame but my own lack of willpower when it came to pussy, but it may have worked in our favour. It might have been enough to convince Frank she was my woman. Maddie didn't look like my type, but she also didn't look like the type to fuck a stranger in a dirty bathroom.

My dick stirred in my jeans at just the memory of being in Maddie, and I cursed it in my head. We were almost at the main part of the bar, and I slowed and stared at Maddie. "Remember what I told you. Keep your mouth shut and do everything I tell you. Do you understand?"

She nodded. After I had fucked her, there'd been a warm,

sated look on her face, but now the same heartbreaking sorrow and fear from earlier had replaced it. I squeezed her hand and gave her a grim look.

"I won't be nice to you. It'll raise suspicions if I am. Don't take it personally."

"I – I won't," she whispered.

She looked close to tears. I surprised the both of us by cupping her face and kissing her roughly.

"Everything will be fine. I promise you'll be warm and safe in your own bed in a few hours."

"Right." She took a deep breath and I silently applauded her when she straightened her back. "I'm ready."

I led her out into the bar. As we crossed the room and I sat down in the armchair, tugging her into my lap, there was a low wolf whistle. Jenkins, the asshole, sauntered toward us and sat down in the chair next to mine.

"You feel like sharing tonight, Riley?"

"No, I fucking don't. Touch her, and I'll send you to the fucking hospital."

Jenkins snorted. "Ease up, boy. What's so special about the fat bitch, anyway?"

Maddie stiffened on my lap. I squeezed the back of her neck in a warning grip before staring at Jenkins. "There isn't anything special about her. I just don't like sharing my toys."

"If you want something better than his puny little pecker, you just say the word, sweetheart. I know how to make you squeal," Jenkins said.

I almost laughed out loud when Maddie looked Jenkins up and down and, in a voice nearly dripping with disdain, said, "Not if you were the last man on earth."

Jenkins flushed, and his hands clenched into fists. He leaned closer, and Maddie shrank back against me. Her pulse was fluttering like a trapped bird beneath my hand, and I rubbed the back of her neck as I glared at Jenkins.

"Stay away from my girl, Jenkins, or that dick you're so proud of will be sticking out of your fucking ass."

"What the fuck has gotten into you, Riley?" Jenkins said with a wounded look.

I shrugged and squeezed Maddie's neck. "Go get me a beer, Kitten."

There was a flash of rebellion in her eyes. I squeezed her neck in silent warning, pulled a twenty from my pocket, and handed it to her. She bit her bottom lip before sliding off my lap. Leaving her shoes on the floor, she limped toward the bar. I watched her go, her ass swaying in that ridiculously skimpy dress and scowled at Jenkins when he reached down and tugged at his obvious erection.

He shrugged. "I like the fat ones."

"Call her fat again, and I'll kick your fucking face in."

"Hey, it's a compliment, man." He grinned at me as Billy sat in the chair next to mine.

"How long you been dating her, Rye?" he asked.

"Not long."

"What's she do for a living?"

"Why?"

"Just curious," Billy said. "Where'd you meet her?"

"At a fucking square dance," I growled. "Is it twenty questions night, and I missed the goddamn memo?"

"Jesus," Billy grumbled, "I was just bein' social. I ain't ever seen you with a woman like her before."

"Hell, we ain't ever seen you with a woman, period." Jenkins laughed. "Was starting to think maybe you liked suckin' cock or somethin'."

I glared at Jenkins as Billy snorted laughter.

"You're really pissing me off tonight, Jenkins."

"That's my job, man." Jenkins glanced at the bar, and I followed his gaze, my stomach dropping when I saw Frank standing beside Maddie. Even from here, I could see the anxiety in her eyes. I shot to my feet and stalked toward the bar, praying she hadn't revealed too much.

* * *

Maddie

I LIMPED TOWARD THE BAR, ENTIRELY TOO CONSCIOUS OF Riley's hot gaze, and smiled at the slender blonde woman standing behind the bar.

"Hi, could I, uh, get a beer for Riley and a glass of water, please?"

The woman looked me up and down, and I shrank back at the anger in her gaze.

"We don't serve water here."

"Just tap water is fine," I said.

"I said we don't serve water. Either order a fucking drink or get the hell out of the bar."

"Fine. I'll take a beer."

I hated beer, but I was too tired to argue with her. She turned away and grabbed two bottles of beer. She removed the caps with an angry twist and threw them into the garbage before slamming the bottles down on the bar so hard that beer sloshed out and puddled on the worn wood.

Without speaking, I handed her the twenty, and she stormed to the cash register. I caught a glimpse of myself in the mirror behind the bar and could barely hold in my groan of dismay. My mouth was still swollen and red, and there were bright red blotches on my face and neck from Riley's stubble. I tried to smooth my hair again as the bartender returned and threw my change into the puddle of beer.

My temper flared. "What's your problem?"

She sneered at me. "Maybe I don't like fat bitches in my bar."

"Call me fat again, and I'll kick your skinny little ass," I said.

I was lying. I'd never been in a fight in my life, and the woman glaring at me might have been half my weight, but I had no doubt she could easily beat the crap out of me. Still, I was having a bad fucking night. I'd be damned if I let a woman I'd never met before insult me.

"You think you mean anything to Riley other than someplace to put his dick? You're wrong," she suddenly snarled.

A lightbulb went off in my head, and I grinned at her. "At least he *wants* to put his dick in me."

Maddie! Shut up! Are you trying to get yourself killed?

"Shut your mouth," she said. "You don't know nothin' about Riley and me."

Ignoring my inner voice, I leaned forward and grinned again. "I know you want him, and he doesn't want you. I know it's killing you that you could hear us fucking in the bathroom."

Maddie! Stop! For God's sake – stop!

Her face went pale, and she stared at me with pure fury. "You shut your fucking mouth."

"Make me," I said.

Her hands clenched into fists, and I stared silently at her. Outwardly, I appeared calm, but my insides were churning, and I was seriously considering just turning and bolting for the door. Before I could, a low voice spoke beside me.

"Whiskey, Deena. Now."

Deena twitched and, with a final glare, turned away. I stared at the man standing beside me.

"Frank." He held out his hand. I shook it briefly, my stomach twisting at the feel of his hard hand.

"Maddie."

"You don't belong here, Maddie."

I stayed silent and tried not to shudder when his gaze lingered on my large breasts. He shook back his long hair and rested his belly against the bar as Deena placed a glass of whiskey in front of him. He took a sip, and I picked up the beers. "It was nice to meet you."

"I'm not finished."

He spoke softly, but every nerve ending in my body lit up like a Christmas tree.

"What's a nice girl like you doing in a place like this?"

I swallowed down my nervous laughter. "My car broke down, and I knew Riley was here tonight. I needed a ride home."

"How long have you and Riley been fucking?"

"Not long."

"Where'd you meet?"

"A bar."

"Which bar?"

"I don't remember. I was pretty drunk." I took a swig of beer, trying not to grimace at the bitter taste.

"Is that right?"

"Yes."

He waited patiently. I smothered another bout of laughter. If Frank thought I would spill my guts just because of a little silence, he was in for a surprise. I'd spent enough time teaching clients to keep their answers short when on the stand that I had the upper hand in this conversation, even if Frank didn't know it.

After a moment, he took another sip of whiskey. "You don't look like his type."

"How many of his girlfriends have you met?"

"Is that what you are? His girlfriend?"

I just shrugged in reply and drank some more beer. It was already starting to affect me. I couldn't remember the last time I drank, and I cautioned myself to slow down. Being drunk was the last thing I needed.

"What do you do for a living, Maddie?" Frank said.

"Office work."

"Secretary?" He looked me up and down again, and I nodded.

"What company?"

"Why do you want to know?"

"Just answer the fucking question, Maddie," Frank said.

Relief flooded through me when Riley appeared. He looped his arm around my waist and reached for his beer, drinking nearly half of it before staring at Frank. "What's going on, Frank?"

"Just chatting with your kitten," he said.

Riley squeezed my waist. "Let's go, Maddie."

"Where'd you two meet, Riley?" Frank asked.

"I told you, we met at the -"

"Shut your mouth, *Kitten*," Frank said. "I ain't talking to you."

I shut my mouth with a snap as Frank stared expectantly at Riley. I slid my arm around Riley's waist and dug my fingers into his hip before deliberately tapping my finger against the bar's top.

I breathed a sigh of relief when Riley said, "At a bar."

"What's she do for a living?" Frank asked.

"Jesus, Frank, I don't fucking know. What do I care what she does? I call her when I want her to suck my dick or need a pussy to fuck, that's it."

"She said she's your girlfriend."

"No, I didn't," I said.

Frank stared at me, and Riley slapped my ass so hard I fell against the bar. "Shut your fucking mouth, Maddie."

I rubbed my stinging ass and glared at him before

26

lowering my gaze to the floor. He grunted with satisfaction and stared at Frank. "What's this about, Frank?"

"We got business to discuss. How do I know she's going to keep her mouth shut?"

"Jesus, I already told you she would. She's a fucking nobody who's scared of her own goddamn shadow half the fucking time. She won't say a word. But if you're so fucking worried about it, I'll take her home right now and be done with it."

Frank stared at him for a long moment before picking up his glass of whiskey. "She stays."

He walked away, and I sagged against Riley while Deena glared daggers at us both. Frank clapped his hands and the men in the bar quieted down as Riley tugged me away from Deena and the bar.

"What do you do for a living?" he breathed into my ear once we were sitting in the armchair again.

I pressed my lips against his ear. "Lawyer."

"Fuck." His hand tightened on my thigh.

"I told Frank I was a secretary."

"Smart. Don't tell anyone in this room the truth."

"I'm not an idiot," I whispered.

He snorted as Frank moved to the middle of the bar. He leaned against the pool table, and I listened silently, trying not to show my shock and dismay, as the gang of men casually discussed the large shipment of drugs they were moving.

* * *

Riley

I HATED TO ADMIT IT, BUT THE WOMAN SITTING ON MY LAP impressed me. Her entire body vibrated like a live wire, but she had arranged her face into a mask of boredom and disinterest as Frank and the boys discussed the details of our biggest shipment of drugs yet.

I wondered what she was thinking. I doubted it was every day that she fucked a drug dealer in a dirty bathroom. No doubt she fucking regretted that now. She had wanted me badly. I could see it on her face – hell, I could almost smell her fucking desire – but knowing what she did now would have snuffed out her desire. My chance to fuck her again was finished.

Are you fucking crazy, Riley? Even if she weren't some fancy-ass lawyer, you wouldn't have a chance with her. She had a moment of insanity in that bathroom, and you're fucking deluded if you think it was anything more than that. She is way too good for you.

Yeah, I knew that, but my dick certainly didn't know or care. It wanted a taste of Maddie's sweet pussy again, and my asshole of a father always said that my dick did most of the thinking. He was wrong about many things, but that wasn't one of them.

I had the sudden urge to tell her the truth. To try to make her understand that I had done what I did in a last-ditch effort to save Andrea. She needed treatment, and mental hospitals weren't cheap. My mother had been barely making ends meet as it was, and she was sick herself. I had joined Frank's merry gang of drug dealers, and three months later, Andrea was dead, and I was trapped in a life I had never wanted.

I was struck by the ridiculous urge to get up and take Maddie out of the bar. To hop on my bike and drive to some all-night diner where I would tell her the truth. I could almost picture myself confessing my sins to her like she was my goddamn priest and responsible for saving my mortal soul.

It was a stupid idea. Even if I told Maddie the truth, it wouldn't matter. A woman like her wouldn't be caught dead with a man like me. Despite how she was dressed tonight, I knew instinctively that the moment in the bathroom was a moment of madness for her and nothing more. Unfortunately, my dick didn't care. It wanted another chance at that warm and oh-so-fucking tight pussy, and I was having a hard time denying it.

I snorted loudly, and Maddie gave me a curious look. I shook my head at her and slid my hand under her dress. I curled my fingers around her inner thigh. It was ridiculous, but I wanted to make her want me again. Despite what she knew about me now, I wanted to bring back that almost feral desire from earlier. I slid my fingers higher toward that tight pussy that was so fucking hot I was nearly drooling for it.

"Behave!" Maddie muttered as she clamped her legs shut, trapping my hand between those smooth thighs. I almost laughed out loud at the prim way she glared at me.

I forced my attention to Frank. He was finishing up, and there was a loud cheer from the boys when the bouncer, Dirk, opened the door and ushered in a group of seven women.

"Entertainment's here, boys!" Dirk shouted. The boys cheered again as Maddie stiffened against me.

"Please, can we go now?" she pleaded.

The women were making their rounds through the bars, laughing and slapping at the hands reaching out to pinch and squeeze.

I shook my head. "Not yet."

"Please," she whispered.

"No." I gave her a harsh look. "We need to stay."

She moaned, and I squeezed her thigh. "It'll be fine, Kitten."

Frank nodded at Deena, and she dimmed the lights in the bar before moving to the sound system. Music blared out of the speakers mounted on the walls, and Maddie jumped nervously. I pulled her back against me and wrapped my arm around her waist. I had a feeling she was close to bolting. I kissed her throat before rubbing her hip.

"You're fine, Kitten. Take a deep breath."

"I'm fine," she repeated. Her face was pale, and her gaze darted around the room. The women began dancing, using the pool tables and chairs to grind their bodies against as the boys watched.

"Look at me, Maddie," I demanded.

She turned toward me obediently, and I cupped her face before kissing her. She tensed against me, and I stroked my tongue across the seam of her lips, urging her to open them. She moaned and parted her lips. I slipped my tongue inside her warm mouth, tasting her and soothing her as her body relaxed against mine.

"Good girl," I murmured against her mouth.

She pressed herself against me as the music swelled. It didn't take long for the fucking to start – it never did. Within half an hour, most of the women were either naked or close enough, and the bar was filled with the sounds of fucking and sucking.

Maddie breathed shallowly, her gorgeous tits moving rapidly under her dress. I did my best to keep my dick under control. A blonde woman, wearing only a pair of panties, dropped to her knees in front of Jenkins. She quickly unbuttoned his pants before pulling out his cock. She sucked enthusiastically at it. I groaned under my breath when my dick hardened at the sight of her lips sliding back and forth over his erect cock.

Maddie instinctively ground her ass against my cock, and I muttered a harsh curse. "Jesus, Kitten. Stop doing that."

She flushed and gave me an embarrassed look before leaning forward. "I'm sorry."

I reached under her and tried to arrange my cock into a more comfortable position. I wondered if she was as turned on as I was. She stared across the room at Frank as he fucked a girl on her hands and knees. After a moment, she turned back to me and gave me a tentative smile. She leaned back against me with her ass pressing against my cock. My entire body jerked convulsively when she whispered in my ear.

CHAPTER 3

Maddie

I stared numbly around the bar. Everywhere I looked, someone was naked and fucking. One of the women made a loud squeal of delight, and my gaze darted toward the sound. She was lying naked on the pool table, her legs spread wide as a man with short blond hair buried his face between her thighs. She crowed again, her entire body arching and fingers scraping against the pool table. I quickly looked away.

I was in the middle of a damn orgy. Me, who had never even had sex with the lights on, was sitting in a room full of people having sex, and the crotch of my panties was so wet I was afraid I was about to leave a damp spot on Riley's jeans.

I shifted and squirmed, trying to relieve some of the ache between my thighs as I scolded myself fiercely for even being turned on. Nice girls didn't enjoy watching other people fuck, and if there was one thing I knew about myself, it was that I was a nice girl.

A blonde woman wearing nothing but a pair of panties

dropped to her knees in front of Jenkins and sucked at his cock. I bit down on my lip as I shifted, and Riley's hard cock pressed against me. Before I could stop myself, I ground my ass eagerly against it. Riley made a harsh groan.

"Jesus, Kitten. Stop doing that."

"I'm sorry," I whispered and leaned forward, trying to ignore the feel of his cock. Across the room, Frank had a redhead on her hands and knees. He fucked her rapidly, his large belly bouncing against her ass as she moaned and squealed. I shuddered when his dark eyes stared at me.

I wondered if he thought it strange that Riley and I weren't doing anything other than watching. My pussy throbbed as I stared at my knees.

Maddie, no. You can't. It's one thing to fuck him in the bathroom, but if you do what you're thinking, you might as well just call yourself a whore and be done with it.

Whore.

I whispered the word, tasted it on my tongue, before leaning back against Riley.

"Will he find it weird that we're not doing anything? Will it make him suspicious?" I whispered into his ear.

I didn't know if I was looking for an out or permission, but Riley's entire body jerked beneath me, and his arm tightened painfully around my waist. He stared at me, his blue eyes burning with a dark desire. I squirmed under the intensity of his gaze.

I didn't know him, hell, he was a complete stranger, but I saw the lie in his eyes when he gave a clipped nod. "Yes."

I took a deep breath as Riley stared at me. He hadn't moved a muscle beneath me, but I could see how badly he wanted me again. A surge of desire, tinged with pride, went through me. What I was about to do was madness – utter madness – and if Jordan could see me now, he would be horrified, but I realized with a wild sense of freedom that I didn't care.

For once in my life, I wouldn't be the good girl. For once in my life, I would do what I wanted and not give one fuck about the consequences of my actions. I wanted to suck Riley's cock in a room full of people, and just for tonight, I wouldn't deny myself.

I leaned forward and kissed him hard on the mouth. He returned my kiss immediately, his tongue sliding into my mouth like it belonged there and his hand reaching up to knead my breast. I arched my back as he trailed hot kisses down my throat and nipped at the top of my full breast.

He reached for the zipper of my dress, and I pushed his hands away. He stared at me in frustration. I smiled at him as I slid from his lap and kneeled between his thighs. I reached for his belt buckle. Despite my desire, my hands were trembling, and he caught them with his and squeezed them briefly.

"You don't have to do this, Maddie."

"I know."

I unbuckled his belt, and he helped me unbutton and unzip his jeans. He pulled his cock out of the opening and stroked it with his rough hand as his other hand stroked my hair. "I want your mouth so much, Kitten."

"I know," I repeated before leaning forward and taking the head of his cock into my mouth.

He groaned, both hands sliding into my hair to grip tightly as I sucked tentatively at his cock. I didn't have a whole lot of experience. Jordan had never really enjoyed it when I went down on him, and I was feeling ridiculously self-conscious despite my desire.

Given Jordan's lack of interest, I had always assumed I was terrible at it. Even now, knowing what I did about Jordan, I could feel nerves creeping in. I raised my eyes to Riley's face, my sucking slowing to a stop as I stared at him. There was a combination of intense need and almost comical relief on his face, and his hands tightened in my hair as his eyes popped open.

"Fuck, Kitten. Don't stop now."

Fresh liquid poured from my pussy, and my nipples tightened into hard, throbbing buds. I licked my lips and plunged my mouth back over his cock. I was determined to make him feel good, determined to do whatever it took to make Riley come. I sucked and licked enthusiastically as I wrapped my hand around the bottom of his shaft and squeezed. I glanced again at his face, and a sense of power rippled through me at his look of desperate need.

I might have been the one on my knees, but I held all the power.

I squeezed his cock, then licked the head, trailing my tongue over the top before sucking hard again. He gasped and moaned, his hips arching up from the chair. I stroked him rapidly as I bobbed my head up and down. He was so much bigger than Jordan, thicker and longer. I took a deep breath and slid as much of him into my mouth as I could. My cheeks bulged, and he moaned again. I sucked as hard as I could, my cheeks hollowing with my effort.

"Oh my fucking God," he groaned, "you are so fucking good at this."

Another tingle of pride went through me. I took a second deep breath and took so much of him into my mouth that I gagged a little. I eased up and glanced at him. "I'm sorry."

He shook his head and said hoarsely, "Keep going, baby. Please, you're fucking killing me here."

I grinned and attacked his cock again. Behind me, I could hear the sounds of the others, their loud moans and cries of pleasure, and it only turned me on more. I was dripping wet. I could feel the moisture escaping my panties and sliding down my thighs as I sucked and licked like a woman possessed. Riley's harsh moans and the way his hips bucked helplessly against my mouth filled me with that weird sense of power again.

I made a low humming noise. My lips vibrated against the velvet skin of his cock, and he jerked before cursing under his breath. Precum coated my tongue, and I licked him clean eagerly, loving his taste, as he stroked and petted my long hair. His cock swelled in my mouth, and he pulled my head away with a painful tug.

"I'm gonna come," he gasped out.

I wrapped my hand around his hard cock and stroked it rapidly. His hips rose and fell with my hand, and I gave him a slow smile that made him groan. His hands clenched on the arms of the chair, his hips thrust upward, and he came with a hoarse shout. Cum surged from the tip of his cock and coated my upper chest and breasts with its warmth. I continued to stroke him, milking every last drop from him until he pulled my hand away.

"Jesus Christ," he whispered.

I climbed into his lap, not caring that his cum covered me. I kissed him eagerly before taking his hand and trying to shove it under my dress.

I needed to come. My pussy was aching and throbbing in a way I had never felt before. I needed to feel his rough fingers against my clit. He traced my inner thighs, grinning at the moisture that covered them, before cupping my breast through my dress. I moaned into his mouth and thrust my pelvis at him.

"Jesus, Maddie. You're going to be the fucking death of me," he muttered.

His gaze drifted across the room, and I made a harsh cry of disappointment when he slid his hand out from under my dress.

"No! Riley, please!" I tried to force his hand back under my dress, not caring how pathetic and needy I looked. He slapped me sharply on one thigh.

"Enough, Kitten."

His entire body had stiffened. I followed his gaze to see Frank, naked and smoking a cigarette, reclining on one of the couches. Even from across the room, I could see the lust in his eyes as he watched us. I shuddered all over, my desire dissipating immediately.

"Go to the bathroom and get cleaned up," Riley said.

I nodded and walked rather unsteadily to the bathroom.

* * *

Riley

ONCE MADDIE HAD DISAPPEARED INTO THE BATHROOM, I zipped up and crossed the bar to Frank. He reclined on a couch with the woman he'd fucked lounging at his feet. I scowled at her when she reached out and stroked my thigh.

"I'm leaving."

"So soon?" Frank blew a smoke ring out, and it drifted lazily toward the ceiling. "Party's just gettin' started."

"I need to get my girl home."

"You sure you don't want to stay? Maybe let one of the others have a go at her while Kassie takes care of you?"

The redhead leaned forward and cupped her breasts before purring, "I know what you need, Riley."

I shook my head. "I'm not into sharing, Frank."

"That's a shame."

"Yeah. I'll see you tomorrow."

I walked away before he could reply. I promised Maddie I

would get her out of this bar and safe in her bed. I intended to keep that promise.

And maybe you'd like to be in that bed with her?

Fuck yes.

I waited impatiently for her to come out of the bathroom. When she did, I took her hand and gave her a quick once-over. My cum was washed away, but I could see the stain on the front of her dress. Satisfaction washed over me. Thinking that just because I'd blown my load all over that pale skin of hers marked her as mine was stupid. But the thought kept pushing into my head as she grabbed her shoes and purse from the floor by the chair.

I hustled her toward the door, nodding to Dirk before nearly pushing her into the cold night air. She started to shiver almost immediately. I hurried her to my bike, grabbing my leather jacket from the seat and helping her into it.

"Th-thank you."

I zipped it up before placing her shoes and purse in one of the leather bags hanging across the bike. I swung my leg over the bike. "Get on."

She hesitated and I gave her an impatient look. "Get on, I said."

"I've never been on a motorcycle before," she said.

Of course she hadn't. I rolled my eyes and tugged her closer. "Swing your leg over and sit down. Feet on the pegs."

"Riley, I don't -"

"Do you want to go home or not, Maddie?" My voice was harsher than I intended.

"Yes," she nearly whimpered.

My stomach twisted at the sound. "It's perfectly safe, Kitten. I promise."

"Okay."

Moving timidly, she climbed onto the bike behind me. Her skirt rode up, showing the top of her stockings. She yanked at it as she placed her feet on the pegs and rested her hands on my shoulders.

"No, around my waist," I instructed.

She wrapped her arms around me, and I surprised myself by squeezing one cold hand to reassure her. "Hang on tight, okay?"

She nodded and recited her address in my ear. I started the bike, and she jumped, her body sliding up against mine more naturally as her arms tightened around my waist. I pulled out of the parking lot and headed down the dark road.

* * *

Maddie

DESPITE MY FEAR, DESPITE THE FACT THAT IT WAS ONE IN THE morning, and I was bone tired and sore, and in a fog of disbelief that I had survived my ordeal, I was still delighted by the ride on Riley's bike.

Hell, delighted wasn't a strong enough word. Exhilarated, maybe.

He drove fast, too fast probably, and the wind was ice cold, but I was still strangely euphoric when he pulled up in front of my small house and cut the engine. Disappointment flickered through me. The night was over, and I would never see Riley again.

I should have been happy about that, but my euphoria faded, leaving me feeling cold and sick to my stomach. Riley was rough, Riley was dangerous, but he had also saved my life tonight, not to mention giving me the best orgasm of my life. I was horrified to realize I was close to tears at the thought of never seeing him again.

Get it together, Maddie, I scolded myself fiercely. *Riley isn't some white knight. He's a drug dealer who happens to have some morals. Don't go thinking there could be something more, you idiot.*

I climbed off the bike and was slightly surprised when Riley climbed off. I pulled out my shoes and purse before taking my hand. He led me down the sidewalk. I limped badly, and he kept the pace slow. We climbed the porch steps in silence. I took out my keys, but my hands suddenly shook so violently I couldn't guide the key into the lock. Riley took the keys from me and unlocked the front door. He swung it open and peered inside as he dropped my purse and shoes on the hallway floor.

It was completely dark in the hallway, so he couldn't have seen much, but he gave me a crooked smile. "Nice place."

I smiled tentatively in return before clearing my throat. "Uh, I – thank you, Riley. I know a simple thank you isn't enough, but please believe me when I say I'll never forget what you did for me tonight."

He stared silently at me as I bit back my urge to give him my cell number. What the hell would I say? *Hey, if you ever feel like fucking, give me a call?*

The man was a drug dealer, and I was a lawyer. No scenario in the world could make us work. Besides, I wanted a relationship, not a quick bang now and then.

Are you sure, Maddie? You had a relationship with Jordan, and look how well that turned out.

I pushed the thought out of my head as Riley stepped closer. His arm snaked around my waist, and I squeaked in surprise when he cupped my ass and squeezed. "You're right, you know. A thank you, even one as sweet as yours, isn't enough."

"Riley, I don't know what you want from me," I said.

"Yes, you do. Invite me in, Kitten. We have some unfinished business."

41

"N-no, we don't."

"We do." He dipped his head and pressed his mouth against my throat, flicking his tongue over my pounding pulse. "Normally, I'm not one to keep score, but I can't walk away knowing that you've only come once, and I've come twice."

I moaned as he said, "What do you say, Kitten? Invite me in, and I'll eat your sweet pussy until you've come so many times we both lose track."

"Oh my God," I moaned again. My pussy throbbed and ached, and Riley nipped at my earlobe before taking my mouth in a hard, possessive kiss.

I returned his kiss, pressing my body against his as our tongues tangled together. After a moment, he pulled back and cupped my face, rubbing his thumb across my swollen bottom lip.

"Do you want me to stay the night, Kitten?"

"Y-yes, I -"

"What the fuck? Get away from her!"

I jerked in surprise at Jordan's voice as Riley pushed me behind him and stared coldly at my fiancé. "Get lost, asshole. This doesn't concern you."

"Like hell it doesn't!" Jordan climbed the steps, and I stared at him in confusion as he ran a hand through his short blond hair. "What the fuck is going on, Madeleine? Who the hell is this dickhead?"

"Watch your mouth," Riley growled. Jordan stepped back and licked his lips as I stepped out from behind Riley.

He frowned and held his arm out, preventing me from moving toward Jordan. "Do you know this asshole, Kitten?"

"Yes, He's my, well, he's -"

I was suddenly at a loss for words. After what I'd walked in on tonight, there was no way that Jordan and I were getting married. Frankly, I was stunned to see him standing on my front porch.

"I'm her fiancé!" Jordan snapped.

Riley stiffened, and his arm dropped as he stepped away from me. I flinched at the odd look of betrayal in his eyes.

"Riley, it isn't -"

"Forget it. Have a nice life." He pushed past Jordan and stalked down the steps.

"Riley, wait!"

I hurried after him, grunting with frustration when Jordan grabbed my arm and hauled me to a stop.

"Riley, please listen!" I shouted as he climbed onto his bike. "He isn't -"

His bike roared to life, drowning out my frantic cry. I yanked my arm from Jordan's grip and glared at him as Riley tore down the street and out of my life forever.

"You fucking asshole!" I shouted before storming into my house. I slammed the door. A hard bite of satisfaction threaded through me when Jordan stuck his arm between the door and the frame, and he howled with pain when the door hit him just above the elbow.

He shoved the door open and stomped down the hallway after me. "What the hell was that, Madeleine? Who was that fucking guy, and why the hell did he have his tongue down your throat?"

I flipped the switch for the kitchen light and yanked open the fridge. I grabbed a bottle of water, twisted off the cap, and downed half before turning to face Jordan. He stared at me, his face a mask of anger and hurt. My temper flared. That he would have the audacity to even question me after what I'd seen tonight brought on a wave of anger so strong I was nearly blinded by it.

Unwisely, Jordan was still talking. "Where the hell have you been? I've been waiting for hours for you to come home.

After you left my place, I was worried about you. Really worried. I tried calling your cell phone, but it went straight to voicemail. I've been sitting in my car since eleven, just waiting for you, Madeleine."

I slammed my water bottle onto the counter, ignoring the water that surged from it to splash against my hand and gave Jordan a look of pure fury.

"First, my fucking name is Maddie, not Madeleine. We've been together four fucking years, Jordan, and I've asked you repeatedly to call me Maddie."

"You know I hate nicknames," he protested. "Besides, Maddie doesn't suit you, you're not -"

"Second, you have no right to question me about anything after what you've done. Why the fuck are you even here?" I snarled. "If you want to get your ring back, I suggest you check somewhere along Route 47. I threw it out the fucking car window."

"You bitch! Do you know how much that ring cost?" He stared at me in disbelief, and I laughed in his face.

"What's wrong, Jordie?" I sneered. "Planning on asking your new lover to marry you? Just ask Mommy and Daddy to buy you another ring. I'm sure they'll happily help out their baby boy."

His face blanched, and I smiled triumphantly. "I guess I'm not the only one who didn't know you were gay, huh?"

"I'm not gay!" he shouted. "I just experiment sometimes, and if you hadn't run off in a huff, I would have told you that."

"Bullshit!" I shouted back. "At least have the guts to admit the truth to yourself!"

"I'm not gay!" he repeated vehemently.

I grabbed my cell phone from the counter and scrolled through my contacts.

"What are you doing?"

"Calling Kurt. The three of us have been friends for years. I'm betting he'll tell me exactly how long you two have been fucking behind my back. What do you think he'll say when he finds out that you're not gay, you're just experimenting with him? Hmm?"

His face paled even further, and he shook his head. "Don't call him, Madel – Maddie. Please."

I paused with my finger over the call button. "Why not?"

"Because I – I love him." His entire body slumped, and he stared at the floor between his feet. "I'm sorry. I didn't mean to hurt you. It's just… if my parents find out I'm gay, they'll cut me off, Madeleine. You know I need that money to live."

"So, you strung me along for four years to keep your trust fund?" I asked.

He winced. "It's not like that, Madeleine. I care for you a great deal. I wanted to make you happy. You have to believe me."

"You could have just told me the truth. You wanted me to be happy?" My anger was tinged with sorrow now. "All I wanted was for *you* to be happy. If being with Kurt is what you want, you should have been honest with me. You made me believe that I – I was terrible in bed. I thought if only I could lose a little more weight or try a little harder in bed, you'd finally want me and love me the way I loved you. I've wasted four years of my life with you. Don't you get that?"

"I didn't mean to hurt you," he repeated. "You have to believe me."

"I don't have to believe a fucking word from your lying mouth. Get out, Jordan."

"Maddie, please, don't – are you going to tell my parents?"

I barked harsh laughter as a wave of exhaustion washed over me. "Get the fuck out, Jordan."

"Please don't tell them. Please, I can't -"

"Get out!" I shouted. "Get the fuck out of my house right now, or I swear I'll call the fucking cops!"

He held up his hands and backed out of the kitchen. I followed him down the hallway, and he stood on the porch and gave me a final pleading look. "I'm so sorry. Please don't tell my parents."

I stared at him, finally seeing for the first time the real Jordan. A frightened little boy who would forever hide his true self to appease his parents and keep the money that was so important to him.

A wave of pity washed over me. "I'm not going to tell them, Jordan."

"Thank you, Madeleine. I can't -"

I shut the door in his face.

CHAPTER 4

Three months later

Maddie

"So the guy forced you to give him a blow job in front of a roomful of bikers?" Roman stared over his cup of coffee at me.

I shook my head impatiently. "No. I told you, Roman, I wanted to do it."

"Jesus." Roman ran his hand through his hair. "I leave for four months to do a med tour in Africa and return to find my sweet little Maddie has turned into a sexy slut."

I blushed and sipped at my coffee. "I'm not a – a sexy slut. It was just a one-time thing."

Roman grinned at me. "You had sex with some random biker in a bar bathroom and then gave him a blowjob in front of a bunch of other bikers – that gives you a lifetime membership into the slut club. From one slut to another - welcome aboard, baby."

He held his fist out, and I rolled my eyes before bumping my fist against his. "Thanks."

His smile faded, and he gave me a somber look. "I'm sorry about Jordan, sweetie."

"Did you know?"

"Why would I? You believe all gay men have the gaydar that alerts them to other gays in the vicinity, huh?"

"Don't you?"

He grinned boyishly. "Some of us are better than others when it comes to gaydar."

"Did you know?" I persisted.

"I suspected. Mostly because I caught him staring at my junk a few times over the years." He reached out and took my hand. "I'm sorry, Mads. I should have told you."

"It wasn't your responsibility to tell me, honey. Besides, I wouldn't have believed you anyway. I was so deep in denial you might as well have called me Cleopatra."

He smiled before drinking more coffee. "So, what about this hot biker of yours? What did you say his name was again?"

"Riley. And he's not my hot biker. I haven't seen him since that night. Jordan showed up on my doorstep after Riley drove me home. He announced he was my fiancé, and Riley left."

"Well, that's a good thing, right?" Roman said. "If this guy is as dangerous as you say he is, if he's part of a gang running drugs, then you can't have anything to do with him. You know that, Mads."

"I know." I stared blankly into my coffee cup.

"Maddie? You don't want to see him again, do you?"

"I don't know. Maybe. For the first time in my life, I felt like a woman. Riley wanted me and made me feel things I never knew I was capable of. Jordan never made me orgasm the way Riley did."

"That's because Jordan likes to ride cock," Roman said. "Riley didn't do anything special, sweetheart. I guarantee you can find a nice, straight guy who will rock your world like this biker did."

"Maybe," I said moodily.

"You're not considering trying to find him, are you?"

"How would I? I don't even know his last name." I cleared my throat and stared at my coffee cup again. Roman would kill me if he knew that a month ago, I drove back to the bar. I parked at the far end of the parking lot, scanning the bikes that were lined up neatly and trying to decide if any of them looked familiar. Ultimately, I had driven away, unsure if Riley was there and too scared to go in to look for him. What if he wasn't there? What if it was Jenkins or Frank who greeted me?

"Mads, you need to stay away from him."

"I know," I said. "I'm not going to try to find him. Besides, if he wanted to see me again, he knows where I live. He hasn't shown up, so…"

I took a sip of coffee as Roman studied me carefully. "It's better this way, sweetheart."

"Yeah, I know." I needed to change the subject before I made a fool of myself and started crying over the fact that a biker I had banged once in a dirty bathroom hadn't tried to contact me. "How was the med tour?"

"It was amazing. It was hot, and the work was difficult but unbelievably rewarding. The people there are so," he paused, "incredible, I guess is the word. They face such hardships in their lives, but they never give up. I treated a child who was brought in with malaria. She was only about four, and we almost lost her a few times, but she just kept fighting back. I found out later that her mother had lost three other children to malaria."

"Oh, Roman." I gave him a sympathetic look, and he shook his head.

"It was good, Mads. The girl survived, and her mother took her home. That's what I went there for – to help, you know?"

"I know." I squeezed his hand. "When do you start back at the hospital?"

"Next week. It will be weird to work in a hospital again instead of hiking through villages with my medical bag."

I smiled a little. Roman and I had grown up together, and he was my best friend. While he slaved away in med school, I slogged through university and studied for the bar exam. We always made time for each other, even rooming together for a few brief years, and I loved him enormously. I had missed him for the last four months. I stood and hugged him impulsively.

"What's that for?" He patted my back as I kissed his rough cheek.

"I love you, Roman. I'm so glad you're home."

"I love you too, Mads."

* * *

I RUBBED MY ACHING BACK AS I DROPPED MY BRIEFCASE AT MY feet and unlocked my front door. It had been a long day in court. Despite it being Friday, I'd worked late at the office, trying to catch up on my never-ending caseload. It was close to nine, and I was tired and hungry. As I opened the door, a low voice spoke to my left.

"Working late, Kitten?"

I bit back my scream and whirled around, squinting into the darkness as a figure emerged from the far end of the porch.

"Riley?"

"Hello, Kitten. You miss me?"

I studied him in the dim light of the moon. His face was pale, and he staggered on his feet as he raised a bottle to his lips and drank deeply.

"What are you doing here?"

He shrugged and winced before taking another drink. "I was in the neighbourhood and thought I'd drop by."

"How did you get here?"

"My bike."

I studied the street. No bike was parked there, and I gave him a questioning look as he moved closer.

"I parked it between your house and your neighbour's house." He stumbled forward another step.

"Were you drinking and driving?"

He snorted laughter and then winced again. "No, Kitten. I didn't start drinking until I got to your place. I've been waiting a while for you."

He perused me slowly, and I felt a tingle of lust when he studied my breasts. "You look fucking hot in that business suit, by the way."

He stood in front of me, weaving unsteadily. I took a nervous step back.

"You afraid of me?" he asked with something that almost sounded like hurt in his voice.

"No. I'm just surprised to see you."

"I'm like a bad penny. I always turn up." He laughed again before hunching over and coughing.

"What's wrong?" I asked in alarm as his tanned face went the fresh white of mountain snow.

"Nothing. This was a mistake."

He started to leave, and I reached for him instinctively. "No, Riley, don't go."

I touched his arm, my hand stroking the soft leather of his jacket. He turned toward me, dropping the bottle to the porch floor. I squeaked in alarm when he staggered forward and collapsed against me, shoving me into the door.

"Riley!" I slipped my hands around his waist to try to steady him and stiffened at the wetness that coated my right hand. I pulled my hand free and studied the liquid dripping from my fingers. "Is this – is this blood?"

"Yeah. Got into a bit of a mess and got myself fucking shot," he slurred.

"Oh my God!" I reached behind me and pushed the door open wide, staggering under Riley's weight as I backed into the house. "You need to go to the hospital."

His hand took mine in a fierce grip as I flicked on the light switch and shoved his jacket from his broad shoulders. I moaned at the bright red blood that coated his left side and reached for my cell phone in my pocket.

He cupped my face. "No! If you take me to the hospital, I'll spend the rest of my life in prison, Maddie. Do you hear me?"

"Riley," I said, "you're bleeding badly. You need surgery, you probably need a blood transfusion and -"

"No!" he repeated. "I can't go to the hospital. Please, Maddie, I need to lie down for a bit, okay? I need a safe place to rest, and when I feel better, I'll leave. Okay?"

"Riley, I don't -"

"Please," he pleaded. "Help me, Maddie."

"Can you walk to my bedroom?"

He nodded, and I slipped my arm around his hips and helped him stagger to my room.

"Put some towels on the bed," he grunted.

"Riley, just lie down. It doesn't matter."

"No." He shook his head wearily. "I'm not wrecking your shit. Get some towels."

I left him propped against the wall and hurried into the hallway, grabbing a stack of towels from the closet before returning and piling them on the bed. He sat down carefully, and I pulled off his boots before helping him lie back against the towels. His face was horrifyingly white, and his large body quaked and shivered as he stared up at me with haunted eyes.

"Don't take me to the hospital, Maddie. Promise me."

"I promise."

"Good, good." He stared blearily around the room. "This is nice, real nice. I like -"

His eyes rolled up in his head, and he passed out cold. I pressed a towel against the bleeding wound. Even unconscious, it made him groan. I bit my lip before reaching for my cell phone.

* * *

"Steady!" Roman said sharply. "Don't pass out on me, Mads."

"I won't." I was standing on a stool beside my bed. The bedroom light was on, the table lamp from the living room had been moved to my dresser - the lamp shade removed to provide Roman with more light - and I shone a large flashlight onto Riley.

"Take some deep breaths." Roman studied the wound on Riley's side.

"I'm fine," I repeated. "How bad is it?"

He wiped away the blood and, with a grunt of effort, heaved the unconscious Riley onto his uninjured side. "It could have been a lot worse. The bullet went clean through him, although I think it probably chipped a rib or two on its way through."

"But you can help him, right?"

He cleaned Riley's back with disinfectant before reaching into the bag at his feet and pulling out a suturing kit. "I can suture him up, stop the bleeding, and prescribe some antibiotics, but he really should be at the hospital. He needs IV fluids and a blood transfusion. He's lost a lot of fucking blood, Mads."

"I can't take him to the hospital," I said. "I promised him I wouldn't."

"Jesus," Roman swore softly as he sutured the wound in Riley's back with small, neat stitches. "What the fuck have you got yourself into, sweetheart?"

"He saved my life, Roman. I owe him."

"I know." He finished suturing the wound and moved Riley onto his back before cleaning the wound on his front. He continued to suture, biting his lip with concentration as he worked.

When he was finished, he bandaged Riley's side and helped me gather the bloody towels. I stuffed them into a garbage bag as Roman cut off the rest of Riley's shirt. I sucked in my breath as Roman whistled.

"Jesus, this guy's abs are amazing."

I studied Riley's upper body. He had never once taken off his shirt the night in the bar, and this was the first time I'd gotten a good look at him. His upper body had tattoos scattered across it, although not as many as I would have suspected, and Roman was right. Riley did have an amazing body.

"Help me take off his pants," Roman said. I tugged off his socks as Roman unbuckled Riley's belt. Working together, we eased his blood-soaked jeans and underwear down his legs.

"Holy fucking shit! This guy has a big dick."

I smacked him on the arm. "Now is not the time."

He studied Riley's body as I threw his clothes into the garbage bag.

"Seriously, girl, I'm beginning to see why you banged him

that night."

"He's not that big," I said. "Is he?"

"Are you kidding me?" Roman asked. "Sweetheart, I'll cut you some slack because the only dick you've seen before this guy's was Jordan's, but unless Jordan is built like a goddamn elephant, this guy's dick is fucking epic. I can't believe you fucked him. I love cock, but I would have run screaming from this monster."

"I didn't exactly see it before he... you know..."

"Fucked the bejesus out of you?"

"Yeah. It hurt a little," I admitted.

"I bet it fucking did. Could you take all of him?"

"Yes. I mean, I think so. It felt like I did – hell, it felt like he was splitting me in two – but, uh, maybe I didn't." I was suddenly ridiculously nervous that I had disappointed Riley when we were fucking.

"Christ." Roman's eyes lit up. "We should measure it."

"Roman - focus! We are not measuring it!" I said. "He's been shot, remember?"

"Right." Roman pulled the covers up to Riley's waist as I gave him a nervous look.

"Is he going to die?"

"I don't think so. There's always the possibility, especially with this much blood loss, but his pulse is strong, and his respiration is normal."

"Thank God," I breathed as we left the bedroom.

"Thank you, honey. Really." I hugged Roman and kissed his cheek as he returned my hug. "I'm sorry to call you so late. Go home and get some sleep, okay?"

"Nope." He shook his head. "I'm not leaving you alone with him."

"It'll be fine. Riley won't hurt me. Besides, he's too weak to do anything."

"I'm still not leaving you alone with him. What if the

people who shot him followed him to your place? Have you thought of that?" Roman asked.

I glanced uneasily at my front door. I hadn't considered that possibility.

"You shouldn't be alone," Roman said. "I'll stay the night. He's stable right now, but that could change. Do you want him dying on you in the middle of the night?"

"God, no." I shuddered before giving Roman a weak smile. "I'll make up the guest room. Thank you, honey."

"You're welcome. Maybe you should stay in the guest room with me."

"I can't. He might wake up in the night and need me."

"He's not going to wake up. I gave him a shot of pain relief, and that, combined with the alcohol, will keep him out for the night."

"Should you have given him that?" I asked worriedly.

Roman shrugged. "It's not a great idea, but I also didn't want him screaming and thrashing around in pain in the middle of the night and ripping open his sutures."

"I'll feel better if I stay in my room, just in case he does wake up." I double-checked my front door's lock before turning off the lights and following Roman to the guest room.

CHAPTER 5

Riley

I climbed the stairs slowly, dread filling my body as I watched the bedroom door grow closer. I was dreaming, the same dream that had plagued me off and on for the last three years. Although I wanted to stop - I knew what was beyond that door - my feet propelled me helplessly forward.

I almost hadn't gone over when Ma called, worried about the noise she could hear upstairs. A creaking, she said. She was afraid it was rats in the walls again, and the real fear in her voice was what finally got my ass off the couch and headed over to my childhood home.

I moaned and tried to stop my dream self from reaching out to turn the doorknob. My body betrayed me, and my hand grasped the knob and turned. The door opened with a soft squeal, and I swallowed down the sobbing scream that wanted to burst from my throat when I saw her feet.

She was barefoot - she had always hated wearing shoes - and her feet swung back and forth in the heavy, cold wind that blew in from the open window.

I tried to back away, tried not to look up at her swollen and black face, and made another harsh, sobbing moan. I didn't want to see her again. I would go crazy if I did. I tried to turn and run as a burning pain shot through my side.

"Andrea," I whispered her name as more pain flooded through me. "No, please God, no."

The pain and the sorrow filled me up. I couldn't move, couldn't breathe, and I really was going to go crazy. I would end up just like her, and there wouldn't be a single person to mourn my death. I wouldn't –

"Riley, it's okay. Stop moving, honey."

Her warm and familiar voice spoke in my ear. I reached out for her like a man drowning. Her hand clasped mine, our fingers linking as I fought to swim out of the darkness surrounding me.

"Shh, honey. You're okay. It was just a dream. Go to sleep."

I wanted to see her, wanted to look into those dark eyes that I hadn't been able to stop thinking about for three long goddamn months, but I was so fucking tired. My side throbbed and burned with a pain that made me sick to my stomach.

Her cool hand stroked my face, and her mouth pressed against my ear. "Go to sleep, Riley. You're safe here."

I squeezed her hand and drifted into the black.

* * *

HER HAND WAS ON MINE AGAIN, WITH HER FINGERS PRESSING against my pulse. I opened my eyes with effort, blinking at the bright light and staring at the unfamiliar ceiling. My eyes wanted to close again. I was tired and weirdly weak. Instead, I rasped, "Hello, Kitten."

I turned my head to smile at her, the smile changing to a

grimace at the sight of the large, dark-haired man sitting next to me on the bed.

"Hello yourself, pussy cat."

Adrenaline pumped through me and lit up my tired body. Ignoring the pain in my side, I reached up with my other hand and wrapped my fingers around the man's throat. I squeezed tightly as the man's eyes widened. He dropped my wrist and clawed at my hand around his throat.

"Where is she? What have you done to her?" I squeezed again, and the man made a gagging sound.

"Riley, no! Let go!" Maddie kneeled on the bed beside me. She yanked at my arm. "Let him go right now!"

I released the man, my arm falling to the bed with a weary thud as I stared at Maddie. Her long dark hair was loose, and its softness brushed against my bare shoulder as she stared worriedly at the man.

He staggered to his feet, coughing and gagging as he rubbed at his throat.

"Roman! Honey, are you okay?"

A surge of jealousy went through me. The prick wasn't her fiancé, so who the fuck was he?

"Just fine," the man said hoarsely before giving me a wary look. "Fuck, he's strong."

"Don't fucking touch me again," I growled.

"Riley, stop it! He saved your life." Maddie frowned at me before reaching out to touch Roman's face. "Are you sure you're okay?"

Another surge of jealousy went through me, and I scowled at the man as he nodded.

"Yes, I'm fine, Mads."

"Good." She breathed a sigh of relief before staring down at me. "Riley, how do you feel?"

"Like I've been shot."

She smiled at my pathetic joke and touched my shoulder. "Do you think you could drink some water?"

I nodded. My throat was as dry and dusty as a desert. I struggled to sit up, and pain shot through me. I was helpless to stop the groan from escaping my lips.

"Don't do that," Maddie said in alarm as I fell back against the pillows, panting harshly.

"You can't move, not yet, okay?" She smiled her thanks to Roman when he brought her a glass of water with a straw in it. "Take small sips."

I sipped at the water, grunting angrily when she pulled it away. She patted my shoulder. "You can't have too much at once."

"How long have I been out?" I asked as Roman pressed a stethoscope to my chest.

"Day and a half." She smiled at me, and I studied her until she blushed. "What?"

"Thanks for saving my life."

"I didn't. Roman did."

I stared at the man listening to my heart. "You a doctor?"

"Luckily for you, yes." Roman smiled at Maddie. "Mads, can you warm up some water? I don't need it boiling, just warm. I'm going to clean Riley's wound."

"Of course."

She slid off the bed. My gaze dropped to her ass automatically as she walked out of the bedroom.

"Is she in danger?" Roman asked.

"What?" I frowned at Roman.

"Is Mads in danger?" He spoke slowly. "The people who shot you – are they going to come after you and now her as well?"

"No."

"Are you sure?"

I glared at him. "Yes, I'm fucking sure."

He didn't cringe away from my angry glower, and I felt a tinge of respect for the man. "Are you fucking her?"

"Excuse me?" His hands, peeling back the bandage on my side, paused.

"Are you fucking Maddie?"

She had a fiancé but hell, that hadn't stopped her from fucking me.

"Not that it's any of your business, but no," he said. "We're friends, nothing more. Hold still."

"You seem like you're more than friends."

He grinned. "Trust me, handsome, I'm more interested in fucking you than her."

A dull blush crossed my face, and Roman laughed. "Aww, I've embarrassed the big bad biker. I take it there aren't a lot of gay men in your circle of friends."

I shrugged and then hissed out a breath when he peeled the bandage from my side. I stared at the neatly sutured gash. "Thanks for saving my life."

"You're welcome." He examined my side carefully, and I grunted when he probed at it with his fingertips.

"Sorry," he said cheerfully. "I bet it's fucking sore, huh?"

"Yeah."

"You got lucky. The bullet went right through. You'll have to take antibiotics for another week, but it should heal nicely."

He reached into a bag on the floor and pulled out a syringe and liquid filled bottle.

"What is that?" I asked.

"Pain relief."

"I don't want it."

"Don't be a hero, pussy cat," he said. "You need this - trust me."

"I don't need it," I insisted as Maddie entered the room carrying a large bowl.

"Don't need what?" She placed the bowl of water on the nightstand and handed Roman a cloth.

"Never mind," I said.

"Your biker babe here doesn't want his pain relief." Roman carefully cleaned my side.

Maddie frowned at me. "Riley, you need to take it."

"I'm fine."

I didn't want my senses dulled around Maddie. I only drank occasionally, and despite what I did for a living, I never actually used drugs. Who the fuck knew what I would confess to her if I were high on meds.

"You're not fine. Give him the meds, Roman."

"Don't, Roman," I said. "You don't get to speak for me, Maddie."

"When you're lying in my bed helpless as a baby, yes, I do."

"Fine, I'll leave."

I tried to sit up and groaned harshly when pain speared through my side. I bit my lip as sweat broke out on my forehead. I was already starting to feel nauseous from the pain, and a dismaying weakness was settling into my limbs.

Maddie pushed gently on my chest, and I collapsed against the pillows. I glared at her when she gave me a smug smile. "You're taking the meds, Riley."

"I don't need -"

"Are you afraid of needles?" Roman asked. "Maybe you should hold his hand, Mads."

"Shut up. I'm not afraid of needles," I snapped, but it was too late. Maddie had already moved around to the opposite side of the bed and climbed onto it. She sat cross-legged beside me and picked up my hand.

"Just look at me, Riley."

"I'm not afraid of needles," I said through gritted teeth.

Jesus, but it was bugging me that she thought I was afraid of something stupid like a needle.

"It's fine if you are." She gave me another smug little smile, and I squeezed her hand before deliberately dropping my gaze to her tits. She wore a loose t-shirt that did a disappointingly good job of hiding them, but I let my eyes wander over her chest anyway.

I didn't flinch when I felt the sharp sting of the needle. I gave her my own smug smile when I finally raised my gaze to her suddenly flushed face. "Have you missed me, Kitten?"

"I… I still have your jacket," she said.

"I've missed you. I've especially missed your sweet little pussy."

"Jesus, dude. I'm right in the room," Roman said.

"Maybe you should leave then," I said.

"Maybe you should be a bit more respectful to Maddie."

"You going to make me, tough guy?"

He rolled his eyes. "Really? You're lying in bed weak as a fucking kitten, and I have shit in this bag that could kill you with a single dose."

"Is that a threat?" I growled.

"Oh, for goodness sake," Maddie said, "Roman, stop threatening to kill Riley."

I grinned arrogantly, and Maddie smacked me lightly on the leg. "And Roman's right – be more respectful, or I'll dump you in the street."

I wanted to reply with a smartass comment, but a weird numbness coursed through my limbs, and my eyelids were incredibly heavy.

"What the fuck did you give me?" I slurred.

"I told you - something to help with the pain." Roman grinned, and I snarled weakly at him as I struggled to keep my eyes open.

"Don't fight it," he advised. "You need to sleep."

I could feel the bright edge of panic biting at the numbness. I didn't want to sleep. With sleep came the nightmares. Over the years, I had gotten used to getting by on as little sleep as possible.

"Maddie," I mumbled, and with great effort, tried to squeeze her hand.

"You're fine, Riley," she said, stroking my forearm. "Go to sleep. Everything's fine."

* * *

Maddie

I WATCHED AS RILEY'S EYES CLOSED AND HIS BODY SLUMPED against the bed.

"He's not exactly Prince Charming, is he?" Roman said.

"I told you he was rough around the edges."

"Rough around the edges? Sweetheart, the man is dangerous."

"No, he isn't." I defended him vigorously, even though I wasn't entirely sure he wasn't dangerous.

"Don't let an amazing body and a giant dick cloud your judgement, Mads."

"I'm not. Riley isn't dangerous."

Roman glanced at his watch. "My shift at the hospital starts in an hour."

"Go. I'll be fine."

"I'm not sure I should leave you alone with him."

"He's not going to hurt me, Roman. If he wanted to hurt me, he would have that night at the bar. He saved me, remember?"

"I remember," Roman replied.

"Do I need to give him more pain meds?"

"No. The stuff I gave him will last twenty-four hours. I'll be back tomorrow to give him another shot, okay?"

"Okay."

"In the meantime, if you need anything, just text me. The hospital is only fifteen minutes away."

"I'll be fine. Stop worrying."

He hesitated. "I asked Riley if you were in danger from the people who shot him, and he said no."

"Thanks, honey."

"Do you believe him?"

"Yes. He wouldn't deliberately put me in danger."

"Mads, you can't possibly know that. You hardly know this guy."

"I know enough," I said. "Go, honey. You don't want to be late."

* * *

I HEARD HIS CRIES FROM MY OFFICE DOWNSTAIRS. I RAN UP THE stairs and into my bedroom. My heart thudded erratically at the pain and fear in his voice, and I climbed onto the bed.

"Riley, honey, it's okay. Shh, it's okay," I whispered into his ear.

"Andrea?" he moaned. "Oh please, no, Andrea."

Every hair on my body stood up at the pure terror in his voice. He was beginning to thrash on the bed. Afraid he would rip the stitches, I pressed my body up against his uninjured side and wrapped my arm around him.

"Wake up, Riley. Please wake up. Come on, open your eyes."

After what seemed like an eternity, his eyelids fluttered open, and he gave me a dazed look of incomprehension. "Maddie?"

"Yeah, it's me. You're okay. You were having a bad dream."

He shuddered, and I stroked his arm and kissed his forehead. "You're fine. Take a few deep breaths."

"Fine," he repeated shakily.

"That's right." I smiled at him and then squeaked in surprise when he lifted his head and pressed his mouth against mine. He kissed me hungrily, and my arm tightened around him. He groaned in pain, and I pushed away from him.

"Riley! I'm sorry. Are you okay?"

"Fine, Kitten. Come back here." He tried to grin cockily at me, but there was a haunted look in his eyes, and his body was still shivering.

"No, you need rest to heal properly."

"I need you to heal properly."

"Flattering but inaccurate." I stroked his bare chest as he stared silently at me. "How do you feel?"

"Fine. What time is it?"

He didn't look fine. He looked pale and afraid. I squeezed his shoulder. "Just before five. Do you want something to eat?"

"I have to piss."

"Roman brought a urinal from the hospital."

He shook his head as I showed him the plastic container. "I am not pissing into that."

"Riley, getting up probably isn't a -"

"I don't care. Help me sit up, Maddie, or I'll hold it until my fucking bladder explodes."

"You're being an idiot, you know that, right?" I said.

"Yes. Help me up."

I pulled the covers back and studiously avoided looking at his dick. I slid my hands behind his back, braced my legs and pulled. He groaned as he sat up and one hand pressed against his side. He cursed under his breath as I helped him swing his legs over the side of the bed.

"Change your mind?" I asked.

He shook his head. "Just give me a minute."

I waited patiently as he sat with his head bowed. After a few moments, he nodded to me. "Ready."

"On three," I said. I counted to three and heaved him to his feet. He weaved unsteadily for a moment, and I slid my arm around his waist.

"Riley, I wish you would just -"

"I'm fine, Maddie," he said. "Let's go."

Moving slowly, we shuffled to the bathroom connected to my bedroom. I helped him into the room and then, at his insistence, stepped back into the bedroom and closed the door. I waited until I heard the toilet flush before opening the door. He was staring at himself in the mirror and rubbed his hand over his face.

"I could use a shower."

"You can't get your wound wet," I said.

He grimaced with disgust as I reached into the medicine cabinet and pulled out a new toothbrush. "Here."

"Thanks." He glanced at the shower. "I'll be quick."

"No," I said. "Tomorrow."

"You could give me a sponge bath," he said.

"I'm not a nurse."

"I know. You're a fancy lawyer."

"Not that fancy." I glanced at my t-shirt and yoga pants as Riley gave me a hopeful look.

"I stink, Kitten."

"Yeah, you do."

He waited, and I couldn't help but give in. "Wait here. I'll be right back."

He was finishing brushing his teeth when I returned with an armful of towels and a chair from the kitchen. I set it in front of the vanity and placed towels on the floor. I helped him to sit down before putting a folded towel across the front of the counter.

"Can you lean back?"

Wincing a little, he leaned back and rested his neck against the towel with his head hanging over the sink basin.

"Good." I reached for the shampoo and used a cup to soak his short hair with water. As I poured some shampoo on his head and massaged his scalp, he groaned loudly.

"I'm sorry. Is it too painful?"

"No, it feels really good."

I rubbed his head as he closed his eyes. "Where's your fruitcake friend?"

My hands stilled in his hair, and he opened his eyes, recoiling a little at the look of fury on my face.

"One, that *fruitcake* saved your life and two, his name is Roman, and he's my best friend. I will not tolerate any gay bashing, and if you're a goddamn homophobe, this ends now. You can get dressed and leave my house. Do you hear me?"

"I'm sorry."

I relaxed a little at the sincerity in his voice and started to scrub his scalp again.

"I'm not a homophobe, Maddie. I swear."

"Good."

I rinsed his hair and helped him to straighten before wetting his upper body and using a washcloth and soap to scrub the dirt and blood from his skin.

I worked silently, trying to ignore the ridiculous tendrils of lust starting in my belly. He cleared his throat. "Where is Roman?"

"He had a shift at the hospital. He'll be back tomorrow to check on you and give you more pain meds."

"I don't want them," he said immediately as I pressed a towel against the bandage on his wound.

"Hold this."

He rested his hand against the towel, and I rinsed his upper body clean.

"Call him and tell him I don't need them."

"I won't. You do need them."

"I don't," he insisted.

I shook my head as I squatted and washed his lower legs. "You do. You don't have to be a tough guy around me, Riley."

He didn't reply and I scrubbed at his upper thighs. "Seriously. You were shot, and it must be incredibly painful. Why be in pain if you don't have to be? It's one thing to try to -"

My breath caught in my throat. Riley's cock had stiffened, and I swallowed down my urge to lean forward and take it into my mouth.

"Behave yourself," I admonished as I rinsed his legs clean.

"I can't help it," he said.

"You can."

I poured water on his crotch and, taking a deep breath, rubbed my hands with soap before gently grasping his dick. He moaned, and I bit my lip as I stroked him.

"That feels really fucking good, Kitten," he said hoarsely.

"I'm not doing this to make you feel good. I'm bathing you, nothing more."

"No? So why aren't you using the washcloth to clean my dick?"

I glanced up, my face burning, and swallowed heavily at the look of desire on Riley's face.

"Why don't you take off those damn pants and climb on, Maddie. I know what you need," he whispered.

My hand tightened around his cock. He groaned before reaching out and cupping the back of my head. "I want to fuck you again, Kitten."

I was tempted.

Fuck was I tempted.

I shook my head to dislodge his hand and let go of his dick. "You've been injured."

"That's never stopped me from fucking before."

"You've been shot before?" I reached for the cup and, my hands trembling noticeably, rinsed his crotch.

"No, but I have very good pain tolerance. Besides, it'll be worth it to feel your tight little pussy riding my dick again."

As he stared at me, I dried him with the towel, perhaps more roughly than I intended.

"I can't, Riley."

"Because of your dickhead fiancé?" he asked.

I twitched in surprise. It had been three months since I'd spoken to Jordan, but I'd spent more than my fair share of time rehashing our four-year relationship in my head. Of course, I hadn't thought of him once since Riley showed up on my doorstep wounded and bleeding.

It wasn't that I wanted Jordan back, but I had spent a lot of time obsessing over my failure at having a normal relationship. What was wrong with me that I couldn't see what was so obviously right in front of my face?

Maybe he wasn't gay before you. Maybe having to sleep with you turned him gay, my inner voice whispered.

I knew that thought was ridiculous, but it didn't stop it from creeping into my head daily. At least, that was until Riley had staggered back into my life.

"Maddie?"

"He's not my fiancé anymore."

"Because you fucked me?"

"No," I said. "Here, you need to go back to bed. You're pale, and you need more sleep."

"I'm fine." He winced as I helped him to his feet. I slipped my arm around his waist, being careful not to touch his bandaged side.

"Yes, I know," I said a bit irritably. "But you're still going back to bed."

I helped him back to the bed and tucked the covers around him. "I'll bring you some soup, okay?"

"I'm not hungry."

"Riley, you need to eat."

"I can't, not now."

I studied him. He suddenly looked exhausted and sick, and I brushed my hand against his forehead, searching for a fever. He was cool to the touch, and I squeezed his shoulder as he stared up at me.

"Get some sleep, Riley."

A boyish look of fear crossed his face for a split second. "I don't want to."

He yawned hugely and shook his head to clear it as his eyelids drifted shut. "I don't want to, Maddie. Please don't make me."

"I don't think you have much choice," I said.

"I don't – I can't stand the nightmares," he muttered.

Goosebumps broke out on my skin at the terror in his voice.

"What nightmares, honey?" I leaned over him and stroked his cheek.

"Andrea," he sighed as his eyes closed again.

When I straightened, his eyes popped open, and he stared blearily at me as he groped for my hand. "Please don't leave me, Maddie."

"I won't." I pressed my lips against his forehead before climbing into the bed beside him and wrapping my arm around his upper chest. "Go to sleep, Riley. I'm right here."

CHAPTER 6

Riley

Her scent surrounded me, and I breathed deeply, a smile crossing my lips. She was all soft curves and warmth against my body. I opened my eyes and carefully turned my head. It was early morning, and I studied her face in the soft light that filtered through the blinds.

Fuck, she was gorgeous. Everything about her just about set me on fire, and I touched her soft hair before tracing my fingers across her pale cheek. The pain in my side was worse this morning but the tiredness was gone. For the first time in days, I had slept well.

My eyes widened. I had slept well last night. I had slept all night and hadn't been jerked awake, sweating and afraid, by a single nightmare. That hadn't happened since the day I found Andrea.

It was the drugs, I decided. The drugs had knocked me out and kept the nightmares at bay.

Are you sure? You had a nightmare earlier. Maybe it isn't the drugs but the woman lying next to you.

I snorted softly. Maddie might make my dick stand at attention every time I goddamn looked at her, but I barely knew her. I wasn't about to get all fucking sentimental about her just because I shared her bed and didn't have a nightmare. It was a coincidence, nothing more.

Whatever, asshole.

I blocked out my inner voice and cupped her breast through her shirt. She was wearing a bra, and I scowled in irritation as I squeezed lightly. She moaned in her sleep, a ridiculously sweet sound, and I squeezed her breast again as she stirred in the bed.

I tried to shift on my side, and pain shot through me. I groaned, and her eyes opened. She sat up straight, knocking my hand away. "Riley? What's wrong?"

"Nothing," I said. I reached out and cupped her breast, and she stared blankly at my hand.

"What are you doing?"

"What's it look like I'm doing, Kitten?"

She sighed and took my hand, pushing it back to the bed. "You have a one-track mind."

"I really do," I agreed.

She slid out of bed and patted nervously at her hair. "I'll make us some breakfast. Do you like pancakes?"

"I do." I struggled to sit up and she hurried around to my side of the bed and helped me into a sitting position.

"How do you feel?"

"Tired and weak." I blinked in surprise. Why the hell had I told her that?

She gave me a sympathetic look. "It doesn't help that you haven't eaten in a couple of days. I'll help you to the bathroom and start breakfast, okay?"

I nodded and tried not to flinch when she helped me to stand.

* * *

"How's the patient?"

Roman stepped into the bedroom and gave me a cheerful smile as Maddie crossed the room and kissed him on the cheek. I swallowed down my jealousy. It was fucking ridiculous to be jealous of Maddie kissing Roman, and I nodded tersely. "Better."

"He's in a lot of pain," Maddie said.

"I'm *fine*," I muttered.

"He isn't. He's just trying to be tough."

"Well, tough guy, let's take a look at your gunshot wound," Roman said.

Maddie took the tray off the bed as Roman gave her a hopeful look. "You made pancakes for him? I don't suppose there are any left?"

She grinned at him. "I made extra for you, honey."

"Mads, if I didn't love dick so much, I'd fucking marry you."

"That's so sweet," she said dryly as she set the tray on the dresser.

Roman peeled back the bandage. I made myself stay perfectly still as he probed at the wound with warm fingers.

"You okay?" Maddie climbed onto the bed beside me, and I didn't object when she took my hand.

"Yeah, I don't need the drugs today," I lied.

"Yes, you do," Roman said. "No need to be a hero, remember?"

He placed a fresh bandage on my side and taped it down. "It's looking good, no sign of an infection, and it's starting to heal. You'll be back on your feet in no time."

"Good," I growled before looking Maddie up and down.

She flushed as my gaze lingered on her hips.

"No sex," Roman said.

"Roman!" Maddie's flush deepened, and Roman laughed.

"Oh please, I recognize an 'I want to fuck you' look when I see one."

He tapped me on the chest. "I mean it, tough guy. You'll rip your sutures."

"Not if she rides me," I said.

Roman cocked his head. "Well, maybe if she did all the work and you didn't move. But what fun would that be?

"For heaven's sake," Maddie said. "I'm not riding anyone. Enough – both of you."

She tugged her hand free and slid off the bed. Roman pulled a syringe from the bag at his feet.

"I don't need it," I insisted, ignoring the panic trickling through me. Jesus, if Maddie knew I was afraid of something as simple as sleeping, she'd dump my ass.

Dump your ass? So now you're dating?

Fuck off.

Ignoring me completely, Roman slid the needle into my arm. The prick of pain was followed by the now-familiar flush of warmth and heaviness in my limbs. The trickle of panic became a hungry claw in my stomach.

"Maddie!" My voice was sharp with fear. She frowned before hurrying back to the bed and taking my hand.

"Honey, it's okay. You need sleep to heal."

"Please," I mumbled. "I don't wanna, I can't…"

My eyelids drifted shut, and I slipped into the dark.

* * *

Maddie

"For someone who does drugs, he has a ridiculously low tolerance," Roman said as Riley's eyes closed, and he slumped against the bed.

"Just because he deals drugs doesn't mean he does them," I said.

Roman rolled his eyes. "Mads, not even *you* are that naïve."

I ran my hand over Riley's forearm before flipping his arm over and showing Roman the crook of his elbow. "No track marks."

"Plenty of ways to do drugs other than shooting up."

"You just said it was weird that he had such a low tolerance. If he did drugs, he wouldn't get knocked out so quickly by the drugs you're giving him."

Roman packed away the supplies in his medical bag. "Why are you so anxious to prove he's a good guy, Mads? We both know he isn't."

"You're wrong." I covered Riley with the quilt. "Besides, he doesn't even want the drugs you're giving him. If he were an addict, he'd be asking for more."

I arched my eyebrow at him, and Roman smiled. "You got me on that one. Still, I don't think he's as completely drug free as you believe him to be. Hell, everyone smokes a little weed now and then."

"I don't." I smoothed the wrinkles out from the quilt over Riley's broad chest. Just the feel of his hard flesh under the quilt made my stomach quiver with lust.

Roman laughed. "True, you are the poster girl for the anti-drug movement."

I stuck my tongue out at him. "I'm not that much of a good girl. I used to smoke, remember?"

Roman laughed again. "You smoked half a cigarette in University before turning green and barfing your guts up. Doesn't count, Mads."

"Whatever." I stroked Riley's forehead. He looked so much younger in sleep, with the anger always visible on his face smoothed away.

"Who would have ever thought a good girl like you would have a bullet-riddled, tattooed, giant-dicked biker in her bed?" Roman said.

"You're awfully obsessed with the size of his dick, Roman."

Roman shrugged, "I love dick, girl. And in case I didn't mention it before, his is fucking epic. A monster of a dick, the dick of *all* dicks, the Dirk Diggler dick of the biker world."

I laughed as Roman wiggled his eyebrows at me. "You going to take another ride on that monster when he's healed?"

My laughter turned to a flush of embarrassment. "Roman!"

"What? It's a simple question. Are you having another go at it or not?"

"It was a one-time only thing for him," I muttered.

"What do you mean?" Roman said.

I sighed and stood before pointing to my oversized body. "Look at me and look at him, Roman."

"I'm looking. I don't see the problem."

"Men like him are not attracted to women who look like me. I have no idea why he even had sex with me that night, other than thinking you're right about him having a drug problem and he was high on something," I said.

Roman laughed so loudly that I shushed him and hurried him out of my bedroom. He trailed after me to the kitchen, and I opened the oven and pulled out the plate of pancakes that were warming in it.

"Here, sit down and have some breakfast."

Roman was still laughing, and I scowled at him. "What's so funny?"

"What's so funny?" he repeated as he sat. Still snickering, he reached for the syrup.

"Well, what?" I poured myself a second cup of coffee.

"You thinking that Riley doesn't want you."

"He doesn't."

"Whatever, Mads. The guy wants to fuck you silly, and if he could, he'd have you riding him right now – gunshot wound be damned."

"Don't be ridiculous, Roman." I sipped at the rich, dark brew.

"No, don't you be ridiculous." Roman suddenly scowled. "You're a beautiful girl, Mads and -"

"I'm a fat girl."

"So fucking what?"

I realized with dismay that Roman's good mood had vanished, and he was giving me an uncharacteristic look of anger. "You think just because you carry a few extra pounds that you're ugly? Worthless?"

"Jordan -"

"Fuck Jordan!" Roman slammed his fist on the table. "I hate that fucking guy, Mads. Always have. The way he tore you down, the way he convinced you that you were worthless just because you don't have a size two body, makes me want to rip off his fucking head. Just because he was too goddamn chicken to admit he liked sucking dick instead of eating pussy, didn't give him the right to fuck you over like he did for four years."

I stared at him in silent shock as he looked moodily at his untouched pancakes. "I spent four years watching him tear you down little by little. I wish to fucking God I had said something, but I wanted you to be happy. I hated that asswipe, but I thought you loved him, so I kept my fucking mouth shut."

"It's not your fault, Roman," I said. "I'm an adult, and I let myself stay in that toxic relationship. It's not your fault it took me four years to get out of it."

He reached across the table to take my hand. "You're not out of it, Mads. I know you think you are, but you're not."

He tapped me lightly on the forehead. "Jordan still lives in there. You're still hearing his voice telling you that you're not worth it, that he's only with you because he feels sorry for you, that you're never going to be pretty enough or smart enough because you're not a size two."

"He never said anything like that or a word about my weight."

Roman sighed deeply. "He didn't have to say anything, Mads. Jesus, you're a bright girl – why can't you get this? Sometimes, the people we love hurt us the most without saying a word."

I blinked back the sudden tears as Roman picked up his fork and cut into the stack of pancakes. "Riley wants you badly. Even a goddamn blind man can see it."

He shoved a bite of pancake into his mouth and chewed noisily before swallowing. "Can I give you some advice?"

"Yeah."

"Once your biker babe is healed, give him what you both want and fuck him senseless for a few weeks. Let him show you exactly what you've been missing in bed with that shit-head Jordan."

"I – we're too different to be in a relationship."

Roman rolled his eyes. "Did I say to start dating him? No, I said to fuck him. There's a difference. Maybe the two of you are dynamite in bed together, or maybe you aren't. The night in the bar could have been a fluke. But if it wasn't, you deserve to be shown just how hot and fuckable you are, and Riley's the guy to do it. The way he looks at you – hell, it makes me a little hot for you."

I blushed furiously. "You keep telling me he's dangerous, and now you're saying I should just let him have sex with me to prove -"

"Fucking," Roman said. "It's called fucking, Mads, and I'm not saying you should let him do anything. I'm saying you should take what *you* want for a change and show Riley the time of his life."

"But he's dangerous, remember?" I scowled at him. "God, Roman. I love you, but you're acting crazy. One minute you're telling me to stay away from him, and the next minute you're telling me to have sex," I held up my hand when Roman opened his mouth, "to *fuck* this dangerous, drug-addicted biker."

Roman's bad mood had dissipated as quickly as it had appeared, and he smiled cheerfully. "I've changed my mind. Is Riley dangerous? Yeah, probably. But I also don't believe he'll hurt you. The two of you aren't going to last – you're like oil and water. But that doesn't mean you can't let him take a week or two to show you exactly what you've missed out on the last four years before you go back to your different lives."

He licked some syrup from his fork. "What do you think is up with his fear of sleeping?"

My head spun from the change in subject. "What?"

"Why do you think he's afraid of sleeping? I'm almost certain he doesn't want the drugs because he doesn't like the way they knock him out."

"He has nightmares," I said. "Twice now, he's almost started crying in his sleep, and he shakes terribly."

My body trembled in sympathy at the memory of the fear on Riley's face and in his voice. It disarmed me to see him like that. Made me feel helpless and afraid for him. "He cries out for a woman named Andrea."

"Any idea who she is?" Roman asked.

"No. A girlfriend, maybe." I ignored the bite of jealousy in my stomach. Why would Riley fuck me - want to fuck me - if he had a girlfriend?

You had a fiancé, and you still fucked Riley.

That was true, but there were reasons for it. I would never have cheated on Jordan if I hadn't walked in on him and Kurt in bed together. And it wasn't like I deliberately set out to retaliate by sleeping with someone else. The sex with Riley had just sort of…happened.

Maybe you could just sort of let it happen again.

I shoved that voice out of my head as Roman finished his pancakes. "I think something bad happened to her, and Riley dreams about it."

"Sounds like it," Roman said. "If you find out who she is, let me know."

I shrugged. "I don't think Riley would tell me. We're not, like, friends or anything like that."

Roman rinsed his plate and stuck it in the dishwasher. "No, you're not. And I don't think you should be. You don't need friendship or love from Riley, do you understand?"

"Yes," I said a little bitterly. "I just need a good fucking from him."

Roman either ignored or didn't hear the bitterness. "That's right, sweetheart. You do, and that ain't anything to be ashamed of. Embrace your sexuality and let a guy give you a goddamn orgasm for once in your life instead of your own hand."

"You're over the top with the crudeness today," I said. "I'm starting to regret sharing details of my sex life with you."

"Non-existent sex life, you mean." Roman kissed my forehead. "I'm out. Are you going to work tomorrow?"

"No. I've already texted my boss and told him I was sick and would work from home. I don't think Riley's ready to be alone yet."

"Okay. I'll be back tomorrow morning to check on your biker babe, but text me if you need anything, okay?"

I nodded, and he kissed my forehead again. "I love you, Mads. I just want what's best for you."

* * *

I PAUSED ON MY WAY TO THE SHOWER AND RESTED MY HAND ON Riley's forehead. I was checking for a fever, not because I had an irresistible urge to touch him whenever I was near him.

I sighed before standing and heading to the bathroom. I shut the door quietly. Although Riley was sleeping so deeply, he wouldn't have heard it even if I'd slammed it shut. I stripped out of my clothes before climbing into the shower. I washed and conditioned my hair, rinsing the long, dark strands before washing my body. My hand lingered between my thighs, and I made a small hiss of pleasure as I rinsed the soap from my sex. I held my breath as I circled my clit with the tips of my fingers. Allowing myself to fantasize about Riley was dangerous, especially when he was lying not twenty feet away, but I couldn't help it.

It was shameful to admit, but I'd been in a constant low level of arousal since the moment Riley had staggered into me on my front porch. I stood under the hot spray of water and gave my clit a little pinch that made me moan. I clasped my hand guiltily over my mouth. I needed to be quiet. If Riley heard me in here, if he figured out that I was touching myself, I'd die of embarrassment. Riley knowing I was so desperate and horny, sent shivers of horror down my back, and my fingers stilled on my throbbing clit.

What would he think if he knew I had masturbated repeatedly over the last three months to the memory of that night in the bar? At this point, I could only orgasm by remembering the sound of Riley's voice in my ear, the feel of his chest against my back, and his hand between my legs, touching and stroking and bringing me to a fevered pitch of need so easily. What had happened between us was permanently seared into my brain. I had a very bad feeling that I'd never orgasm again without remembering that single, scorching night when Riley had made me his.

I moaned again and resumed my touching. He'd claimed my pussy that night and forced me to say it belonged to him. I should have been horrified by that. So why exactly did I use it to make myself climax? Why would Riley's claim of ownership be the thing that made me so fucking hot I could barely think straight?

The shower curtain drew back with a rattling clang. I froze with my fingers in my pussy and stared guiltily at Riley. He was naked, his magnificent cock erect and brushing against his abdomen, and he had one hand clamped over the wound on his side.

"R-Riley, what are you doing?" I said as he stepped into the shower with me. "You can't get your wound wet and -"

My voice cut out in a breathless moan when one large hand wrapped in my wet hair and pulled. My head fell back, and Riley placed a hot kiss on my throat as he backed me up against the slick shower wall.

"I could smell your sweet pussy from the bedroom," he growled against my wet skin before nipping at the sensitive flesh on my throat.

I moaned, my pelvis pressing against him helplessly when he rubbed his erection against the curve of my belly.

"Did you really think I'd allow you to touch what's mine?" he asked.

My pussy throbbed as I stared defiantly at him. "I… it's not yours."

"Isn't it?" He used his thigh to push my legs apart, and I made a sharp cry of need when he reached down and thrust two fingers deep into my aching core.

I rose to my tiptoes before pushing myself desperately against his thick fingers.

"You like that, Kitten?" he rasped in my ear. "You like having my fingers fucking you?"

"Yes!" I gasped. "Oh God, yes."

"This belongs to me." His deep voice was making my insides melt. "And no one, not even you, is allowed to touch it without my permission."

He slid a third finger in, stretching me in a delicious combination of pleasure and pain, before rubbing his thumb against my swollen clit. "Do you understand?"

I panted and moaned, pumping my hips so rapidly against his thrusting fingers that the sound of my wet skin slapping against the shower wall echoed in the small room.

He pinned me against the wall, stopping my wild movements as his fingers slowed. "Do you understand, Kitten?"

"Riley, please," I whimpered. "I need it."

"Need what?" He licked the line of my jaw, clearing the wet drops from it. "Tell me exactly what you need."

"I need you to – to fuck me!" I gasped and then blushed at my crudeness.

A tight grin crossed his face, and he rewarded my answer with a slow stroke of his fingers. "I know you do. Tell me what I want to hear, and I'll fuck you until you can't stand up, Maddie."

I tried to wiggle against him and force him to move his fingers, but I was no match for his strength.

"Tell me," he repeated.

"I understand!" I nearly shouted. "Please, Riley, I understand."

"Understand what?" He thumbed my clit again, and I was so fucking close, needed it so badly, I couldn't stop my shrill cry.

"My pussy belongs to you!"

"That's my good girl," he whispered. "Your pussy is for my cock and only mine. Say it."

"Only your cock," I moaned desperately. "Only yours."

He kissed me, his mouth slanting over mine to force it wider, to accept the proprietary touch of his tongue as his hands moved to my hips. My eyes widened when I realized what he meant to do, and I tore my mouth from his.

"Riley, no! You're hurt, and I'm too heavy and -"

He lifted me easily, my back sliding against the slippery wall and my legs instinctively wrapping around his hips as he grinned fiercely at me.

"Riley, your side! Please put me -"

My plea was lost the moment I felt the blunt head of his cock spear my entrance. He pushed his way in roughly, giving me no time to adjust to his thick length. I threw my head back and moaned in sheer delight. The air was thick with steam, Riley was nearly hidden within it, and I clung desperately to his wet body as he thrust hard and fast.

His hand was back in my hair, his thick fingers clenched tightly around the wet strands. "Is this what you need, Kitten?"

"Yes!" I gasped. "Yes, I need it so badly, Riley."

"I know, Maddie," he said hoarsely. "I have what you need."

"I'm going to come!" I screamed. "Riley, I'm going to -"

Riley's hoarse cry of fear and pain shook me from my fantasy. My hand stopped its furious rubbing between my thighs, and I froze in place. The water had begun to cool. I stepped away from the spray, stuck my head outside the shower curtain, and listened. My pussy was practically screaming at me to finish what I had started, but I was certain I had heard Riley cry out. I was certain that –

His second cry was louder and filled to the brim with heartbreaking fear. I shut off the water and stumbled out of the tub as he groaned and whimpered. I snatched my towel from the counter, wrapped it around my wet body and hurried into the bedroom as Riley screamed.

"Riley!" I ran to the bed and nearly fell onto it as Riley twisted and turned.

"Andrea! NO!" he screamed again, and my blood ran cold.

"Riley, wake up!" I pinned his body down with mine and slapped him lightly on the cheek. "Riley, open your damn eyes! Please!"

His hands, which were clenched in the quilt, sank into my towel-covered hips. I bit back my groan of pain as he twisted under me.

"Riley, stop!" I shouted and then slapped him again. "Wake up!"

He woke with a start, his eyes popping open, and his face twisted in pain. Tears ran down his cheeks, and he stared wide-eyed at me as I stroked his thick, dark hair.

"You're okay, honey. Ease up on your grip, please."

He stared blankly at me, and I said, "Riley, you're hurting me."

Shame flashed across his face, and he released my hips. "I'm sorry."

"It's okay," I said. "You didn't mean to."

He shook and shivered, and I rolled cautiously to my side beside him before wiping the tears from his face. "You had a bad dream."

"Yeah," he said hoarsely and then winced when a particularly violent shiver wracked his entire body.

I eased back the quilt, almost afraid to check his bandage. I breathed a sigh of relief when no blood oozed through the white. "I'm going to take a quick look, okay?"

He nodded, and I peeled back the bandage. The stitches hadn't torn, and I taped the bandage down before sitting up.

"No!" His hard hand grabbed my wrist in fresh panic.

"I just want to check your back," I said.

He shook his head. "It's not bleeding."

"Just let me look to be sure."

"No," he said. "It's not bleeding, Maddie."

I bit my lip before nodding. "Okay. Do you – do you want to talk about your dream?"

* * *

Riley

I STARED AT MADDIE'S SWEET FACE AND WILLED THE IMAGE OF Andrea's swollen face with her tongue protruding grotesquely from between her lips out of my head. Christ, it had been awful. Normally, I could wake myself up before I saw her face, but this time…

Another shudder wracked my body, sending such a bad bolt of agony down my side that I had to clamp my mouth shut against the cry of pain.

"Riley? Do you want to talk about it?" Maddie repeated before stroking her soft fingers over my naked chest.

For a moment, I almost blurted out everything. The horror I had felt when I'd seen Andrea's body swinging from that rope, the all-engulfing panic that swallowed me when I heard my mother's footsteps on the stairs. I could feel tears threatening to fall, and I blinked rapidly.

Maddie will make it better. Tell her, and she'll make it all go away.

I opened my mouth, ready to spill the whole goddamn story to her, when my common sense kicked in. I couldn't tell Maddie something like that. If she found out how badly I'd failed my sister and realized that I'd been so wrapped up in my own problems that I couldn't see how Andrea was practically screaming for help, she'd think I was a monster. I didn't want that. Seeing the look on her face as it turned from compassion to repulsion would destroy me.

"No," I said. "I don't want to talk about it."

"Are you sure?" she asked. "Sometimes talking about it, even if it's scary and painful, can help."

"I'm fine."

"You're not fine. I heard you crying out from the shower. Riley, you should talk about it."

My eyes drifted from her face to her body. Jesus, she was almost naked. Her body, her soft, luscious body, was warm and damp and wrapped in nothing but a towel. My cock hardened, tenting the sheet and the quilt as I stared at her breasts. The towel had slipped, and I could see part of her areole and just a hint of one pink nipple.

"Riley?" She glanced down at her body. Her face flushed, and she grabbed for the towel.

"No," I growled.

Her hand hesitated at the edge of the towel as I said, "Let me see them."

"Riley, I can't -"

"Yes, you can. Loosen the towel, Kitten, and show me those beautiful tits."

Her tongue slipped out to moisten her lips, and I groaned inwardly. If I weren't so fucking weak, if the goddamn pain meds weren't making me feel dizzy and tired, I'd pin her to the bed, push my body between her thighs and make her feel exactly how much I wanted her.

"Do it, Maddie," I demanded.

Her fingers tugged at the towel, and it slipped to her waist. I sucked in a harsh breath. I'd been seeing her tits in my head for three long months, but it was nothing compared to the real thing.

"So fucking beautiful," I murmured before reaching out and tracing one nipple with my finger. It hardened immediately, and she made a half-groan and half-whimper. I glanced up at her. Her face flushed, and she bit compulsively at her bottom lip.

"Have you missed my touch, Kitten?"

She nodded, and I cupped one full breast, testing the weight of it in my hand as I rubbed her nipple with my thumb. "I've missed your soft skin. You have the prettiest tits I've ever seen, Maddie."

"Thank you," she whispered, and I had to hide my smile.

She was so fucking beautiful, so sweet and pure. To know that someone like her wanted someone like me – it was a fucking wet dream come true.

"Come closer, Kitten."

"Wh-why?" she asked nervously as I squeezed her warm breast.

"Because I want to taste your nipples again."

"Riley, I don't want to hurt you. You -"

"You won't." I wrapped my hand around the back of her neck and pulled. "Lean over me and let me suck on those gorgeous nipples."

She flushed again, and I cocked my head at her. "Did your dickhead fiancé not talk about how fucking amazing your tits are?"

She shook her head. "He, uh, he didn't say much in bed. And if he did, it wasn't, um…"

I grinned wickedly at her. "Dirty?"

"Definitely not dirty," she mumbled. I tugged again at her neck, and she wiggled a little closer.

I wasn't surprised. I had only a brief look at the dickhead, but he'd looked like the type of guy who wouldn't have a fucking clue what to do with a woman like Maddie.

"What about before him?" I asked. "Any of your previous boyfriends like to talk about your perfect tits or what it felt like to be balls-deep in that hot, wet pussy of yours?"

She closed her eyes, and my grin widened when I felt her pelvis press against my hip. My little kitten liked the dirty talk. Probably a good thing. I'd had more than one woman tell me I talked too much when I was fucking, but hell, I couldn't help it. I got chatty when I had a wet pussy wrapped around my cock. I wanted them to know just how good it felt to fuck them.

"Answer me, Maddie," I said.

"There weren't any others," she whispered.

My eyes widened in disbelief. "Are you telling me that dickhead is the only guy you've fucked?"

She nodded. "Yes. Well, until that night in the bar when we, well, when we…you know."

"When we fucked, Maddie. Say it."

She cleared her throat. "When we fucked."

I stared silently at her, my hand tightening on the back of her neck when she looked embarrassed and tried to pull away. "Let me go, Riley."

"In a minute, Kitten. I still need to taste your nipples."

"That's not a good idea," she breathed, but her nipples were still tight, and I could see her pulse thudding in her throat.

"You're not leaving this bed until I've sucked your nipples," I said. "Lean over me."

I watched conflicting emotions war across her face, cheering silently when desire won. Holding the towel around her waist, she sat up and leaned over me. Her hair was wet and sending little trickles of water down her chest. I watched a drop slide slowly down her breast and caught the drop in my mouth when it fell from her nipple. She was already panting lightly, and I cupped both of her breasts, pushing them together before nuzzling my mouth against her left nipple.

Her soft little moan made my dick throb, and I licked her

nipple in a nice, slow stroke before sucking it into my mouth. She cried out, her back arching, and I growled happily as I sucked her nipple until it was dark red and swollen. I kissed the tip of it before turning my attention to her right nipple. I was determined to give it the same treatment despite the pain that was starting to radiate up and down my ribs. I kissed and sucked and rubbed my tongue across her nipple.

Maddie made harsh gasps and moans, and she pressed her tits so eagerly against my face that the perfect, pale globes were nearly suffocating me. I didn't give a shit. I could think of worse ways to go than suffocating between Maddie's perfect tits.

I pushed the quilt and sheet off my throbbing dick and groped blindly for her hand. She didn't resist when I guided her hand to my dick.

I stared at her flushed face. "Touch me, Maddie."

She bit at that bottom lip again, and I groaned when I felt her tiny hand wrap around my dick. Fuck, her hand was as soft as velvet. I could barely stop from blowing my fucking load when she rubbed her thumb over the head.

"Your mouth," I said roughly. "Give me your mouth."

She started wiggling down the bed, and I wrapped my hand in her wet hair and tugged. "No, kiss me, Maddie."

"Oh," she said as embarrassment flickered across her face again. "I'm sorry."

"Don't be sorry, Kitten," I said. "Trust me, you'll have your hot mouth wrapped around my dick soon enough."

Her pelvis gave a little thrust against my hip as she leaned over and pressed her mouth against mine in an oddly sweet and timid manner.

I forced her mouth wider and slipped my tongue into her mouth. I brushed it delicately against her teeth before tracing it over the roof of her mouth. She moaned, and I sucked on her bottom lip for a moment before whispering, "Do you like my kisses?"

"Yes." Her hand stroked and rubbed my aching cock. "You taste good, Riley."

"You taste good too, Kitten."

Her hand tightened around my dick and squeezed. I arched my back, needing more of her touch, and a truly ball-shrinking stab of pain flared in my side. I groaned loudly, my hand flailing to press against my wound. Maddie let go of my dick and gave me a horrified look.

"Oh, Riley, I'm so sorry!"

"It's fine. Just give me a minute, and we'll start again."

"No!" She yanked up the towel. Even with the pain lancing through me, I felt a pang of loss at the disappearance of her tits. She scrambled off the bed and hurried into the bathroom as I took shallow breaths and tried to ignore the way my side burned. She returned a few seconds later, her perfect body wrapped up in a thick robe that did a dismayingly good job of hiding her curves.

"Let me see," she said.

"It's fine. Ditch the robe and get back in the bed, Maddie."

"No." She tugged at my hand. "Move your hand."

With a harsh sigh, I dropped my hand and let her peel the bandage back. She studied it closely before giving me a look of relief.

"It's not bleeding."

"Of course it isn't. Now climb back into bed so we can finish what we started," I said. "I want to fuck you."

I was lying. Well, not exactly lying. I really did want to fuck Maddie, but my side throbbed, and my sudden burst of energy had disappeared. Exhaustion seeped back in, and my eyes burned with the need to sleep. Panic bloomed in my stomach. I couldn't sleep. I would see Andrea in my dreams again, and I was so fucking tired of reliving her death night after night.

My body started to shake, and alarm crossed Maddie's face. "Riley, what's wrong?"

"Nothing. I just need to fuck you. Get in the bed."

"No," she said. "I shouldn't have done that. Besides, you heard Roman – no sex."

"Could you maybe just -"

I stopped abruptly. Jesus, I sounded like a fucking whiny baby, and I was horrified by it. The last thing I wanted was to look weak in front of her. I stared grimly at the ceiling, hoping Maddie hadn't heard the pleading in my voice, and closed my eyes when she leaned over me.

"Riley? Look at me," she said.

I refused to open my eyes, twitching a little when her fingers touched my cheek.

"Do you want me to lie down with you while you sleep?" she asked.

Now I was the one flushing with embarrassment. How the fuck did she see through me so easily?

"No," I snapped. "If you're not going to fuck me, then just go. I don't need a fucking babysitter to watch me sleep."

She sighed, and I swallowed my bitter disappointment when she moved away from the bed. I wanted her to stay. I wanted her – fuck, *needed* her – to lie in the bed beside me. It was ridiculous, but I had already begun to think of her as a talisman against the nightmares. The warmth of her body and the sound of her soft breathing would keep the nightmares away and allow me to sleep.

I threw my arm across my eyes, blocking the early afternoon sun and trying to stay awake. I couldn't sleep, didn't dare to sleep, and I tried to remember the taste and feel of Maddie's soft lips in a desperate attempt to keep the sleep at bay. I grunted in surprise when the bed dipped. Maddie crawled into bed beside me, wearing a short, cotton nightgown.

I glared at her. "Change your mind about fucking me?"

She shook her head but pressed her warm body against mine before I could tell her to leave. Her hand stroked my chest soothingly, pressing down when I started to move.

"What are you doing?"

"I want to lie on my side," I muttered. "I can't sleep on my fucking back."

She helped me turn toward her - I bit back my grunt of pain like a fucking man for once - and allowed me to wrap my body around hers like a vine. She slid one arm under my neck and slung the other across my shoulder. Her hands stroked my back, and she didn't object when I lifted her thigh and put it over my hip.

I nestled my cock in the juncture of her thighs. My erection was long gone, chased away by the pain and the weariness, but it still felt right to have my dick pressed against her warm pussy, separated only by the thin barrier of her panties.

I wanted to say something sexual, something that would let her know that I wasn't a goddamn pussy who couldn't keep it up. Instead, I buried my face in her throat and breathed deeply. She smelled good, a delicious combination of vanilla and coconut. My arms tightened around her until she gasped.

"Sorry." I loosened my grip.

"It's fine. Go to sleep, Riley."

"Will you stay?" The pleading was back in my voice, but I was too tired to care this time.

"Yes," she promised. "Now sleep."

CHAPTER 7

Riley

When I woke, we were in the same position. I tilted my head back and stared blearily at Maddie.

"Hey, how are you feeling?" she asked.

"Better. What time is it?"

She craned her head to stare at the alarm clock. "Just about five. Are you hungry?"

"A little."

She eased away, rubbing at her arm as she sat up in bed. I frowned. "What's wrong with your arm?"

"Pins and needles."

"You should have woken me so you could move." I was feeling embarrassed again, but Maddie just shrugged it off.

"You were sleeping deeply, and I didn't want to disturb you. You need rest, Riley."

"Yeah. I gotta take a piss."

She helped me sit up, but I could swing my legs out of bed and, bracing my hands on the mattress, stand up on my own.

"Good job." Maddie clapped, and I rolled my eyes as I walked slowly toward the bathroom.

"It's not that impressive. Fuck, I hate being this weak," I said.

"You were shot. You're lucky you're not dead." She slid off the bed and grabbed her ridiculously thick robe. "I'm going to start dinner."

She left the room, and I used the bathroom before brushing my teeth. In all honesty, I was feeling much better. I had slept deeply and nightmare free for nearly four hours, and I couldn't believe what a difference it made in how I felt.

I stretched gingerly and left the bathroom. I didn't want to get back into bed. As comfortable as Maddie's bed was, I was tired of the invalid routine. I glanced at my naked body before checking out Maddie's closet. My clothes were gone. Maddie had told me earlier that they were soaked in blood, and she had thrown them in the trash. I searched through her clothes. Plenty of business suits and t-shirts and yoga pants - my cock stirred at the memory of her ass in those tight yoga pants - a few pairs of jeans and not much else.

I couldn't ignore the small trickle of relief at not finding a single item of men's clothing. Not that I thought she was lying about her fiancé, but I didn't want to see even a single piece of evidence that another man had once shared her bed.

Why is that? She doesn't belong to you, asshole. Stop acting like she does.

I ignored my inner voice and concentrated on finding something to wear. I was perfectly comfortable strolling around naked, but I was confident Maddie wouldn't care for it. I was starting to think that my only choices were nudity or a towel around my waist when I caught sight of a wicker basket on the closet shelf. Holding my side, I stretched for it and tested its weight. It wasn't heavy, and I eased it off the shelf and peered into it.

"You've been holding back on me, Kitten." I pulled the sheer pink nightie out of the basket. I held it up to the light, picturing how Maddie would look in it, before setting it aside. A scrap of lace that was the matching panties came out next. I looked around almost guiltily before pressing the panties against my face and inhaling. They smelled like laundry soap, and I placed them on top of the nightdress before pulling out the robe. It was soft and silky and pale pink. I shrugged and tried it on. It was snug across the shoulders and barely fell past my ass, but it at least covered my dick. I tied the silk belt around my waist and placed the lingerie back in the basket before heading slowly to the kitchen.

* * *

Maddie

"THAT SMELLS GOOD," RILEY SAID.

"Thanks," I replied without turning around. I'd heard him shuffling down the hallway and almost left the kitchen to help, but I had a feeling it wouldn't be appreciated. Being weak and relying on others was as foreign to Riley as a life peddling drugs was to me, so I'd left him alone. He could always call for me if he needed me.

"It's just reheated lasagna." I opened the oven door and added a loaf of foil-wrapped garlic bread next to the lasagna. "I work late so often that I usually cook a bunch of meals ahead of time and freeze them."

I closed the oven door and swung around. "Do you want something to…"

My mouth dropped open. Riley, wearing the pale pink robe from the lingerie set I had bought on a whim and only worn once, sunk carefully into one of the kitchen chairs.

"What?" He grinned at me and smoothed the robe down as I giggled.

"That's quite the look."

"I look good in pink, Kitten. Admit it," he said.

"The colouring does go well with your skin tone."

"Thanks," he said with another grin.

"Do you want a drink?" I asked.

"Do you have any beer?"

"No, afraid not. You can't have it anyway. You're on pain meds, remember? I have water, milk and juice."

"Water is fine."

I sat a glass of water in front of Riley, and he watched silently as I set the table. I took the lasagna and the garlic bread out of the oven and sliced the bread before dishing up a piece on each plate.

"Careful, it's hot." I sat down across from him.

He ate a bite and closed his eyes in delight. "Jesus, this is fucking delicious, Maddie."

"Thank you. I like to cook."

He was attacking the lasagna and the garlic bread, nearly shoving the food into his mouth. I placed another piece on his plate without comment when he was finished. He took his time with the second helping, then leaned back with a soft sigh when his plate was clear.

"Christ, I haven't eaten food that good since my mother died," he said.

"Did she pass away recently?" I was insanely curious about his life.

"About two years ago. Cancer."

"I'm sorry. Were you close to her?"

"Yeah."

"What about your dad?" I asked.

"He took off when I was a teenager."

I gave him a look of sympathy, and he scowled. "It was a good thing."

"Do you have any siblings?"

Pain crossed his face before he shook his head. "No."

I instinctively knew he was lying, but his face had closed over, and he stared mulishly at his empty plate.

I stood and started to clear the table. "Are you still hungry?"

"No. It was delicious. Thanks, Maddie."

"You're welcome."

"What about you?" he asked abruptly. "Your folks still alive?"

"They are. They live in North Carolina, but we usually see each other once a year or so. I'm not super close with my dad, but my mom and I often text and video chat."

"Your dad a dick?"

I smiled and shook my head. "No. He just really wanted a boy, but my mom had a difficult pregnancy with me and nearly died in childbirth. She was advised not to have any more kids. My dad loves me but is sad about not getting the son he always wanted. It made our relationship a bit strained when I was a teenager."

"You like being a lawyer?"

"I do. I work for a pretty big firm, and I haven't been a lawyer for that long, so I sometimes get the shit work, but I don't mind."

"You work with criminals, shit like that?"

"Oh God no," I said. "We're a family law practice. Divorces, child support, that sort of thing. We take on a lot of pro bono work. The head partner of the firm had a rough childhood, so he takes on a lot of cases for single moms who don't have much money. It's a good firm to work for. I feel like I'm making a difference, you know?"

He shrugged. "No, I guess I don't."

I cleared my throat and glanced at the pink robe. "How long have you been, uh…"

"A drug dealer?"

"Yeah," I said.

"A few years."

"What did you do before that?"

"Construction, mostly. I had to drop out of high school when my dad left. We were broke, and Ma's job at the grocery store didn't pay enough to support us. I was big for my age, and they believed me when I said I was eighteen."

He was giving me a sullen, almost embarrassed look. "Bet your parents would shit themselves if they knew you fucked a man who doesn't even have a high school degree."

I shrugged. "My dad isn't invested enough in my life to care, and my mom, well," I paused and smiled a little, "she sees the good in almost everyone."

He didn't reply. I tugged nervously at the collar of my robe as he shifted and winced.

"Are you tired? Maybe you should lie down again."

"I'm tired of lying in bed."

"Why don't we watch TV in the living room?"

"Sure." He stood gingerly and followed me out of the kitchen.

Riley

"How's that?" Maddie asked anxiously. "Do you need another blanket?"

I shook my head. Maddie's sofa was a small sectional, and she helped me stretch out on the chaise part before tucking a blanket around me. "Are you sure? I can grab another one from the closet."

"I'm fine," I said. "Stop fussing over me." I gave her a surly look, but she ignored it.

She sat on the far end of the couch and turned on the TV. Truthfully, I was kind of enjoying her fussing. Not that I wanted her to be my goddamn mother or anything, but it was nice to have someone worry about me. She'd think I was a fucking pussy if she knew that, though, so I glared again at her as she flipped through the channels.

"I'm not watching some ridiculous woman show," I said.

She laughed. "Well, it's my house and my remote control, so I guess you're watching what I want to watch. Unless," she arched her eyebrow at me, "you want to wrestle for the remote?"

I grunted in annoyance, and she grinned cheekily at me as a man in a tux popped onto the screen. He stood before a large group of women dressed in evening gowns with a tray of roses beside him.

"What the hell is this?" I asked.

"It's *The Bachelor*. It's a reality show about finding love."

I snorted loudly.

"It is," she insisted. "He dates all of those women, and each week whittles them down until he finds his true love."

"Sounds like a way to fuck as many women as possible and get away with it."

"They don't have sex!"

"Yeah, right. You're telling me that guy doesn't bone those chicks?" I said.

"Well, not always," she replied. "Now be quiet. I want to see who he picks."

"You seriously watch this every week?"

"Yes," she said without a single bit of shame. "Well, actually, I record it. I'm about eight episodes behind so don't be watching ahead while I'm at work and spoiling it for me."

I snorted again. "Like I'd be caught dead watching this show."

"Oh hush, you might like it."

"Doubtful," I grunted before relaxing against the couch.

Nearly two hours later, she paused the TV and studied me closely. "You're pale, Riley."

The pain was bad, and I was tired, but I didn't want to admit it. It was barely eight, and I was sure Maddie wouldn't climb into bed with me. The thought of going back to bed without her, of falling asleep without her, made fear curl in my belly.

"I'm fine," I said. "Let's watch another episode of your stupid show."

"No." She shut off the TV. "C'mon, it's time for bed."

"You always go to bed at eight?" I muttered as she pulled off the blanket and helped me to my feet.

She shrugged. "I'm not much of a night owl, but even eight is early for me. I'll lie in bed with you and read for a while."

I tried to hide the relief on my face. "I don't need you to go to bed with me."

"I know." Her voice was carefully neutral. "Listen, I can sleep in the guest room if you don't -"

"No," I said a bit too quickly, "I'm not kicking you out of your own damn bed."

This was the part where I was supposed to offer to sleep in the guest room, but I couldn't bring myself to do it.

"Then let's go to bed," she said.

She shut off the lights, and we walked slowly to her bedroom. I brushed my teeth and used the bathroom before taking off her robe and easing carefully into the bed. Maddie had already disappeared into the bathroom, and I tucked my hands behind my head and stared at the ceiling as I listened to her hum softly to herself. She came out of the bathroom ten minutes later and shed her robe before climbing into the bed beside me. She leaned over me.

"You okay?" Her breath smelled minty, and her soft skin gleamed in the light from the bedside lamp.

"Yeah, good night," I said.

"Night." She reached for her iPad and relaxed on her back. I stayed where I was for nearly five minutes before sliding closer and rolling to my side. I nosed under her arm like a goddamn dog looking to be petted and molded my body against hers.

She stroked my hair as I buried my face in her neck. I cupped one firm breast through her nightgown, and she tugged lightly at my hair. "Behave."

"I am."

"Riley?"

"Yeah?"

"If you give me the address of your place, I'll go over tomorrow and pick up some clothes and personal items for you."

I stiffened against her, and she made a soft, soothing noise under her breath. There was no fucking way I wanted Maddie to see my shithole of an apartment in the bad part of town. Besides, I was behind on rent, and by now, my land-lord would have changed the locks and tossed my shit. Not that I cared. None of my stuff was worth anything. The only thing that ever meant anything to me was Andrea's necklace and that had been buried with Ma.

"No," I said.

She frowned at me. "You must want some of your stuff, Riley. I don't mind."

"No," I repeated. "I don't live in a good neighbourhood. It's too dangerous for you to go there alone."

"I can take Roman with me."

"I said no, Maddie," I snapped. "I don't need anything from there."

"You can't walk around naked or in my robe forever."

She wasn't going to let this go. "I'm behind on rent, and my landlord will have changed the locks and threw away my shit, okay? There, are you happy?"

"Why would that make me happy?"

"I don't know," I said wearily. "Jesus, Maddie, do we have to talk about this right now? I'll buy some new clothes."

With what, I didn't know. I had maybe fifty bucks to my name. That asshole Frank had taken most of the proceeds from our drug deals and funnelled it back into the club, but I would slit my own goddamn throat before I admitted to Maddie that I was broke.

"Okay," she said quietly.

Although nothing in her voice suggested my anger hurt her, I gave her a guilty look. "Fuck, I'm sorry. I didn't mean to snap. I'm just really tired, and my side hurts."

"I know. Go to sleep."

I was bone tired, and her soft body felt a little like heaven. She traced lazy circles on my bare back as she read, and I tucked my face into her throat and closed my eyes. For the first time in my life, I was cuddling with a woman and enjoying it. Hell, I was fucking loving it. I really was going soft.

"Good night, Riley," she said.

I was already half asleep. I squeezed her breast before saying drowsily, "Good night, Maddie."

* * *

Maddie

"Mads? You decent?" The front door slammed, and Roman's voice called down the hall.

"Yes, I'm in the kitchen."

Roman strolled into the kitchen and sniffed the air. "Oh my God, you're making French toast, aren't you?"

I nodded and flipped the piece of bread in the pan. "Yes, sit down and help yourself."

"You're the best, Mads." Roman kissed me on the cheek before grabbing a plate and silverware. He stabbed a piece of French toast from the stack on the table, poured a liberal amount of syrup, and stuffed a piece into his mouth.

"Delicious, Mads. Thanks."

"You're welcome."

"How's your biker babe feeling this morning?"

"Better, I think," I said. "He seemed to sleep better last night."

"It doesn't look like I can say the same for you."

I shrugged. "I'm just not used to having someone sleep in the bed with me. It's been a few months since I shared my bed with Jordan, and even then, he always slept on the far edge of the bed. Riley likes to, um, sleep close."

That was the understatement of the year. Riley had clung to me the entire night, and the man was as warm as a damn furnace. I woke up sweaty and too hot at one, but when I wiggled free of his tight grip, Riley frowned in his sleep and followed me across the bed. I was back in his arms and plastered against his hard body in less than thirty seconds. If he kept that up, I'd have to sleep naked just to keep from overheating. My face flushed a little as I thought about my bare skin pressed against Riley's firm, hard flesh.

"Aww, the big bad biker likes to cuddle." Roman laughed. "Who would have thought?"

"Keep that to yourself," I scolded.

"My lips are sealed." He snagged another piece of French toast. "Where is your biker babe anyway?"

"In the bathroom, I think. What time does your shift start?"

"Holy shit," Roman said.

I turned and followed his gaze. Riley, wearing my short pink robe again, stood in the kitchen doorway.

"That is way fucking hotter than it should be," Roman said.

Riley flushed and tugged self-consciously at the hem of the robe. "My eyes are up here, buddy."

Roman laughed, and Riley studied me. "You look tired."

I added two more pieces of French toast to the stack on the table. "I'm fine. Sit down and eat."

"Feeling better?" Roman asked.

Riley helped himself to some food. "Yeah. Best I've felt in a few days."

"Good. Once we're done eating, you can untie your pink robe, and I'll check the wound."

Riley glared at him, and Roman grinned cheekily. "Don't look at me like that. I like the robe, and I think you look stunning in it. It goes well with your colouring."

Riley's mouth twitched upward, and he glanced at me as I joined them. "That's what I told Maddie, but she didn't seem to think so."

"No, I told you that," I protested with a grin. "As lovely as my robe looks on you, I'll run out and get you some new clothes tomorrow. I'd go today, but considering I'm supposed to be at home sick, it's probably best if I don't leave the house."

"You called in sick?" Riley said.

I nodded, and he scowled in disapproval. "You didn't need to do that. I'm not a complete invalid."

"I don't mind," I said.

"I don't want you getting fired because of me."

"I won't," I assured him. "I'm allowed sick days, and I think this might be the first one I've taken in two years. Stop worrying about it. Besides, I'll do some work from home."

"I've got a short shift at the hospital today." Roman popped the last piece of his French toast into his mouth. "I'll buy Riley some clothes and bring them by later this evening."

"I don't need you to buy me clothes," Riley said.

"Why not?" Roman asked. "Listen, this will sound cliché as hell, but I have an amazing sense of fashion."

"He does," I said. "He helped me buy all my work clothes."

Roman eyed Riley thoughtfully. "You're in serious need of a makeover, dude."

Riley stared at me in panic, and I giggled. "He's just kidding, Riley."

Roman shrugged. "Maybe I am, maybe I'm not. Anyway, I'll pick you up some nice dress shirts, a few pairs of khakis, and -"

"I just need a couple of pairs of jeans and a few T-shirts," Riley said a bit desperately. "Nothing else, Roman."

"Are you sure? Maybe you could branch out a little and try wearing a shirt that buttons," Roman said teasingly.

"T-shirts and jeans," Riley said.

"Fine." Roman sighed. "Write down your sizes after breakfast, and I'll pick up your boring clothes."

"Where's my wallet?" Riley asked me.

"It's in the top drawer of the nightstand," I replied. "I can grab it for you."

Roman shook his head. "Nah, don't worry about it. You can pay me back later once I have the total cost."

Riley scowled. "Nothing too expensive. Just hit a Walmart or something."

I almost laughed out loud at the look on Roman's face. My best friend had particular tastes, and I doubted he'd ever purchased a single item of clothing from Walmart. My urge to laugh faded when I caught the look on Riley's face. His face had an odd combination of shame and anger, and his hands were clenched into tight fists. Before Roman could say anything, I changed the subject hurriedly.

"Roman, maybe you could look at Riley's wounds now. He was a bit restless yesterday afternoon and I'm worried that he might have, I don't know, stretched the stitches?"

Roman laughed. "You can't stretch stitches, Mads. Stand and drop your robe, Riley."

Riley stood and untied the robe. He held it self-consciously around his waist as Roman, suddenly all business, peeled away both bandages. He studied the wounds before nodding with satisfaction.

"Damn, I do good work. It's looking good, big guy."

"It feels better," Riley said.

"Good. I think we can do without the shot today. What do you think?"

The look of relief on Riley's face was unmistakable. "Yeah."

"You can take Tylenol or Advil for the pain," Roman said. "If it's not enough, just let me know, and I'll prescribe some Tylenol 3. Still taking the antibiotics?"

Riley nodded, and Roman clapped him on the back. "Good. Make sure you finish the bottle, even if you're feeling fine."

He bent and studied the neatly sutured gashes again. "I think we can leave off the bandages as well."

"Can I have a shower?" Riley shrugged into the robe and belted it.

Roman nodded, and Riley immediately turned and started out of the kitchen.

"Hey, give me your sizes," Roman said. "I've got to get to work."

Riley recited his clothing sizes, and Roman tapped them into his phone. "Okay, good to go."

Riley held out his hand. "Thanks, Roman."

Roman shook it. "You're welcome, man."

"Towels are in the closet next to the guest room," I called as Riley left the kitchen.

I smiled at Roman. "Thanks for picking up some clothes for Riley, honey."

Roman nodded. "Out of curiosity, why aren't we going to his place and picking up his clothes?"

I glanced at the doorway of the kitchen before lowering my voice. "Riley told me last night that he was behind on his rent, and his landlord would have changed the locks and tossed his stuff by now."

"So, the guy's homeless?"

"Yeah, I guess. I get the feeling that he doesn't have much money."

"Kind of odd for a drug dealer, isn't it?" Roman asked.

"I don't know. He's the only drug dealer I know," I said peevishly.

Roman frowned. "What's wrong?"

"Nothing. I'm just tired."

"Are you sure?"

I nodded. "Anyway, I don't think he has a lot of money, and he's embarrassed about it, so don't go crazy with the clothes purchases, okay?"

"I won't," Roman said. "I've got to run. I'll see you tonight."

"Come for dinner," I urged as he kissed me on the cheek. "I'm making chicken stew."

"Sweet," Roman said cheerfully. "Thanks, Mads. See you later."

CHAPTER 8

Maddie

M y fingers hovered over the keyboard of my laptop as I cocked my head and listened carefully. Faintly, I could hear the TV. After taking the world's longest shower, Riley retreated to the living room, and I went to my office to do some work. That was nearly three hours ago, and honestly, I hadn't accomplished much. I hesitated and then quickly typed a few sentences into Google. It didn't take long to find what I was looking for, and I clicked the news link, my breath catching in my throat as I stared at the article's title.

Local Bike Gang Gunned Down in Drug Deal Gone Bad.

I skimmed the article, my gaze drawn repeatedly to the pictures that were scattered throughout.

Jesus, that's Frank. I stared at the large-bellied man, his long white hair partially covering his face, sprawled on the floor. A dark pool of blood was under his body, and nausea swept through me. At least a dozen men were lying dead on the floor of the very bar I had stumbled into a few months ago.

That could be Riley lying there.

I shuddered all over. How he escaped, I had no idea.

I forced my gaze away from the pictures and started to read the article in detail. Before I made it past the first paragraph, Riley's drawn-out cry had my blood freezing in my veins. I jumped up and ran to the living room as his cries grew louder. He had stretched out on the chaise and fallen asleep. His face was pale, and his hands plucked restlessly at the blanket that covered him as he moaned.

I hurried over and wedged my body next to his on the chaise. "Wake up, honey."

I rubbed his chest and patted his face as he made another sharp cry of fear. He sounded like a wounded and trapped animal. I winced – God, I hated hearing him sound like that – and shook him lightly.

"Wake up, honey. Open your eyes."

He woke up abruptly like he always did and clutched at me as I rubbed his chest. "Just a bad dream, Riley."

He shifted to his uninjured side, flinching and making a grunt of pain before flattening his broad body against mine. He rested his head on my breast in a mute plea for comfort, and I held him close until his shivering eased.

"Better?"

He nodded, and I kissed the top of his head. "Do you want to talk about it?"

He shook his head, and I squeezed him. "I think you should. It'll help, Riley."

When he remained silent, I rubbed his back. "It will, honey. You can't keep having nightmares like this. Talk to me."

He took a deep, shuddering breath. "Yeah, okay."

I held my breath and waited, more anxious than I would

admit to hearing who Andrea was. To my surprise, he cleared his throat and said, "Frank was smart and could read most people, but for whatever reason, he didn't have a fucking clue how crazy Richie was."

"You were dreaming about Frank?"

"Dreaming about the night I got shot."

I held him a little closer as he sighed deeply. "Richie and his, I guess gang, for lack of a better word, were some of our regulars. Only, he had started to lose it, you know? He was doing too much coke, not sleeping, and starting to get real paranoid. The guy had money to burn, some family inheritance, I think, and that blinded Frank to how dangerous and unpredictable he was becoming. The night before we were meeting up with Richie, I tried to convince Frank to call it off. Tried to make him see how fucked up the guy was, but Frank refused."

He scrubbed his hand across his face. "Our club wasn't doing well financially - Frank wasn't great with money - but he had big plans for us. He wanted to expand our distribution, as he called it, and for whatever reason, he believed that Richie was the key to making that happen. I think he thought he could bring Richie in as a silent partner or some shit like that."

He fell silent, and I rubbed his back briefly before saying, "What happened?"

When Richie got there, he was already high as fuck. He was talking crazy shit. Frank tried to calm him down, got him and his boys a few drinks and tried to talk to Richie about his business proposal. I don't know exactly what Frank did or said to piss him off, but the next thing you know, Richie and his guys pulled out fucking automatic weapons and just... started killing us."

"How did you survive?" I asked in a horrified whisper.

He grinned in bitter amusement. "I had to take a piss. I was in the bathroom when they started shooting."

I could hear the dry click in his throat when he swallowed. "When I heard the gunfire, I ran out of the bathroom and down the hall. There was an emergency exit near the bathroom, but I was going back for Billy."

"You were close with him?" I asked.

He shrugged. "I guess. Billy was just a kid, and I'd been trying to convince him to leave the club. His mama lived in Alabama. Billy's stepdad kicked him out when he was thirteen, but I guess he had died, and his mama wanted him to come home. They were starting to text and shit like that, and she was talking about sending him some money to take the bus home. Billy hadn't started doing the hard drugs yet. He could still get free, you know? Frank wouldn't have bothered to look for him."

"Riley?" I patted his back until he raised his gaze to mine. "Do you do hard drugs?"

"No. I've never done anything stronger than weed." He gave me an oddly vulnerable look. "Do you believe me?"

"Yes," I said. "I do."

A brief look of relief crossed his face before he laid his head back on my chest. "I didn't reach the bar's main part to find Billy. One of Richie's men came into the hallway. He had a gun, and he shot me."

"Oh, Riley," I whispered.

"I tackled him. I knew I'd been shot, but there wasn't any pain. We wrestled on the floor, and I got the gun away from him."

He fell silent, and I said, "What happened then?"

"I shot him in the head, and then I turned and ran like a goddamn chicken out the back door, got on my bike and got the fuck out of there." His voice was flat. "I threw the gun in the east river."

His hand squeezed my hip compulsively, and his voice was hoarse when he said, "You want me to get the fuck out of your house now, or wait until it's dark so the neighbours don't see me?"

"Why would you say that?" I asked.

"You got a murderer living in your house, Maddie."

"I don't. Killing a man who was trying to kill you isn't murder. It's self-defense."

His tense body relaxed a fraction, and he blew his breath out in a harsh rush. "I haven't watched the news or checked online. Maybe Billy made it out of there."

"He didn't. I'm sorry, honey, but I was looking online, and there were no survivors."

"I shouldn't have run out of there like that. If I hadn't been so afraid, Billy might still be alive," he said in a low voice.

"You would have died in that bar if you had tried to save him. You did the right thing by leaving."

He grunted in reply. We lay on the chaise in silence for a few moments before he said, "You're right, Maddie. Talking about it helped."

"Good, I'm glad." I gathered my courage. "Who's Andrea?"

His body stiffened, and he eased away from me. "How do you know that name?"

"You cry her name during your nightmares," I said.

"No, I don't."

"You do. How else would I know her name? Was she your girlfriend?"

"I don't want to talk about her."

"I think you should," I said. "It'll help."

He glared at me. "No, it won't."

"Riley, you just said that talking about the shooting helped. Tell me about Andrea. It'll -"

He suddenly cupped my head and pulled it down until my

mouth was pressed against his. He kissed me hard, pushing his tongue past my lips until I was breathless and making small moans.

"I don't want to talk about it," he muttered before kissing me again.

"Riley," I gasped, "we can't -"

"We can!" he said angrily. "I need you, Maddie. I need this."

He pushed up my shirt and sucked on my nipple through the lacy fabric of my bra. I moaned again, my hand clutching helplessly at his head as he bit my nipple lightly. He pulled the cups of my bra down and made a harsh noise of approval at the sight of my naked breasts. His lips tugged at my nipple, sending shivers of need down my spine, and I arched my back as he teased and tormented both of my nipples into hard peaks.

His cock was hard and heavy against my stomach. I gasped when he shoved the silky material of the robe aside and rubbed the head of his cock against my bare flesh. It leaked precum, and I stared at the smear of liquid on my stomach as he slid his hand past the waistband of my pants and into my panties.

"Riley, wait. You're still injured and…"

My protest turned into a soft moan when his hand cupped my sex. His rough fingers parted the wet lips of my pussy, and I cried out when he rubbed my swollen clit.

"You like that, Kitten?" he panted against my breast before slicking his tongue across my nipple. "You like having my fingers touching your sweet pussy?"

"Yes," I moaned. The flex of his fingers had my body on fire, and I pressed against him eagerly. His cock was trapped between us, and it rubbed against my smooth flesh. He groaned before kissing me again. I returned his kiss, sucking at his tongue and his lips as he rubbed my clit.

"You're going to come all over my fingers, Kitten," he rasped, "and then you'll ride my dick with that tight pussy of yours."

"We can't," I gasped. "You – you'll rip your stitches."

"I won't." He tugged on my clit, grinning fiercely when I cried out and nearly climaxed. "We'll just go real slow, Kitten."

"Oh God," I whispered. "Riley, you're driving me crazy."

"Good."

I closed my eyes and arched my back as Riley sucked and pulled on my nipples with his hot wet mouth, and his fingers rubbed my clit. I was so damn close, my body shuddering with the need for relief, and my brain temporarily short-circuited by the feel of Riley's hard body against mine.

"Oh," I said, "oh God, Riley, I – I'm so close, I -"

The sound of the doorbell nearly jarred me from the chaise. I teetered on the edge before grabbing Riley's broad shoulders for balance. He winced, and I gave him a horrified look.

"Fuck! Riley, are you okay?"

"Just fine, Kitten." His fingers were still pressing and stroking my clit, and he bent his head toward my breast again.

"There's someone at the door," I said as he circled my nipple with the tip of his tongue.

"Ignore them," he grunted as the doorbell rang again.

His fingers pinched my clit, and I clapped my hand over my mouth to muffle my moan of pleasure. "Riley, I think -"

"Stop thinking, Kitten." He kissed between my breasts.

The doorbell rang for a third time, and I tugged at Riley's arm. "Stop, Riley."

He sighed in frustration and pulled his hand from my pants before glaring at me. I ignored it and scrambled off the couch, tucking my breasts back into my bra and straight-

119

ening my shirt before walking unsteadily out of the living room. I wiped my hand across my lips, which were swollen and sensitive from Riley's kisses, and cleared my throat before opening the door.

"Tim? What are you doing here?" I stared in surprise at my co-worker.

"I heard you were sick, and I thought I'd stop by during lunch and bring you some chicken noodle soup." Tim held up the brown paper bag. "Can I come in?"

"Oh, um…"

He shouldered past me and handed me the bag before taking off his jacket and hanging it on the hook. "Do you have a fever, Maddie? Your face is red."

I blinked in surprise when he pressed his hand against my forehead. "You're warm."

"Tim," I tried again, "it's nice of you to drop by, but you shouldn't have wasted your lunch like this. I'm fine, just a bit of a stomach bug."

"I don't mind," he said. "I was worried about you. You're never sick. Why don't you show me the way to the kitchen, and I'll heat your soup while you sit and rest? I picked it up from that deli down the street. I know you love their soup, don't try to…"

Riley, wrapped in the blanket from the couch, had appeared in the hallway. Riley stared silently at him as Tim cleared his throat. "Oh, I didn't realize you had company."

"Um, Riley, this is Tim. He's a lawyer at my firm. Tim, this is Riley, my, um," I hesitated – what the fuck was Riley to me anyway?

Tim stared at me, one blond eyebrow arched, and I smiled weakly. "He's my roommate."

"Oh! I didn't know you had a roommate, Mads," Tim said before holding his hand out to Riley. "Tim Macklin. Nice to meet you."

Riley's gaze darkened at his casual use of my nickname. He stared with distaste at Tim's outstretched hand before lifting his eyes to mine. In his gaze, there was anger and something else – it almost looked like hurt, but that was ridiculous.

"Nice to meetcha," he grunted to Tim. He turned and walked down the hallway to my bedroom, slamming the door behind him, and Tim glanced at me.

"He's…interesting."

"Yes," I said nervously. "Listen, Tim, I appreciate you bringing me soup, but I don't want you to get sick and -"

"I won't," he said. "I never get sick. I drink this juice concoction every morning to keep everything away. I invented it myself. You should let me make it for you some-time. I guarantee it'll keep you healthy. Is this the way to the kitchen?"

He wandered down the hallway and disappeared into the kitchen. I followed him, and he smiled at me before pointing to one of the chairs. "Sit down, and I'll heat this up for you."

Feeling shell-shocked, I dropped into a chair as Tim found the bowls and poured soup into one before popping it into the microwave. We waited silently as it heated, and he handed me a spoon before setting the soup in front of me.

"Eat, Mads," he urged.

I took a sip of the soup to be polite and smiled at Tim. "Thanks, it's good."

"You're welcome." He sat beside me and crossed one leg over the other, tugging on the leg of his pants. "Do you think you'll be back to work tomorrow?"

"Yes."

"Good. I missed seeing your face at the office today."

"Tim, I -"

"You know, Maddie, I've wanted to get to know you better for a long time."

I blinked in surprise. Until today, Tim had never shown anything but professional interest in me. He was handsome enough, but his blond hair and slender body did nothing for me. I probably outweighed him by seventy pounds, and I couldn't imagine dating him or, hell, having sex with him.

You'd snap him like a twig the first time you were on top.

I smothered my sudden bout of hysterical laughter.

"Tim, I'm not looking to date anyone right now. I just got out of a pretty serious relationship and -"

"You and your fiancé broke up three months ago. A pretty girl like you shouldn't be sitting home alone night after night."

"Pretty girl?" I raised my eyebrows at him. Being called a girl, like I wasn't a grown woman with a law degree, made my hackles rise.

He gave me a sheepish look. "Sorry, a beautiful woman like you deserves to have a little fun in her life."

"Well, that's nice of you to say, but like I said, I'm not looking for -"

"Don't say no right away. Just think about it, okay? We have lots of things in common."

"Like what?" I couldn't hide the disbelief in my voice. "Until today, we've never spoken outside of work."

His smile oozed smarmy charm. "We're both lawyers, aren't we? We're both intelligent and passionate about our jobs. Hell, you're a much better lawyer than me – I could learn some things from you. And," he smiled again, "I can show you how to eat properly."

"Show me how to eat properly," I repeated.

"Yes." He leaned forward eagerly. "I'm a bit of a health nut and know of so many ways to improve your body and health with nutrition and exercise. You're a gorgeous girl, but I could help you be the best, leanest, and healthiest version of yourself."

I stood. "I think you should go. The soup has upset my stomach, and I need to lie down."

"God, I'm sorry." Tim stood, and I shuffled backward as he tried to take my hand. "I didn't mean to make it worse, Mads. I thought the soup would help."

"Yeah, I know. I'll see you tomorrow at the office, okay?"

"Sure." He followed me out of the kitchen and grabbed his jacket from the hook. "I'll email you my cell number. Just call or text me if you need anything, okay? I don't mind at all."

"Thanks, but I'll be fine."

"Right. Okay, well, take care of yourself, and I'll see you tomorrow," Tim said as I opened the door and he stepped out onto the porch.

"Bye, Tim. Thanks again." I shut the door and leaned against it, shaking my head in disbelief, before returning to the kitchen. I poured the soup down the drain and threw away the container. Riley was still in the bedroom, and I waited a few minutes before joining him.

"Riley?"

He was lying in the bed with his back to the door. I touched his blanket-covered shoulder gingerly. "Riley, it's lunchtime."

"I'm not hungry," he grunted.

"You need to eat. Come to the kitchen, and I'll make you a sandwich."

"That asshole still here?" he asked.

"No. He had to go back to work. C'mon, Riley, you need to eat something."

"I said I wasn't hungry. Leave me alone, for God's sake, Maddie."

"Fine." I stormed from the bedroom.

123

Riley

I LAY IN MADDIE'S BED AND STARED AT THE CEILING. I COULD hear the low murmur of Roman and Maddie's voices and smell the delicious scent of chicken stew. My stomach growled, but I ignored it. I had stayed in the bedroom all afternoon and refused to come out when Maddie knocked on the door to tell me dinner was ready.

I was being an asshole. I knew I was, but I was still reeling from hearing Maddie call me her roommate. Her fucking roommate – as if I hadn't had my fingers in her pussy not two minutes before that.

I shifted, muttering a curse under my breath at the twinge of pain in my side, and continued to pout. I hated that asshole, Tim, from the moment I saw him. His stupid hair gelled to perfection, and wearing a fucking suit that probably cost more than my bike. Why the hell he thought he could walk into my woman's house and –

Your woman? Maddie isn't your woman, so don't start thinking she is. Her little roommate comment made it clear that she doesn't want her coworkers and friends to know that someone like you could be more than just a friend to someone like her.

I uttered another curse. Of course she didn't, and why would she? I was lucky she hadn't called the cops the minute I showed up on her doorstep with a fucking gunshot wound. She had a fucking law degree, and I was a high-school dropout who dealt drugs for a living.

You can change. Frank and everyone else in the club is dead. You could return to working construction, maybe even get your GED, and show Maddie you're a good guy.

Except I wasn't a good guy, and a normal job and diploma wouldn't make me one.

I sat up gingerly and threw the covers back before heading to the bathroom. Starting to think that I could have something more than a fuck session or two with Maddie was a bad idea. My life was fucked up, and I had no right to drag her down with me.

I was easing back into the bed when there was a knock on the door.

"You decent, pussy cat?" Roman called through the door.

"Go away."

The door opened, and Roman stuck his head into the room. "Nope."

He kicked the door open with his foot, and I stared at the tray in his hands. A bowl of chicken stew, a salad, and a glass of water were on the tray. He carried it to the bed, setting it on my lap. A large plastic bag dangled from his wrist, and he sat it on the floor before shutting the bedroom door and leaning against it.

"Thanks," I muttered. The food smelled amazing and, my stomach growling again, I dipped the spoon into the rich broth and started to eat.

"I wanted to let you go to bed without dinner. I mean, if you're going to act like a spoiled little brat, we should treat you like one, right?" Roman said.

I ignored him, hoping it would shut him up and make him leave, but he stayed where he was and snorted laughter. "You're lucky that Mads is tender-hearted. She's in the kitchen worried sick about you right now, by the way."

"I'm fine. She doesn't need to worry about shit."

"That's what I told her. I told her that life always seems to work out for dickheads like you."

"Work out for me?" I barked harsh laughter. "In case you forgot, I was fucking shot a week ago and nearly died."

He shrugged. "Yet here you are, playing the big bad biker routine and treating the only person who probably ever cared about you like a piece of shit."

"Fuck you, Roman!" I snarled.

"What's the matter? Don't like hearing the truth?"

"If you think I'm so bad for Maddie, then why the fuck did you help me? Why the fuck haven't you called the cops?"

"I didn't say I thought you were bad for Mads. I said you're treating her like a piece of shit, and you need to apologize or leave."

"Fine, I'll leave." I shoved the tray to the side, slopping stew over the edge of the bowl and climbed naked out of bed, holding my hand against my side.

"Where are you going to go? Huh?" Roman asked. "You're homeless and broke. You need Maddie."

"I don't fucking need anyone! I'll be just fine."

"Bullshit," Roman said. "You're going to run because you're afraid to say sorry to Maddie for acting like a dick? Jesus, find your fucking balls, dude."

I glared at him, and Roman sighed loudly. "Listen, man, I know your life has been tough, and I understand -"

"No, you don't. You couldn't possibly begin to know or understand. Not someone like you."

He studied me for a moment. "No, I suppose I can't. But here's what I do know – Maddie, for whatever reason, cares about you and is beating herself up, thinking she's hurt your feelings somehow. You need to put on your big boy panties and apologize to her. She's done nothing wrong, and even if in your mind she has, you fucking damn well suck it up and apologize anyway. That woman out there didn't just save you from a prison sentence. She saved your goddamn life, and you'd better not forget that."

"I haven't," I said.

"Good. Then it should be easy for you to apologize." He gestured to the bag sitting on the floor. "I picked you out some clothes and some toiletries. Razor, antiperspirant, that sort of thing."

He pointed to the beard sprouting on my face. "You should shave that off. You're much prettier without it."

I rolled my eyes. "Thanks. How much do I owe you?"

"Don't worry about it."

I scowled at him. "Tell me how much it was."

"I said not to worry about it."

"I don't need your damn charity," I said.

"Think of it as my way of saying thanks for saving Maddie at the bar that night."

"Fine."

He suddenly grinned at me. "See you later, pussy cat."

He grabbed the doorknob and stared at me over his shoulder when I called his name.

"I'm not good enough for her," I said hoarsely.

"No, probably not. But you can give her what that douchebag of a fiancé never did."

"What's that?"

"You're a smart guy - you'll figure it out," Roman said. "Good night."

* * *

I LOUDLY CLEARED MY THROAT AND STEPPED INTO THE kitchen. Maddie was standing at the sink, scrubbing at a pot, and she didn't turn around. I'd waited until I heard Roman leave before leaving the bedroom. He was right – I needed to apologize to Maddie, but I was oddly nervous. What if she didn't forgive me? What if she told me to leave? I had been ready to storm out less than two hours ago, but truthfully, I didn't want to go. It wasn't just the fact that I was homeless and broke. Knowing that if I walked out the door, I would never see Maddie again made me break out in a cold sweat. I was fucking losing it.

I took a deep breath. While waiting for Roman to leave, I

mulled over what he'd said about her fiancé. What hadn't he given her that I could? I was lying on the bed, staring sightlessly at the ceiling, when the answer hit me.

Respect. I had only met the little twerp for a few minutes, but even I could hear the dismissive way he had spoken to her, see the barely hidden disdain in his gaze. Although I found it hard to believe that a strong-willed woman like Maddie would ever let her man disrespect her, it didn't mean it wasn't true. Love had a way of making people do stupid things. It's why I had no fucking use for it.

I was no better than him in how I treated her, though. Always panting after her, acting like she was nothing more than a warm place to stick my dick. She was so beautiful, it made me ache, and I imagined her fiancé felt the same way. He probably treated her the same way – how the fuck couldn't he have? Those curves of hers could bring a man to his goddamn knees. I wanted to fuck her, wanted to be in her warmth so badly it hurt, but she deserved better than that. I would give her the respect that her fiancé never had, be her friend, and forget how much I wanted her.

I cleared my throat again. "Maddie?"

"Yes?" She continued to scrub at the pot.

"I'm sorry. I was being a dickhead earlier."

"Yeah, you were."

"I know. I'm sorry. I have no excuse for it."

She sighed, and some of the tension left her body. "Apology accepted."

Relief flooded through me. I grabbed the dishtowel and dried the pots she had already washed.

"Thanks."

"You're welcome. Thanks for dinner. It was delicious."

"Are you still hungry?"

"No."

She gave me a quick once-over. "Your clothes fit okay?"

I glanced at my T-shirt and jeans. "Yeah, Roman did a good job."

She rinsed the pot and handed it to me for drying. "How's your side?"

"It's fine. I took some Advil earlier."

"Good."

She put the pots away, bending to tuck them into one of the lower cupboards. I forced my gaze away from her ass in her tight yoga pants. Shit, just being Maddie's friend was going to be more difficult than I thought.

She glanced at the clock on the wall. "Do you want to watch some TV?"

"Sure. As long as it isn't that stupid Bachelor show."

She smiled a little. "I guess I can find something else to watch tonight."

I returned her smile and followed her to the living room.

CHAPTER 9

Maddie

I walked toward the bedroom, acutely aware of the way my ass jiggled – hell, the way my entire body jiggled – as Riley followed me. We had watched TV for a few hours, me on one end of the couch and he on the other, and despite Riley's apology, I was tense and anxious. There was something different about him, but I couldn't quite put my finger on what it was. I smiled nervously at him as he lingered in the doorway.

"What's wrong?"

"Nothing," he said. "Listen, Maddie, I'll sleep in the guest room tonight. I'm feeling much better, and your bed is a bit small. We'll both probably sleep better this way."

Dismay bloomed in my belly. I had hoped that the weird tension between us would disappear once he was tucked against me in bed. I was even planning to see if he wanted to finish what we had started earlier today, rationalizing to myself that Riley was right. If we went slow, if I rode him and did all the work, we could have sex without hurting him.

You can't ride him, Maddie. Remember what happened when you were on top with Jordan?

My face flamed as Riley watched me cautiously. Fuck, it didn't matter anyway. How could I have been so blind? The difference in him was so obvious now. He hadn't once looked at my body, hadn't once made a sexually suggestive or dirty comment the entire time we were watching TV together. The previous desire he felt for me was gone.

Tears pricked at my eyes, and I turned away hurriedly before Riley could see. I didn't know what had changed Riley's mind, but deep down, I wasn't surprised. Men like him weren't attracted to women like me, I reminded myself. Be happy his attraction to you lasted for as long as it did.

"Maddie?" Riley said almost tentatively.

"That's fine," I said. "You're right."

There was silence behind me, and I blinked rapidly. The tears fell anyway, and I bit the inside of my cheek so hard I could taste the bitter and metallic tang of blood.

Keep it together, Maddie. So, Riley doesn't want you anymore. Get over it, for God's sake. You knew it would happen sooner or later.

"Good night, Maddie. I'll see you in the morning."

"Good night, Riley." I was proud of how steady my voice was.

The door shut. I walked to the bathroom to blow my nose and wipe my streaming eyes before changing into my night-gown and crawling into bed. I stared miserably at the ceiling, trying to ignore the hurt feelings. Once Riley felt better, he'd leave, and I'd never see him again. It was better this way.

* * *

HIS CRIES WOKE ME ONLY A FEW HOURS AFTER I FELL INTO A restless sleep. I bolted out of bed and was standing in front of the guest room door before I was fully awake. I knocked, his moans of fear cut out abruptly, and I opened the door.

"Riley? Are you okay?"

"Yeah," he gasped out. "I'm fine."

I took a tentative step into the room. He was a dark lump under the bedcovers, and I took another hesitant step toward him. "Do you want me to lie down with you?"

"No. No, I'm okay. I'm sorry I woke you."

"Are you sure? I don't mind."

God, I hated how pathetic and needy I sounded, but I wanted to feel Riley's arms around me so much it hurt.

"No," he repeated. "Go back to bed. I'm good."

"Riley, the nightmares aren't -"

"I said go back to bed, Maddie."

The harshness in his voice had returned. I retreated to the hallway. He didn't even want me near him now, and I had never felt more fat or ugly in my entire life.

"Good night, Riley. I'm sorry," I whispered as the hot tears dripped down my face.

"Good night."

* * *

"Maddie? What's wrong?" Roman stared at me in alarm.

"Nothing," I said. "Just a long week at work. I'm glad it's Friday."

Roman stared suspiciously at me, and I forced myself to smile. The last week had been awful. Riley was still treating me in an odd and distant manner, and with each day that passed, he looked worse and worse.

His side seemed to be healing. He never flinched when he moved now, and last night, I caught him doing a few cautious pull-ups in the kitchen doorway. I'd freaked out a little, but he'd shrugged off my worry.

Unfortunately, although his body was healing, his mind was fracturing. It was the nightmares. He woke me nightly with his loud cries of fear, and it took every ounce of my willpower to stop from going to him to try to soothe him. I had tried to talk to him about the nightmares last night while we were watching TV, but he had denied even having them.

"Riley," I finally said in exasperation. "I can hear you crying out."

He flushed bright red and stared at the TV as I leaned toward him. "How much sleep have you gotten since Sunday night?"

"Enough. Don't worry about it, Maddie. I'm fine. I'm used to not getting much sleep."

"You're not fine," I insisted. "You can't survive without sleep. You need to -"

"I'm getting enough sleep. Let it go, would you?"

"Fine," I retorted. "Excuse me for trying to help."

"I don't need your help."

"Of course, you don't. You don't need anyone's help," I'd muttered.

"Maddie, are you sure?" Roman touched my arm, jarring me back to the present.

"Yes, just tired," I repeated. "How was your week?"

"Fine. We had a guy come into the ER yesterday with a glass soda bottle stuck in his ass."

"You did not!"

"Swear to God. He said he sat on it accidentally. Don't you hate it when that happens?"

I laughed, and Roman kissed me on the cheek. "There's my girl. You had me worried for a minute, Mads." He sniffed the air. "What is that delicious smell?"

"Riley made potato soup for dinner."

"Your biker babe can cook?"

I nodded. "Yeah, and he's damn good at it. He's cooked

dinner every night this week. It's nice to come home from work to a hot dinner."

"Any of that delicious soup left over?" Roman asked.

I laughed again. "Yes. Would you like a bowl?"

"Fuck, yes. I'm starving. Now, where's your biker babe? I'm here to remove his stitches."

"He's in the living room," I said.

I started toward the kitchen and stopped when Roman caught my hand. "Mads? Are you sure you're okay?"

"Yes," I lied. "I'm fine."

* * *

Riley

"HOLY FUCK, DUDE. YOU LOOK LIKE SHIT."

I jerked on the couch and stared blearily at Roman. I had been nodding off, my head throbbing and my eyes burning from lack of sleep. I said a brief prayer of thanks that Roman had woken me before I could fall asleep.

"Nice to see you too, Roman."

He sat down beside me. "Seriously, dude. You look terrible."

He reached for my forehead, and I jerked away from him.

"Relax," he said. "I'm checking for a fever."

"I don't have a fever. I'm tired."

"Does your side hurt? Do you feel achy or warm?" he asked.

"No. I haven't slept well the last few days."

"Have you always had trouble sleeping?" Roman asked.

Before I could answer, Maddie walked into the room carrying a bowl of soup. "He has nightmares every night. He's barely slept at all since Sunday night."

"Maddie," I snapped, "he doesn't need to know that."

"He does. He's your doctor."

She set the bowl of soup on the coffee table. "I think he needs something to help him sleep."

"No, I don't. I'm not taking goddamn sleeping pills."

"Do you have trouble falling asleep or staying asleep?" Roman asked.

"What does that matter?"

"If it's trouble falling asleep, you could try taking melatonin. That can help with insomnia," Roman said.

"He doesn't have trouble falling asleep," Maddie said. "He has terrible nightmares that wake him up."

"What are they about?" Roman asked.

"None of your goddamn business," I said. "You're my doctor, not my fucking shrink."

"Harsh but fair," Roman said cheerfully. "Well, sleeping pills won't help. It sounds like your problem isn't in the actual sleeping but the nightmares. Have you tried meditation before bed? Sometimes that can help relax the mind, and the nightmares may not be as bad if you're feeling relaxed and calm."

"I'm not a fucking hippie," I growled.

Roman laughed so hard he nearly fell off the couch. I could feel my lips turning up, and even Maddie smiled. Fuck, she was gorgeous when she smiled.

"Well, I'm going to recommend seeing a psychiatrist," Roman said. "Talking about it will help, and a good psychiatrist will help you get to the root of your nightmares."

"I keep telling him that," Maddie said.

I glared at her, and she stuck her tongue out at me before smiling at Roman. "Eat your soup before it gets cold, honey."

"Let me take out Riley's stitches first." Roman rummaged through his bag and snapped on gloves before pulling out a pair of small, sharp scissors. "Stand up and take off your shirt, handsome. Let me see that rippling six pack."

I rolled my eyes and stood easily before pulling my shirt over my head.

"Roman, are you sure you should remove the stitches?" Maddie asked a bit anxiously. "It's only been a week."

"I'm sure. It looks really good – Riley's a fast healer."

He studied the healed gashes on my side and back before snipping the stitches with the scissors. Using tweezers, he pulled each one free with a sharp tug and dropped them on a tissue on the coffee table.

"How often do you work out, Riley?"

"Before I got shot, every day. One of the club guys had a gym set up in his garage, and he let me use it," I said.

"Jesus, I wish I had that kind of dedication," Roman said. "I'd rather eat Lucky Charms and watch *The Bachelor*. I've got a home gym, but most of the equipment is just gathering dust."

"He was doing pull-ups last night," Maddie said disapprovingly.

"Fuck, you can do a pull-up?" Roman said.

"They're not difficult," I replied.

"Yeah, well, not all of us have rippling muscles and bodies of steel like you do, Superman."

"You seem to be in pretty good shape," I said.

Roman shrugged as he dropped the last stitch in the tissue. "I have a good metabolism, and I do a lot of cardio – running that sort of thing. I want to get into some weight training, though. I tried before and pulled my fucking hammie. I could barely walk for a goddamn week."

"You've got to start with lower weight and more reps." I shrugged into my shirt. "Build up to the heavier weight."

"Now that you're feeling better, maybe you could drop by my dusty home gym and give me some tips. You can use the equipment as well," Roman said.

I shrugged. "Sure, if you want."

"We'll give it another week or so to ensure you're fully healed. Even then, you'll have to take it easy for a bit. Deal?"

I nodded as Roman removed his gloves and sat down on the couch. He spooned some soup into his mouth. "Damn, this is good."

A tingle of pride went through me when Maddie said, "Riley's a great cook."

"I'm not disagreeing," Roman mumbled around a mouthful of soup. "Hey, have you watched *The Bachelor* finale yet?"

"No!" Maddie said. "No spoilers, I have it recorded."

"I haven't watched it either," Roman replied. "Why don't we watch it together tonight?"

"Can we make it tomorrow night instead? I'm beat and want to have a hot bath and go to bed," Maddie said.

I gave her a furtive, guilty look. I had no doubt that I'd woken her up every night with my nightmares, but she didn't come to my room. More than once, I'd been tempted to go to her, to ask her to hold me so I could get some sleep. But if that didn't make me the biggest fucking pussy on the planet, I didn't know what did.

"Sure," Roman said. "I'll come by around seven."

He scraped the last soup from the bowl before carrying it to the kitchen. He returned, kissed Maddie on the cheek, and grabbed his medical bag. "See you later, guys."

"Bye, Roman," Maddie said.

"Thanks for taking out the stitches," I said.

"Don't mention it." Roman left, and Maddie and I stood in uncomfortable silence.

"Well, I know it's early, but I think I'll have that hot bath and go to bed. Good night, Riley."

"Night, Maddie," I said. I watched her leave before collapsing on the couch and flipping aimlessly through the channels.

I should have been going to bed, but the thought of falling asleep and seeing Andrea's dead face in my dreams again made me shudder helplessly. I didn't know what the hell was happening to me. The nightmares were no worse than before, and the lack of sleep was nothing new, but now, for whatever reason, it was like I couldn't handle it anymore.

It's because you finally remembered what getting a full night's sleep was like. No bad dreams, no waking up in a cold sweat. Maddie did that for you. Stop being such a fucking moron and go to her. She has what you need.

I shook off the thought and, my eyes burning, stared grimly at the TV.

* * *

I WATCHED IN HELPLESS HORROR AS MY HAND TURNED THE *doorknob of Andrea's room. My feet carried me into the room. The cold breeze from the window blew through my hair, and I stared numbly at her bare feet. She hated wearing socks, always had, and I moaned loudly as I raised my gaze to her face.*

Her beautiful, sweet face was swollen and black. Her tongue protruded from her mouth, and her light blue eyes bulged obscenely. I stared in frozen terror at her familiar but suddenly horrifying face as the rope she had used to hang herself creaked back and forth. She was so skinny, her always thin frame wasted away to the point of being skeletal, that her body swung lightly in the breeze.

"Andrea? Oh, Andrea, no," I moaned as tears flowed down my cheeks. "Oh, baby, I'm so sorry. I'm so fucking sorry."

It was my fault she was dead. I had ignored the warning signs and convinced myself she would be fine. My blood froze in my veins when I heard Ma climbing the stairs.

"Rye? Rye, is it rats making that noise?"

"Ma! Stay downstairs!" I tried not to scream, but even I could hear the panic and terror in my voice.

"Riley? Honey, what's wrong?"

Ma's voice drifted closer, and I turned and screamed at her as she crested the final step.

"Don't come up here, Ma! Get back downstairs – right fucking now!"

She cringed back, looking so much like she did when Dad screamed at her, and my heart broke. "Ma, I'm sorry. Just – just go downstairs, okay? I'll be right down."

"Okay, Rye," she whispered.

She walked slowly down the stairs, and, taking a deep breath, I turned around again. I needed to call 9-1-1. Harsh laughter brayed from my lips. It was way too fucking late for 9-1-1. My baby sister was dead, and it was all my fucking fault.

I didn't want to look at her again, but I couldn't help it. Steeling myself, I stared up at her, and fresh horror gushed through me. Maddie, my sweet, loving Maddie, was hanging from the ceiling. Her dark eyes stared accusingly at me. The blood vessels in her eyes had burst, turning the white into a bright, gruesome red. I screamed when she turned her dead gaze toward me.

"This is your fault, Riley." The rope shifted against her throat as she spoke, revealing the harsh burns on her soft skin. I screamed again as she raised one pale hand toward me.

"All your fault I'm dead," she moaned. "You killed me, Riley."

"I'm sorry, Maddie! I'm sorry!" I screamed. "Maddie, I'm so sorry! Forgive me! Forgive –

I jerked awake with another harsh scream, my heart beating as quickly as a runaway train in my chest, and my entire body covered in a thin film of sweat. Adrenaline pumped through my veins, and although the rational part of me knew it was only a dream, it couldn't stop me from stumbling out of bed and running to the door. I needed to see Maddie. I needed to make sure she was alive. I fled into the hallway and straight into Maddie. She cried out with surprise, staggering back and tripping over her own feet. I caught her before she could fall and crushed her against my chest.

"Maddie!" I shouted, and she threw her arms around my waist.

"It's okay, honey. Shhh, it's okay," she said. She was crying, and I rested my sweaty forehead against hers.

"Are you okay?" I asked in a panic.

"I'm fine," she said. "Are *you* okay?"

"Yeah," I said.

I wasn't. I shook like a goddamn leaf, and I couldn't stop touching Maddie, her soft skin, her silky hair. The nightmare had been so fucking vivid, and I was terribly afraid I would always have the vision of that rope cinched around her neck.

We stood in the hallway, holding each other as I tried to stop my shuddering.

"What are you doing out here?" I finally asked.

"You were screaming my name," she said. "It was so awful. I know you don't want me to comfort you anymore, but I couldn't stand it, Riley. You sounded so afraid and so..."

She burst into tears. "It scared me so much."

"I'm sorry," I mumbled into her hair. "I'm sorry, Maddie."

"Don't be." Her hands stroked my naked back. "You're cold, Riley. You should get back into bed."

"No!" My arms tightened around her in a panic. "Don't leave me. Please."

I hated how weak I sounded, but the thought of being alone in the dark sent fresh waves of terror through me. I was so goddamn tired, but I didn't have a chance in hell of sleeping again tonight. Fuck that – I would probably never sleep again.

"I won't. Come with me, honey." She took my hand and led me to her bedroom. She climbed into bed and patted the spot beside her. I nearly fell into the bed next to her and pressed my head against her breast as she pulled up the sheet and quilt and tucked them around us both.

"Go to sleep, Riley. You're safe."

* * *

Maddie

I STARED AT THE CEILING, PETTING RILEY'S BACK IN LONG, soothing strokes. His shaking had finally stopped, and I was certain he was close to sleeping or already asleep. He was still clutching me tightly, but his breathing was deep and even.

I suppressed my shudder of fear as I remembered the sound of Riley's voice screaming my name. God, it had frightened me so badly to hear it. I was out of bed and running to the guest room before I could stop myself. I hadn't cared that he didn't want my comfort. I couldn't lie in the dark and listen to him scream.

I closed my eyes and tried to relax. I wouldn't sleep. Hell, I might never sleep again after hearing Riley scream like that, but I would try to rest.

I twitched in surprise when Riley's voice drifted out of the dark. "Why did you and your fiancé break up?"

"You should try to get some sleep," I said.

"I can't. Was it because of me?"

"No, it wasn't because of you."

"Then why?" He raised his head and squinted at me.

I touched his face, feeling the rough stubble under the palm of my hand, before sighing. "That night in the bar, how I was dressed – it's not normally how I dress."

"Yeah, I figured."

I sighed again. "Jordan and I were together for just over four years. I loved him, and I thought he loved me too. The funny thing is – I think he did love me. Just not the way that I loved him."

I licked my lips, feeling a dull blush heat my cheeks. "Our sex life was never that great. Jordan didn't have a high sex drive, and he just never seemed that interested in me. He said I – I wasn't very good at sex, and I suppose I'm not. I don't have a lot of experience, and sex with Jordan was often weird and uncomfortable. He never said anything, but I knew my weight was an issue. He was thin and fit, and he thought my breasts and butt were too big."

"Idiot," Riley muttered. He was starting to sound like his normal self, and a thin thread of relief went through me.

"I tried a few different things, but he never seemed into it. I would... I would go down on him, and after only a few minutes, he was tapping me on the head and making me stop. He never wanted to perform oral sex on me. He said that I..."

My cheeks flushed again, and I ground to a halt. I couldn't tell Riley what Jordan said.

"He said what, Maddie?" Riley asked.

"Never mind, it doesn't matter," I said.

He cupped my face and frowned at me in the dim light. "Tell me, Mads."

"He said that I smelled weird and tasted strange," I whispered miserably.

"Motherfucker," Riley said.

I closed my eyes, embarrassed beyond belief, and Riley stroked my cheek.

"Go on."

"Our sex life was getting worse. It had been over three months since we'd slept together. I made up my mind that I would do something about it, that I would seduce Jordan and show him that we were compatible. I bought that stupid black dress and ridiculous lingerie and went to Jordan's place to seduce him. I wasn't supposed to go over there that night, but I wanted to surprise him."

"What then?" Riley prompted when I lapsed into silence.

"He wasn't alone," I said dully.

"He was screwing another chick?"

I laughed bitterly. "Not quite. The house was dark, but there was a light on in the bedroom, and when I opened the bedroom door, Jordan was having sex with our friend Kurt."

Riley stiffened against me. "Jordan was gay?"

"Yeah," I said. "The three of us stared at each other, and then I just ran. I got in my car and I started driving. I was crying and shaking and freaking out, and then my stupid car died, and I walked to the bar to look for a phone."

I sat up and stared at him. "I'm not a whore, Riley, and I didn't have sex with you as some retaliation against Jordan, I swear it. When you started kissing me and touching me, for the first time, I felt, well, I felt pretty and wanted, and after what I'd seen, I needed to feel that way. I know deep down that it isn't my fault. Jordan hides who he truly is because his parents are rich, and he lives off a trust fund. If they found out he's gay, they would cut him off from the money. I know the truth, I do, but there is still a part of me that thinks it's my fault. Do you understand?"

"It wasn't your fault," Riley said.

"I know," I said. "But I can't help the way I feel. Part of me thought, still thinks, that maybe it was my body and my poor sex skills that turned Jordan gay. It's ridiculous, I know."

He didn't say anything, and I stared shamefully at him. "I wasn't trying to purposely use you that night. I swear it. But being with you, feeling how much you wanted me, made me feel good. I wanted to hold on to that. It's why I let you fuck me in that bathroom, why I – I gave you a blowjob in front of everyone."

He continued to stare silently at me, and I flushed again.

"I'm sorry for that, by the way. I know I'm not very good at giving blowjobs. Jordan always said that -"

"Jordan is a fucking idiot. It was the best blowjob of my life, Maddie."

My mouth dropped open. "You're just saying that to make me feel better."

"No, I'm fucking not," he growled. "It was incredible. Even now, all I have to do is think about your hot little mouth on my dick, and I'm hard as a fucking rock."

"You – really?"

"To be fair," Riley continued with a small grin, "I'm a bit of an exhibitionist and knowing that the guys in the club were watching as the hottest woman in the room sucked my dick – might have made it even hotter."

I blushed furiously, a small part of me embarrassed but a bigger part ridiculously pleased. God, if people knew that I liked the idea of Riley being turned on by others watching me give him a blowjob, they'd –

They'd what, Maddie? Think you were comfortable with your sexuality? Think you were a slut? Either way, who fucking cares? It's no one's business, but your own, and most people won't give a shit about your love life. Get over yourself.

"Anyway," I said, "as you know, Jordan was waiting for me that night. I broke up with him about five minutes after you left and haven't spoken to him since."

"Maddie?" Riley said.

"Yeah?"

"Do you ever think about that night at the bar?"

"All the time."

"Me too."

"Why did you help me?" I asked.

"Because you were hot as fuck," he said teasingly.

I made myself smile at him. "Tell the truth."

"I am telling the truth," Riley said. "You made my dick

hard just looking at you. I wanted you from the minute you stumbled into that bar, Maddie."

His hand stroked my side through my nightshirt, soft strokes with the tips of his fingers, and I trembled against him.

"I wanted to fuck you so bad," he whispered into my ear. "I couldn't believe my luck when I looked at you in the bathroom and realized you wanted to fuck me too."

I inhaled sharply as his hand slipped under my nightshirt and cupped my bare breast. My nipple was a tight bud, and he made a noise of approval before rubbing it.

"Sliding into your tight pussy, watching your face as I fucked you, made me want to come almost instantly. You have no idea how difficult it was to hold back, Kitten." He traced my jaw with his tongue, and I moaned.

"Your asshole fiancé was wrong, Mads." He nipped my earlobe and pinched my nipple until my back arched. "You're fucking amazing at sex."

I shook my head, my desire dying. "No, I'm not, Riley. Don't start thinking that I am, okay? You'll just be disappointed."

Fuck, this was a bad idea. Riley had this way of making me forget that I sucked in bed, made me so damn hot for him that I wanted to forget my dismal lovemaking skills and let him do whatever he wanted to me.

"I've fucked you, Maddie, remember? I know exactly how good you are." He squeezed my breast lightly.

"You fucked me once," I argued. "I was with Jordan for four years and -"

"How often did you have sex?" he asked.

"I don't know, maybe once or twice a month."

He swore under his breath. "Fine. Let's give the little pencil-dick the benefit of the doubt and say it was twice a month. Four years with him, that's what," he paused and thought for a moment, "ninety-six times you had sex?"

"Yeah, I guess. So what?"

"So, that means I'll need to fuck you ninety-seven times to make an accurate assessment of the situation."

I laughed. "Riley, that's ridiculous. It's not a competi -"

He cut me off by slanting his mouth over mine and sliding his tongue into my mouth. I moaned and clutched at his broad back as he curled his tongue around mine and urged it into his mouth. He sucked on my tongue, his fingers pulling on my taut nipple, and I made a low whimper of assent.

"I want to fuck you, Kitten. I need to fuck you," he whispered raggedly into my ear. "Will you let me?"

"Yes," I said. "I want to – to fuck you too."

He immediately tugged my nightshirt over my head, dropping it over the side of the bed before dipping his head and sucking one nipple into his mouth. I threaded my fingers through his dark hair and held him tightly as he circled the tip of it with his tongue before sucking again.

"Riley," I panted, "maybe we shouldn't do this tonight. You're tired and still not completely healed."

He growled against my soft flesh before biting lightly at my nipple. "I can't wait any longer. Don't ask me to."

"I don't want you to get hurt," I gasped as he slid his warm hand into my panties. He touched my pussy, a grin crossing his face at the wetness.

"You can't wait any longer either, Mads. Let me give you what we both need."

"Your side," I moaned again. "You were shot and -"

"I'm fine. I'll go slow."

"Do you promise?"

He stared down at me before suddenly shaking his head.

"No, I'm going to fuck you hard and fast. I can't be slow – not tonight."

Fresh wetness dripped from my pussy. He gave me a slow grin. "My kitten likes that idea."

"Riley, I -"

He kissed me until I was panting and moaning before nuzzling my ear. "I'll make it slower and better the next time, Mads. I promise. I just need you too much tonight."

As he spoke, his fingers were rubbing my wet clit, and I was shamefully close to an orgasm already. "Riley, I – I'm going to come if you don't stop that."

He grinned, and I cried out when his fingers strummed my clit harder and faster. "Now, why would I want to stop that from happening, Kitten?"

"Riley!" I arched against his hand, my hands clinging to his thick wrists helplessly as he sucked one throbbing nipple. "Oh fuck!"

My orgasm washed over me in a tidal wave of hot, wet pleasure, and I moaned and twisted wildly as Riley pressed warm kisses against my throat.

"Oh my God," I moaned, "Oh my God, Riley."

"Do you have any condoms?" he muttered into my ear.

"Nightstand," I gasped.

He reached across me and rummaged in the nightstand. He ripped open the foil package and rolled the condom onto his cock before nudging my thighs.

"Open your legs, Kitten."

I spread them eagerly, and he pulled off my panties before propping his large body between my thighs.

"Wider," he rasped.

I spread my legs until I could feel the burn in my thigh muscles as he repositioned and his cock nudged at my wet entrance. I tensed nervously, why I didn't know, and he leaned down and pressed an oddly sweet kiss against my mouth.

"Relax, Mads. I'm not going to hurt you."

"I know," I said.

He pushed into me, his thick length stretching me until I gasped. There was a twinge of pain – fuck, I had forgotten how damn big he was – and he stopped when I tensed up again.

"Okay?" he said hoarsely.

"Yeah, I – I forgot how big you were."

A small grin crossed his face, and I smacked him lightly on the back. "No need to look so smug."

I braced my feet on the bed as he pushed. Slowly, inch by inch, my pussy took his cock until he was seated completely inside of me, his heavy balls pressing against my ass.

"You are so fucking tight, Kitten," he suddenly moaned. "I'll be lucky if I last more than a few goddamn strokes."

Now it was my turn to smile, and he grinned before kissing me. "No need to look so smug, Mads."

I giggled, and my inner muscles tightened around his thick cock. He groaned before thrusting hard in response. I gasped and dug my hands into his back as he pumped his hips in and out. He moved harder and faster, his breath tearing in and out of his lungs in harsh gasps. I watched in utter fascination as his head fell back, and his entire body shuddered wildly against mine.

"Jesus," he muttered before rolling off of me. "I'm sorry, Kitten."

"For what?" I asked as he pulled off the condom and threw it in the wastebasket next to the bed.

"I barely lasted two fucking minutes," he said.

I stroked my hand across his chest as he tugged on a piece of my hair and said, "I'm blaming you. Your pussy was too fucking hot and tight."

I gave him a mock scowl, and he grinned before turning to his side. I bit my lip and sat up when he winced and pressed his hand against his ribs.

"Oh God, you hurt yourself, didn't you?"

"No," he said. "Lie down, Mads."

"Maybe I should call Roman. Have him come over and -"

"No," he repeated before pulling me into his arms. "I'm fine. Just tired and ready to sleep for the next fifty years."

"Are you sure?" I persisted.

"Yes." He was already half asleep, and I curled up against him. He pressed his face into my throat and draped his arm around my waist.

"Good night, Riley."

"Night, Mads." He lapsed into soft snoring.

CHAPTER 10

Riley

Bright sunlight streamed into the bedroom when I opened my eyes. I stretched, wincing a little at the dull pain in my side before checking the clock. It was two in the afternoon, and I felt better than I had in days. There'd been no nightmares, and I rubbed the stubble on my cheek. I couldn't deny it any longer – sleeping in Maddie's bed and lying in her warm embrace kept the nightmares away. I muttered a curse to myself as I rolled over to face Maddie. Relying on other people was a completely foreign concept to me, and –

My pulse sped up, and adrenaline pumped through my veins. Maddie wasn't lying beside me. I scrambled wildly out of the bed. Where was she? Had she left? I was at the bedroom door when I heard the shower. Relief swept through me, and my heart slowed its panicked thudding. She hadn't left me.

What the fuck, Riley? You're acting like a scared little boy – get it together, for fuck's sake. What's happening between you and

Maddie isn't going to last forever. Sooner or later, she'll grow tired of you. You have nothing to offer her beyond a good fucking, and your abilities in bed will only keep her interest for so long. She'll ask you to leave and find a good guy to marry and raise babies with. It's what women like her do.

Yeah, it was. And I needed to ignore the surprisingly large wave of jealousy that flooded through me at the thought of Maddie with another man. Maddie and I weren't going to last. Besides, I didn't want a relationship. The only two people I had ever loved were both dead – one because of me and, while Ma's doctors listed cancer as the official cause of death, Ma had died from a broken heart. The death of her child had been too much for her. I knew that as well as I knew my own fucking name.

People I cared about died – it was as simple as that.

Of course, knowing we weren't going to last didn't stop my dick from hardening at the thought of Maddie naked and wet in the shower. I didn't hesitate as I strode to the bathroom and slipped into the room. I might mean nothing more to Maddie than a good time in the bedroom, but I would take what she offered for as long as she let me.

I pulled back the shower curtain and grinned at Maddie when she gasped. She crossed her arms over her chest as I stepped into the shower and crowded her against the tile wall.

I let my gaze drift over her naked body before announcing crudely, "You are sexy as fuck."

She blushed and stared at my chest. "Good morning to you, too, Riley."

I ducked under the hot spray of water, soaking my hair and body before tugging her arms down and pressing my chest against her breasts. Fuck did I love the feel of her tight, hard nipples rubbing against my skin.

"More like good afternoon." I nuzzled her neck.

"Good point." Her voice was already breathless, and her soft little moan when I rubbed my dick against her belly, made my pulse jump. "How are you feeling?"

"Fine." I licked some drops of water from the top of her shoulder before nipping at her soft skin. She jerked in my arms, and I pressed her more tightly against the wall before kissing my way to her neck. I sucked on her flesh where her neck became her shoulder. She moaned again before tilting her head to give me better access. I studied the soft pink mark my mouth had left on her pale skin before dipping my head and sucking hard. Her body twitched against mine, and she gasped my name.

"Riley? Wh-what are you doing?"

"Nothing," I growled before licking her skin. The pink mark had darkened to a deep red, and a wave of satisfaction crept over me. This one would leave a mark – my mark. I had the sudden urge to mark her again, but some common sense trickled past my caveman-like attitude.

A hickey? Really? Are you fucking thirteen years old?

"Riley?" Maddie's voice was hesitant. "We can't have sex in the shower."

I grinned. "That's pretty presumptuous of you, Kitten. Maybe I was just worried you would use all the hot water."

Her face fell immediately, and I cursed to myself. Teasing Maddie about sex was a bad fucking idea, and I knew it. Her asshole fiancé had convinced her she wasn't good at it and that her body was something to be ashamed about.

I stiffened as Roman's words echoed in my head. What Maddie needed - what her fiancé had never given her – was to be shown just how fucking desirable she was.

And I was absolutely the man to do it.

She wiggled her wet body away from mine and grabbed the shower curtain. "I'm finished. You can have the shower to -"

I wrapped my arm around her curvy waist and pulled her back into my embrace. "Where are you going?"

She frowned. "Well, I - you said you wanted to shower."

"That's true." I kissed her perfect mouth. "But I'll need your help."

Her eyes widened, and she stared at my side. "Oh shit, is your side okay? I knew we shouldn't have had sex last night. I'm such an idiot! I need to call Roman and -"

I stopped her nervous babbling by slanting my mouth across hers and shoving my tongue deep into her mouth. By the time I was finished kissing her, she was circling her hips against mine, and her fingers were digging into my naked ass.

"My side is fine, Mads," I rubbed my erection against her wet stomach, "but I want to keep it that way, so you'll have to help me shower."

I handed her the soap and grinned at her. "Get to it, woman."

She rolled her eyes but soaped her hands before running them over my chest. "Fine, but we aren't having sex in the shower, Riley."

"Is that something you've thought about?" I asked as I lifted one heavy breast and kneaded it roughly. "Me fucking you in the shower?"

Her cheeks turned pink, and she shook her head. "No, of course not."

"Liar." I sucked on her bottom lip. "You want me to fuck you in the shower."

"Don't be ridiculous." She turned me around and briskly washed my back. "Our height difference makes it completely impossible, and you can't lift my fat ass to -"

I turned around and threw an arm around her hips before glaring at her. "Call yourself fat once more, Kitten, and I'll spank that delectable ass of yours."

"You wouldn't dare."

"Wouldn't I?"

I slapped her ass, and she made a little squeal of surprise. "Riley!"

"I mean it, Kitten. Your body is fucking amazing. It makes me so damn hot I can barely think straight, and if you put yourself down again, I'll spank you and then fuck you senseless. Right here in the goddamn shower."

She stared silently at me, and I squeezed her ass. "Say your body is amazing."

She bit at her bottom lip, and I gave her a softer tap on the ass. "Say it."

"My – my body is amazing."

"That's right, it is. Fucking amazing. Now," I pushed the soap back into her hands, "keep going."

I kept my arm around her hips, kneading and squeezing her ass as she washed my arms and stomach. She swept her hands carefully over the healing scar in my side before, biting her lip again, sliding one hand around my dick.

I released my breath in a sharp hiss as she stroked me. I widened my stance, and she slipped her hand between my legs and carefully washed my balls. I was panting now, my hips thrusting against her as she touched and caressed my cock again. I was stupidly close to coming all over the soft skin of her stomach. I took an unsteady step back, ducking under the spray of water and rinsing the soap from my body.

"All done." Maddie's nipples were rock hard, and I knew if I put my hand between her thighs, I would find her wet and ready for me.

I shook my head. "Not quite, Kitten. My legs."

"Oh, right." She giggled nervously. "Um, okay. I'll, uh…"

She drifted to a stop, and I grinned at her as she rubbed more soap into her hands.

"Something wrong, Mads?"

"Uh, no, I…"

A stubborn look crossed her face before she kneeled in front of me. She rubbed the soap over my thighs and calves, her face flushed pink. When she was finished and tried to stand, I pressed my hands against her shoulders. She looked up at me, and I smoothed her wet hair back before grasping the base of my dick.

"Open, Mads." I cupped the back of her head and drew her toward the head of my dick.

She moaned and immediately opened her mouth. I slid my cock past her full lips and groaned at the feel of her tongue. She sucked at my aching dick, and I pushed until I touched the back of her throat.

A look of panic flickered across her face, and I pulled out of her mouth before stroking her hair. "I won't give you more than you can take."

She licked her already swollen lips and nodded, and I pressed the head of my cock against her mouth again. She opened, and I closed my eyes and let my head fall back as she sucked me.

"Suck harder, Kitten," I demanded as I threaded my fingers through her hair and held her head.

"Fuck, that feels so good," I moaned when she sucked enthusiastically at my cock. "You are so fucking good at this."

I wasn't lying to her. She was good at it, not tentative or unsure like so many women seemed to be. She sucked my dick like she was starving for it, and I couldn't get enough of the feel of her hot, wet mouth.

My hips thrust back and forth, and I barely felt the sting of her nails digging into my thighs. Jesus, I could watch her suck my dick all day. My balls tightened, and I was close to coming in Maddie's mouth. My entire body shuddered with pleasure at the thought, and I stepped back. She immediately leaned forward, trying to suck my cock back into my mouth.

Just the sight of her eagerness nearly made me come all over her soft skin.

"Mads, wait," I said, my hands tightening in her hair.

"What's wrong?" she asked. "Did I – did I do something wrong?"

"No," I tugged her to her feet, "but I want to fuck you, and if you keep sucking my dick like that, I'm going to come in your mouth."

A shiver went through her, and her nipples tightened visibly. I grinned at her. "You like that idea."

"Yes, I do."

Her straightforward answer almost made me push her back to her knees and shove my dick into her mouth. I controlled myself with effort and rinsed the soap from my legs before shutting off the rapidly cooling water.

"Back to the bedroom." I drew back the shower curtain. "I need to fuck you."

"How is your side?" she asked as we dried each other's bodies with towels.

"Fine." I deliberately avoided drying between her legs. If I touched her there, I wouldn't make it back to the bedroom. I'd bend her over right here and fuck her until she was screaming my name.

"Are you sure?" she said. "Maybe we should –"

"I'm sure." I took her arm and pulled her a bit roughly into the bedroom. "Get on the bed, Mads, before I lose my fucking mind."

She sat on the side of the bed, and I pushed her onto her back before raking my hot gaze over her. I wanted to fuck her – hell, I *needed* to fuck her - but as my eyes lingered on the small patch of dark hair between her thighs, I decided fucking her could wait a little longer.

I dropped carefully to my knees beside the bed as Maddie stared at me. "Riley? What are you doing?"

"I need to taste you, Kitten."

She tried to scramble away from me. "Wait! Riley, I - I don't think I want that. Okay? Please, not right now."

If I were a good man, I would have stopped immediately and said something comforting. I would have taken her in my arms and kissed away her protests and worries before I buried my tongue in her sweet pussy.

I wasn't a good man.

Before she could squirm away, I slid my arms under her legs and draped them over my shoulders, then clamped my hands around her soft thighs and dragged her toward me. Her cries of protest and her struggle to get away stopped the moment I licked from her wet opening to her swollen bud of a clit.

"Riley!" She stiffened, her hands clutching at my head as I licked just her clit again.

"Yes, Kitten?" I said before licking her perfect clit with a wide stroke of my tongue.

"OH! Oh my God!" Her hips thrust into my face, and her heels dug into my back.

I sucked her clit into my mouth, rubbing my tongue over it as she squealed, and her body shuddered under my touch.

"You taste so fucking good, Kitten," I growled before burying my tongue in her wet core.

She screamed my name, her hands pulling painfully at my hair as she twisted beneath me. I could barely keep her on the bed. Her reaction to having my tongue in her pussy was so hot I was close to shooting my load all over the damn quilt.

Her legs slipped from my shoulders, and I grabbed her calves and forced her legs up until her feet were resting on the bed. My fingers tightened on her ankles, and I pushed her legs apart until she was completely open to me. I stared at her pink clit and the liquid dripping from her hot core. I kept her legs open when she tried to close them. There was nothing I loved more than the taste of pussy, and Maddie's pussy was so sweet tasting I could eat her all fucking day.

"Riley? What's wrong?" She lifted her head and gave me a hesitant look tinged with embarrassment. I suddenly wanted to break her ex-fiancé's legs with a fierceness that surprised me.

"Nothing, Kitten," I said with a slow grin. "Just admiring your pretty pussy and thinking about how good it tastes."

She flushed, and I kept my gaze on her as I leaned forward and deliberately licked her swollen pussy lips. "Sweet as honey, Mads. You're so wet. Your sweet honey is dripping all over you."

"Riley, I – you shouldn't say things like that," she said.

I grinned again. "Shouldn't say what? That your pussy tastes good? That every day I'll eat this hot, little pussy until you're begging me not to stop?"

"Every day?"

"Every fucking day, Mads. And you'll be a good girl and let me. Do you know why?" I asked.

She shook her head, but something flickered in her eyes. I nodded like she'd answered me. "That's right. Because your pussy belongs to me, and if I want to eat it every day, I will."

Fresh liquid dripped. I bent my head and licked her clean before raising my head again. She was moaning with her eyes closed and her fingers tugging at her nipples. I groaned before taking a deep breath.

"It's mine. Say it, Mads."

"Yours," she said immediately. "Please don't stop, Riley. I'm so close."

"You like having my tongue in your pussy, Kitten?"

"Yes!" she shouted. "Goddammit, Riley, yes!"

I grinned at her sudden anger. As she raised her head and glared at me, I bent my head back to her pussy and went to work. It took only a few minutes of my tongue sliding across her clit before her back arched, her nails dug into my scalp, and she screamed my name.

I grinned smugly and stood as she panted and shuddered on the bed. I reached into the nightstand, snagging a condom and rolling it onto my dick before lying on my side next to her. I sucked at her nipple, making her cry out and her back arch again before reaching between her legs and cupping her pussy.

"No," she gasped and tried to push my hand away. "I can't – not yet."

"I know, Kitten," I murmured into her ear. "But I want to touch the pussy that belongs to me, and you're going to let me."

I kept my hand still, not rubbing or caressing in any way, and after a moment, her tense body relaxed. "I'm sorry."

"Sorry for what?" I asked.

"I – well, I kind of lost control," she said. "Did I hurt you?"

"Hell, no. Besides, I'm used to that reaction." I winked at her, and she smacked me lightly on the chest.

I kneaded her breast before licking just below her earlobe. "Did you like having your pussy eaten, Mads?"

She shuddered again and nodded as I traced her ear with my tongue. "Tell me."

"I – I liked it."

"Liked what?"

She made a harsh noise of frustration, and I traced my thumb over her lower lip before giving her an expectant look.

"I liked having my pussy eaten," she said.

My cock throbbed, and I turned onto my back and patted my flat abdomen. "Climb on, Maddie."

She shook her head. "No way. My legs are, um, way too weak."

I laughed and patted my abdomen again. "You've had time to recover. Straddle me."

She continued to hesitate and sighed when I arched my eyebrow at her. "I'm too heavy. I'll squish you and hurt your side and -"

"You're getting dangerously close to talking shit about your body again."

"I'm not," she protested. "I'm just being realistic. I hurt Jor -"

"Don't say his fucking name," I growled. "I mean it, Mads."

She glared at me. "I hurt *him* the one and only time I tried being on top. He was hobbling around for a week with a sore back, and I had to drive him to the physiotherapist."

"He was faking."

"He wasn't."

"He was," I said. "Even if he wasn't - if he was just a fucking weakling who couldn't handle your curves - I'm not. Now stop arguing and slide that hot pussy onto my cock."

"Fine!" She sat up and straddled me. "But don't say I didn't warn you."

I watched as she grabbed my dick - non too gently either, but I wasn't fucking complaining - and pushed it into her tight pussy. She had to stop about halfway, a slight frown crossing her face, and I smiled at her.

"Go slowly, Mads."

"Thanks for the tip," she grumbled.

I laughed and tucked my hands behind my head as she eased up and down repeatedly, taking a little more of my cock each time until it was swallowed completely by her wet core, and she sat fully on me. I groaned at having my entire dick in her tight pussy, and she stared at me in alarm.

"Am I hurting you?"

"Hell, no. It feels fucking incredible."

She stared uncertainly at me. "Are you - are you going to move?"

"Nope. Remember what Roman said? You need to do all the work, sweetheart."

She rolled her eyes, and I laughed again. "Get to work, Kitten. I'm waiting."

She braced her hands on my stomach. "You'll tell me if I'm hurting you, right?"

"Yes. Fuck me, Mads."

She moved up and down gingerly, and I moaned under my breath. "Harder."

Biting her lip, she moved a little faster.

"Touch your clit," I demanded.

She rubbed delicately at her clit with the tips of her fingers. I watched my cock slide in and out of her wet warmth. I smiled with hard satisfaction when, after a few moments of rubbing her clit, she forgot about hurting me and rode my cock with hard and furious strokes. I lasted maybe two minutes before my hips started to thrust, my entire body screaming out for relief. She bounced on my cock as she rubbed her clit.

I cupped her breasts, pulling on her nipples until her back arched and, with another scream, she came all over my cock. The surge of wetness made my balls tighten. I gripped her hips and pumped my pelvis repeatedly until my orgasm rushed through me. I cried her name, my own back arching, and ignored the faint pain in my side before shuddering and collapsing against the bed.

She eased off of me and curled up against my side, resting her head on my chest as I panted. I kissed the top of her head, and she stared shyly at me. "I didn't hurt you, did I?"

"No, Mads."

"Are you sure?"

"Yes," I said. "Now, get to the kitchen and make me a sandwich, woman."

"You make me a sandwich. I was the one who did all the work, remember?"

"Good point," I said before sitting up. "Come to the kitchen and keep me company while I make your damn sandwich."

* * *

Maddie

"I'M TELLING YOU, MADS," ROMAN THREW A HANDFUL OF popcorn into his mouth as he stretched his long limbs out on the chaise, "he's choosing Jana. She's perfect for him."

"He isn't," I objected as I hit play. "He's choosing Arlene. He connected really well with her family, remember?"

"So, that doesn't mean anything. He's not marrying her family," Roman countered. "Besides, he -"

"He's choosing Marilyn," Riley said. "She's the only one who banged him on their individual date. That automatically puts her miles ahead of the competition."

Roman and I turned and stared open-mouthed at Riley. He was sitting at one end of the couch, and he shrugged. "What?"

"Nothing," Roman said with a grin. "It's just amusing as hell that Mr. 'I hate this stupid show' is as secretly obsessed with it as the rest of us."

"I'm not obsessed with it," Riley said. "I'm only watching it because Maddie makes me."

"Uh-huh, sure." Roman tossed another handful of popcorn into his mouth and chewed loudly. "You keep telling yourself that, big guy."

Riley snorted under his breath and then scowled when I started to sit next to Roman. "Sit beside me, Mads."

I sat down next to him. He put his arm around me and pulled me against him before dipping his hand into my bowl of popcorn.

"Hey, you said you didn't want any, remember?" I said.

"Changed my mind." He kissed the tip of my nose. "Now quiet, it's starting."

I leaned against him, feeling warm and secure, and then realized Roman was staring at us.

"What?" I mouthed.

Roman just shrugged and gave me a look I didn't understand as Riley moved his big hand to the back of my neck and kneaded it.

He had been like this all day, bestowing small touches and caresses that set my skin on fire with need. He hadn't asked for sex again, but I had the feeling it had more to do with his side than not wanting me. I shivered all over. The way he had kissed and licked my pussy, pinning me to the bed with his large hands and forcing me to not only accept his tongue but crave it, had made me feel more alive than I ever had with Jordan.

My face flushed. I hadn't wanted him to kiss me so intimately - Jordan's declaration that I tasted funny had embarrassed me more than I could ever admit – but Riley had seemed to love it, and the enthusiastic way he...

Ate your pussy, my mind whispered. *Fuck that, Riley didn't just eat it, he devoured it, girl.*

Yeah, he had and even now, hours later, just recalling the memory made my stomach tighten with anticipation and need. He had said he would do it every day, and a small part of me believed – hoped - that he meant it. One session with his tongue in my pussy had turned me into a damn addict.

"You okay?" Riley murmured into my ear.

His hand dipped inside my shirt, and his fingers stroked the hickey he'd left at the base of my neck. I'd scolded him when I discovered it, but he'd given me a boyish grin and cupped my breast before kissing me until I was breathless and clinging to him. I supposed it should have bothered me that he could distract me with nothing more than a few kisses and a bit of groping, but it didn't. After four years of feeling unattractive to the man who was supposed to love me, it was a relief to know that Riley wanted me.

"You okay?" Riley repeated.

I nodded and ignored the way my pelvis throbbed as his fingers moved to trace my collarbone. I hoped like hell Roman didn't glance over. My nipples were hard and poking against the thin material of my t-shirt. I wondered if there was any way I could grab the blanket and cover myself without attracting attention. God, I would have to start wearing three layers of clothing just to hide my arousal whenever Riley touched me.

"After Roman leaves, you're going to take off your shirt and bra so I can suck on those hard nipples," Riley breathed into my ear.

I stifled my soft moan, my hand squeezing the bowl of popcorn as Riley sucked briefly on my earlobe.

"Would you like that, Kitten?" he breathed again.

I nodded and kept my eyes glued on the TV screen as his finger dipped lower and stroked between my breasts for a brief moment before retreating.

I released my breath in a shuddering sigh. Riley tugged playfully on my hair before nipping at my earlobe again. "Then, I'm going to pull your pants down, spread your soft thighs and slide my cock into your sweet little pussy."

I closed my eyes as Riley's hot breath tickled my ear, and his fingers traced small circles on the back of my neck.

"Fast-forward, Maddie."

Roman's voice was distant as I clenched my thighs together and tried to stop the maddening ache between them.

"Maddie? Earth to Maddie!"

A couch pillow smacked me in the face, and Riley glared at Roman. "Watch it, or I'll kick your ass."

"Relax, it was just a pillow," Roman said airily before throwing popcorn at me. "Fast-forward, Mads. I hate the commercials."

"Sorry." I hugged the pillow to my chest, hiding my hard nipples, and quickly fast-forwarded.

Riley shifted and placed his hand on my thigh. I stared at his long fingers as they pressed against my leg. If I spread my legs, if I moved just a little, Riley could slide his hand between my legs and give me some relief from the ache.

Uh, Maddie? In case you've forgotten, you're not alone.

Right. Not alone. I loved Roman, but I could have easily kicked him out of my house at that moment. I took a deep breath. I needed to rein it in. I'd had sex with Riley a total of three times, and I was suddenly a sex addict.

"Getting antsy to have my cock, Kitten?" Riley muttered into my ear.

I shook my head no as Riley made a low chuckle. "Are you sure? It's been nearly six hours since you've had my dick. My kitten feels empty, doesn't she? Misses having my cock filling her, stretching her, making her come."

"Stop talking," I said under my breath.

"Admit that you can't wait for Roman to leave so you can be fucked, and I will," Riley murmured.

I glared at him before glancing at Roman. He was absorbed in the show, and I turned back to Riley and pressed my mouth against his ear. "Yes, I want you to fuck me again, and yes, I can't wait for Roman to leave."

He grinned, returned his hand to the back of my neck,

and squeezed it in a friendly manner before settling back and watching the TV. I sat stiffly beside him, my entire body still throbbing with lust, and waited for my best friend to get the hell out of my house.

* * *

"Thanks for having me over, Mads," Roman kissed me on the cheek before shrugging into his jacket.

"You're welcome, honey. Any time."

Roman laughed. "Normally, I'd believe you, but I think I'll stay away this week."

"What do you mean?"

"Oh, please." Roman glanced over my shoulder. "When did you and your biker babe start having sex?"

"Roman!" I looked behind me. Riley had disappeared after saying goodbye to Roman, but I didn't know if he was in the kitchen or the bedroom. "Keep your voice down."

He ruffled my hair affectionately. "Don't hurt his side, you sexy little slut. He's not completely healed, even if he pretends he is."

"I'm not – I mean, we're not... how did you know we're having sex?"

"You're walking funny," Roman said.

"I am not!"

"I don't blame you for walking bowlegged, the guy's got a monster dick, and I'm still impressed that you don't run screaming from it."

"Okay, out – that's it!"

I pushed him toward the front door, and he laughed and grabbed me around the waist before kissing me on the mouth.

"Playing 'hide the bishop' with a hot-as-hell biker isn't something to be ashamed of, Mads," he said cheerfully. "I'm proud of you. You deserve to find out just how fucking fantastic fucking can be."

"Go, Roman!" I opened the front door and gave him a pointed look. "I love you. Goodnight."

"Goodnight, Mads. Have fun dipping the wick!"

I flipped him the bird, and he blew me a kiss before sauntering down the porch to his car. Muttering under my breath, I locked the door before straightening my T-shirt. There was still no sign of Riley, so I headed into the kitchen. It was empty, and I piled the popcorn bowls into the dishwasher. Riley must have gone to the bedroom.

I jumped about a foot when I turned and saw him leaning against the doorframe, his large body filling most of the doorway. He had taken off his shirt, and my mouth went dry as I stared at his naked chest.

"You scared me," I said.

"Sorry." He didn't look sorry at all. He stepped into the kitchen, and I took a nervous step back. Why did I suddenly feel like a rabbit stalked by a large, dangerous wolf?

"Where are you going, Kitten?" He grinned at me, and I tugged at my shirt.

"Nowhere." I was dismayed at how needy I sounded. Jesus, why didn't I just strut around naked with a sandwich board that said, 'Please fuck me, Riley'?

"Are you, um, ready for bed?" I asked. "Or did you want to watch some more TV?"

Bed, please say bed.

I couldn't stop thinking about his promise to suck on my nipples. They were already hard and tingling with anticipation. I made myself stand perfectly still when Riley's gaze dropped to my breasts.

"Take off your shirt, Mads."

My hands trembling, I pulled my shirt over my head and

placed it on the counter. Riley took a step closer. "And your bra."

I reached behind me. My hands still trembled, and it took me longer than usual to unclip it, but Riley stayed where he was, waiting patiently until I placed my bra on the counter with my shirt.

I automatically covered my breasts with my arms, and Riley arched his eyebrow at me. "You know that's not allowed. Show me your gorgeous tits."

I dropped my arms, trying not to blush as Riley studied my breasts.

"So beautiful." The appreciation in his voice warmed my entire body.

"Riley, are you – you said you would…"

"Suck your nipples?"

I nodded, feeling an odd combination of bold and shy, as he smiled and leaned against the table. "Come here, Kitten."

I walked a bit unsteadily toward him. Riley's eyes darkened with lust as he watched the sway of my large breasts. When I stood next to him, he reached out and pulled the elastic from my hair. He threaded his fingers through the strands before raising a lock to his face and pressing it against his cheek. He traced one finger between my breasts, and I uttered a soft little moan of need.

"Sit on the table and lie back, Mads," he said.

I did what he asked, my hands clenching and unclenching with anticipation as he bent over me. I arched my back when he licked a circle around my left nipple. It beaded into a hard point, and he sucked it into his mouth before blowing on it.

I cried out, and he pushed my breasts together and alternated between sucking on each nipple. His teeth pulled on them, and I gripped the sides of the table as my pelvis pressed rhythmically against his erection.

"You have the prettiest tits I've ever seen, Mads. Did you know that?" he breathed against my wet nipple.

I shook my head as he sucked again, rubbing the tip of my nipple against the top of his mouth. When both my nipples were throbbing, and I was moaning, he straightened and sat me up. He stroked my back as I wrapped my legs around his hips and rubbed against him like a cat.

"Stand up, Mads," he urged, and I slid off the table.

He turned me around, and I ground my ass against his erection as he unbuttoned my jeans and slid his hand inside my panties. He rubbed my clit briefly before sinking two fingers into my aching core.

"Oh, please, Riley," I begged shamelessly. "Please."

He jerked my jeans and panties down until they pooled at my ankles and pushed me down against the table. He stroked my ass, running his hands over my skin as I rested my heated cheek against the table.

He unzipped his jeans, and I looked over my shoulder. "Condom, we need a condom."

He pulled one from his pocket before unwrapping it and rolling it over his dick. "Spread your legs."

I spread them and moaned happily when he sank his cock into my pussy. He pulled out and pushed in again as we both groaned.

"Christ, you're so fucking tight." He planted his hand on the small of my back and thrust forward. When he was completely sheathed, he placed one hand on my hip and wrapped his other in my hair. He pulled on my hair until I stared at the ceiling and drove in and out. My pussy clung wetly to him, and I met each of his thrusts, pushing my ass against him as he fucked me hard and rough.

"Oh God," I moaned as heat built in my belly. He shifted slightly, the head of his cock brushed against the front inside wall of my pussy, and the resulting burst of pleasure took my breath away.

"Holy fuck," I panted. "What the fuck was that?"

He chuckled. "That, Kitten, is your g-spot."

"Do it again," I begged. His hand tightened in my hair, and he thrust rapidly back and forth.

I squealed as every nerve ending in my body lit up, and I writhed against the table. I moaned and panted, and my fingers scraped uselessly at the wood as he quickened his pace. I clenched around his cock, the muscles of my inner walls clinging to and gripping his cock in a desperate need for relief. He muttered a curse under his breath before fucking me so hard the table scraped across the floor.

I closed my eyes as colours burst across my vision, and my entire body shook with the force of my orgasm. I had never had an orgasm without touching my clit. Before I could come down from the first one, Riley reached under me and rubbed and pulled on my clit as he pumped in and out.

"Riley, wait!" I shouted. "I can't – wait. I need -"

I screamed again as my second orgasm, hard and intense and utterly perfect, rolled through me. Riley stiffened behind me. His hand clamped almost painfully around my pussy as he thrust a final time and made a hoarse shout of pleasure as he climaxed.

He collapsed on top of me and pressed kisses against my sweaty back while I panted and shuddered beneath him.

"Holy shit," I said. "Holy fucking shit."

Riley kissed my back again before straightening. He pulled out and tugged my panties and jeans up before stepping away and disposing of the condom. I leaned weakly against the table and stared wide-eyed at him.

"Come to bed, Mads." Riley held out his hand.

I took it and followed him to the bedroom. He shoved off his jeans and briefs and folded back the quilt and the sheet.

"Mads?" A look of worry crossed his face. "You okay?"

"Am I okay?" I mumbled. "I just had the best fucking orgasm – *orgasms* – of my life, and you want to know if I'm okay?"

He grinned and helped me out of my jeans and panties before leading me to the bed. He climbed in behind me and pressed his warm body against mine before cupping my breast.

"You're welcome. Now go to sleep."

I craned my head to stare at him. "Seriously, Riley. The best orgasm of my life."

He brushed my hair back before pressing a kiss against my forehead. "We'll see about that. Good night."

"Good night, Riley." I pressed against him and closed my eyes as he squeezed my breast and kissed the back of my shoulder.

CHAPTER 11

Maddie

I dropped my laptop case on the hallway floor and kicked off my shoes before trudging into the living room. The delicious smell of spaghetti wafted down the hallway, and I sat on the couch with a soft sigh before rubbing at my temples. Today was an absolute nightmare at work, and it was only Monday. I was tired, I had the beginning of a headache, and my entire body ached. Sex with Riley was unbelievably good, but after the marathon amount we'd had this weekend, it felt like every muscle in my body screamed at me. I rubbed gingerly at my thighs.

Riley had incredible stamina, even with an injury, and I wondered if I should join the yoga class that Casey at work always raved about. It would help me be more flexible and give me a better chance at keeping Riley's interest once the initial obsession wore off and he realized how bad I was at sex. In fact, I really should go back to the gym and –

Why are you so worried? Riley's just using you. As soon as he's healed and finds a new place to live, you'll never see him again.

Playing house with him doesn't mean a damn thing. You two are oil and water, remember? There's no future beyond what's happening right now and –

"Mads?" Riley stuck his head into the living room. He wore my 'kiss the chef' apron with a dishtowel slung over his shoulder. I smiled briefly. For a drug-dealing biker, he was adorable.

"I didn't hear you come in," Riley said.

"Just got home. How was your day?"

"Fine. How was yours?"

I hesitated. For a second, I considered telling him just how shitty my day was and how badly I'd fucked up. I wanted to tell him how, for the first time since starting my career, I questioned whether I'd made the right choice. But my common sense kicked in - Riley wasn't interested.

"Fine. Busy."

I stood, suppressing the urge to wince at the ache in my thighs. Riley walked toward me and pushed me gently back onto the couch. He knelt between my legs and slipped his hands under my skirt before rubbing my aching thighs.

"What are you doing?" I asked.

"Every day, Kitten. Have you forgotten?"

A trickle of need slid down my spine, and I stared at him uncertainly as he grasped the waistband of my nylons.

"Lift your hips."

I shook my head. "Riley, no. I need to shower first and -"

"Lift your hips, or I'll rip off your damn nylons."

"You will not."

He grinned. "You know I will."

I sighed but lifted my ass off the couch. Riley tugged down my nylons and panties, and I cleared my throat as he inched up my skirt.

"I really need to shower first."

"No, you really need your pussy eaten."

I made an undignified squeal when he suddenly yanked my skirt up around my waist and pushed my thighs apart. Cool air washed over me, and he lightly slapped the inside of one thigh when I tried to close them.

"Riley," I protested, "I'm uncomfortable with…"

My protest died in a whispery moan when Riley buried his head between my thighs and licked the lips of my pussy. My hips arched, and Riley growled his approval as my hands clutched at his dark hair.

"Riley," I moaned. "Oh God, Riley."

He didn't reply. His tongue, his lovely and oh-so-fucking-talented tongue, was already licking at my clit. I closed my eyes and concentrated on nothing but the feel of his rough stubble against my thighs and his warm tongue. I forgot about my shitty day and my aching muscles as Riley reached under me, cupped my ass and dragged me further down the couch. I thrust my hips against his face, silently begging for more as he sucked on my clit.

I opened my eyes and stared at our reflections in the living room window. I looked almost obscene. My skirt was bunched around my waist, my legs were spread wide, and my hips pumped madly against Riley's mouth. Instead of being embarrassed, a fresh wave of lust swept through me. I made a harsh cry of need as Riley slid one thick finger into my aching core.

"Oh fuck!" I cried. I was shamefully close to coming, and I barely heard Riley's groan when my thighs clamped around his head, and my entire body arched off the couch. I rode his face through my entire orgasm, his tongue licking away the flood of fresh liquid before collapsing in a boneless heap against the sofa. He raised his head and grinned as I stared at him.

"Better, Kitten?"

I nodded. The hell of it was, I wasn't lying. I did feel

better. My slight headache was gone, and my entire body tingled pleasantly. Even my dismay at fucking up so badly at work had lessened.

He kissed one bare thigh, then stood and leaned over me. He cupped my breast through my suit jacket and squeezed lightly before giving me a quick kiss. "Go and get changed. Dinner will be ready in five."

* * *

Riley

"Dinner was really good. Thanks," Maddie said.

"Was it?" I stared pointedly at her plate of barely touched food.

She sipped at her glass of wine. "It was. I'm just not super hungry tonight."

I started to clear the table, waving her away when she stood to help. "Just relax and drink your wine."

She sank back into her chair, and I smiled briefly as I loaded the dishwasher and put the leftovers into a container. If the guys from the gang could see me now, they'd be busting my balls over cooking a woman dinner and cleaning her kitchen.

Of course, Ma would have been proud as hell. If she were here, watching me treat a woman with respect rather than just as a warm place to stick my dick, she would have been tickled pink. I'd done a lot of shit over the years that had broken her heart, and I knew she'd been disappointed in me.

A sudden bout of grief washed over me, and I squeezed my eyes shut as my hands clamped around the edge of the sink. Fuck, I missed Ma. She'd been the only person who gave one shit about me, and in some ways, I mourned her loss more than I mourned Andrea's. I supposed a lot of it had to do with the fact that there was no guilt over Ma's death. There was no way I could have prevented it.

Andrea, on the other hand, was one hundred percent my fault. I wondered if there would ever be a day when I wouldn't feel that gut-wrenching stab of guilt.

You deserve to feel guilty. Andrea would still be alive if you hadn't been so selfish. If you hadn't decided that drinking and whoring and partying with your friends was more important than your own goddam family. It's your fault she's dead. Your fault, and I'm never going to let you forget that. You're not a good guy. Sooner or later, Maddie will realize that, and you'll be alone again.

"Riley? Are you okay?"

I twitched wildly at the touch of Maddie's hand on my back before putting my arms around her and burying my face in her neck like a little kid looking for comfort.

"Tell me what's wrong." She hugged me tightly.

I was tempted, fuck was I tempted. The urge to just tell her everything, to tell her how I had fucked up so badly and the guilt of my sister's death was eating me alive, was nearly overpowering. I straightened and stared down at her. She smiled and touched my jaw.

"Tell me," she urged. "You'll feel better, I promise."

Yeah, tell her. Watch the look in her eyes change when she finds out just how bad of a guy you really are. See what she thinks of you when you tell her you were so selfish that you didn't have a clue how tormented your sister was.

My stomach clenched, and I swallowed my urge to confess. One – she'd had a bad day at work, I could tell even if she wouldn't admit it, and didn't need to hear my fucking problems. Two - it was madness to tell her anything about my past. She'd kick me out of her life, and I'd never see her again. The thought sent panic through me, and my arms tightened around her until she winced.

"Riley? Please tell me," she said. "I want to know why you -"

I cut her off with a rough kiss before sliding my hand under her shirt and squeezing one firm breast. She had changed into yoga pants and a T-shirt before dinner, and I took advantage of the loose waistband and slipped my other hand into her pants to cup her ass.

"Riley, we can't always have sex to avoid -"

"I need you."

She bit at her bottom lip uncertainly and then moaned when I bent my head and sucked on her lip. "The bedroom, Mads, right now."

Before she could argue, I herded her up the stairs and into her room. I had her shirt and bra on the floor and her pants around her ankles before we were barely in the room. I cupped her breasts, pulling firmly on her nipples, and her soft moan of pleasure made my dick press painfully against my jeans.

I pushed her toward the bed, catching her when she stumbled, and she muttered a curse.

"My pants," she said.

I grinned and helped untangle her pants from her feet before raking her panties down. She kicked them off as I stripped out of my clothes. I cupped her pussy, rubbing my thumb over her clit before tracing small circles on her inner thighs. She leaned against me, her breath already quickening, and I kissed behind her ear.

"Look how wet you are, Kitten. You're ready to be fucked, and I've barely touched you," I whispered into her ear.

Her cheeks glowed, and I gave one hard nipple a light pinch before sliding my finger into her tight core. She moaned and widened her legs as her pelvis thrust back and forth.

"Please, I need more, Riley," she begged.

I pushed a second finger into her. "Better, Kitten?"

"You know it isn't."

"Tell me what you want then."

She bit at her bottom lip again before reaching between our bodies and giving my dick a firm tug. "This. I need this."

"Say it," I insisted. I didn't know why, but hearing sweet, conservative Maddie talking dirty just about did me in. It was one of the hottest things I'd ever heard.

She hesitated and then squeezed my dick again. "I need your cock, Riley. I need you to fuck me with your cock."

My dick jumped in her hand, and precum coated the tips of her fingers. She craned her neck to stare at me, and a wicked grin crossed her face before she slipped one finger into her mouth and sucked it clean.

"Fuck." I yanked my fingers from her pussy and pushed her toward the bed. I stopped to grab a condom from the nightstand and tore open the foil before rolling it on hurriedly.

"On your hands and knees," I ordered.

She lowered herself to the bed, and I pushed my way between her thighs. I grabbed her hips and hoisted her a bit higher before pressing the head of my cock into her wet pussy. She moaned and shoved her body back eagerly. I watched her pussy take my cock inch by inch and slapped her on the ass when she tightened around me.

She glared at me over her shoulder, and I rubbed the pink mark on her pale ass. "Stop trying to make me come, Kitten."

"I'm not," she said innocently before squeezing again.

I slapped her other ass cheek, groaning when it made her clench around me, before wrapping my hands around her upper arms and pulling her up. She moaned with pleasure when I pumped in and out, and I quickened my pace. Already, she was growing close. I could tell by her soft cries and the way her pussy squeezed rhythmically around my cock. I thought about stopping, about slowing down to prolong both her pleasure and mine, but she turned her head and gave me a pleading look that I was powerless to resist.

I tightened my grip on her arms and thrust rapidly. My balls tightened, and a deep, aching pleasure radiated through my lower body.

"Fuck, Maddie, oh, fuck," I muttered. "You feel so fucking good around my cock. Your hot, little pussy drives me fucking insane."

She made a soft cry and arched her back. My cock was flooded with wetness, and I shouted her name before grabbing her hips and holding her steady as I climaxed. She trembled and collapsed on the bed in a little heap. I tossed the condom before lying next to her and pulling her into my arms. She rested her head on my chest, and I kissed her forehead.

"You make a guy come faster than a teenage boy getting his first feel of pussy."

She laughed. "I'll be sure to add that to my list of skills on my resume."

We relaxed in silence for a few minutes before Maddie raised her head and rested her arms on my chest. "What's your last name?"

I blinked at her. "What?"

"What's your last name? I've fucked you I don't know how many times now and -"

"Eight."

"What?"

"You've fucked me eight times."

She laughed again. "You've been counting?"

I nodded solemnly. "Ninety-seven times, Kitten. Remember?"

She blushed, and I tugged playfully on her hair. "I thought

about putting notches in your bedpost but figured you'd kick my ass if I marked up the wood."

She slapped me on the chest as I grinned at her. "Should we try to make it an even ten before tomorrow?"

"As delightful as that sounds, I need to be able to walk tomorrow," she said.

"Oh c'mon, Kitten, I'm big but not that big."

"It's my thigh muscles that are sore," she said tartly. "But it's good to know that your ego is as big as your dick. Seriously though – what's your last name?"

"You didn't look in my wallet when I was drugged up?" I asked.

"Of course not," she said. "I wouldn't rummage through your personal belongings like that."

She stared at me suspiciously, and I grinned again at her. "Don't worry, Kitten. The only thing I rummage through while you're at work is your panties drawer. It's not weird that I spread them all out on the bed and nap on them, is it?"

She stared wide-eyed at me before bursting into giggles. I tugged again on her hair as she rubbed her hand across my chest hair. "You're nuts, Riley."

"Yep," I agreed, "and it's Walker."

"Your last name is Walker?"

I nodded, and she repeated my name softly before smiling at me. "It's a good name."

"Thanks. What's your last name?"

"Smith."

"Really?" I cocked my eyebrow at her, and she giggled again.

"Yes, really."

"I'm going to need to see one of your fancy-ass lawyer business cards to confirm it," I said teasingly.

A shadow flitted across her face before she gave me a strained smile and rested her head on my chest again.

"Tell me what happened at work today," I said.

"Nothing happened." She tried to get up. I tightened my arm around her and pulled her back against my chest.

"Tell me, Mads."

"Why?" she asked.

"Because I want to know."

"I want to know who Andrea is, and you won't tell me," she said quietly.

I stiffened against her, and she stared up at me. "I'm sorry. I shouldn't have said that. It was a rough day at work, but that doesn't mean I can be a jerk to you."

I almost laughed out loud. "If that's you being a jerk, I think I can handle it. I once dated a woman who tried to stab me when I wouldn't introduce her to Ma."

"You're kidding me?"

"I wish I was."

She smiled faintly, and I stroked her hair back from her face. "Tell me what happened at work today, and I'll tell you who Andrea is."

A look of surprise crossed her face before she said, "I have a client – let's call her Jane – who's going through a nasty divorce with her husband. They have four children. She's been a stay-at-home mom for the last ten years, and her husband left her and the kids for his secretary."

"You're joking," I said. "There's no way that happens in real life."

"You'd be surprised. Anyway, Jane has been fighting tooth and nail for child support and alimony. Her asshole of a husband hired an expensive and experienced lawyer, and, long story short, he kicked my ass at the hearing today to discuss child and spousal support. Because of me, Jane isn't going to get nearly as much child and spousal support as she should."

I rubbed her back as she sighed loudly. "The worst part?

She isn't even upset with me. My boss accepts a lot of pro-bono cases, and Jane was one of them. After the hearing, she thanked me for helping her and getting her at least a little child support. She should have been angry with me, should have gone to my boss and had me fired, but she thanked me. I'm pretty sure she feels like she can't complain because it was pro bono, and that makes me feel like shit."

She wiped discreetly at her eyes, and I squeezed her waist. "I'm sure it wasn't as bad as you think."

"It was," she said morosely. "Bad enough to make me wonder if I'm in the right career."

I rubbed her back, wishing I could think of something comforting to say. I wasn't good at shit like this, never had been, and until this moment, I had never really felt the need to be.

"I think you're a great lawyer," I finally said. "One bad day doesn't mean you need to rethink your career choice."

"Maybe not," she sighed before looking at me expectantly. "Your turn."

"Andrea was my sister," I said.

"You said you didn't have any siblings."

"I lied."

"Why?"

"Because she's dead."

"I'm sorry. Why do you have nightmares about her?" she asked.

"That wasn't part of the deal."

"It might help if you talk about it," she said.

"No. Let it go. I agreed to tell you who Andrea was, and I did. The rest of it is none of your business."

A look of hurt flashed across her face. "No, I guess it isn't. I know it's early, but I'm exhausted and think I'll call it a night."

She turned her back to me and pulled the covers up to her

chin. I laid on my back and stared at the ceiling, listening to her soft breathing for nearly ten minutes. I didn't feel guilty, I told myself. There was nothing to feel guilty about. Maddie didn't need to know the details, and it would do more harm than good to share it with her. Her feelings were hurt, but she would get over it. I wouldn't say sorry. I had nothing to be sorry about.

Another ten minutes passed. I'd spent the last few nights curled up against Maddie with her arms around me and her warm body tucked into mine. I wondered bleakly if the nightmares would return. If she wasn't touching me, if I couldn't feel her soft skin, would a dead Andrea invade my dreams again? Worse, would it be Maddie?

I shuddered all over. The thought of the nightmares returning was bad, but knowing that I had upset Maddie made me feel fucking awful. She'd been nothing but nice to me, and I, like usual, had acted like a real asshole.

I slid over to Maddie's side of the bed and wrapped my arm around her waist, pulling her stiff body against mine and nuzzling the back of her neck.

"I'm sorry, Mads," I said into her hair. "I'm sorry, but I can't talk about it."

She sighed before turning and putting her arms around me. "I'm sorry, too. I shouldn't pry."

I buried my face in her throat and rubbed her back. "Good night, Mads."

"Good night, Riley."

* * *

Maddie

I CLOSED THE FRONT DOOR AND HUNG MY JACKET ON THE

hook. I was incredibly happy it was Friday and even happier to be home. I was hungry and tired and –

Horny.

I smiled wryly to myself. Yeah, I was. Every night for the last week, I'd barely be in the door before Riley was leading me to the couch or the bed, tugging off my panties and burying his face in my pussy. I'd start to feel the pulsing ache of need as I drove home, and I was wet by the time I walked in the door. I found it embarrassing, but Riley loved it.

He would tease me gently about my wetness, kissing my inner thighs and licking me clean with his tongue before bringing me to orgasm. Frankly, it never took long – another embarrassment – and I had begun to crave Riley's daily ritual with a fierce need I'd never experienced before.

I paused and listened intently for a moment. Unlike the past few nights, there was no smell of dinner cooking, and Riley didn't appear in the hallway.

"Riley? Where are you?"

There was no answer, and adrenaline shot through my veins. I hurried into the kitchen. It was empty and I checked the living room as dismay built in my stomach. Riley had left. He'd finally grown tired of me and left. I blinked back the sudden tears.

Maybe he would still be here if I hadn't given in so easily each night. He wanted sex from me, and I had given it to him willingly every night. I should have played hard to get. I should have denied him what he wanted at least once or twice. Maybe he would have stayed if I had.

What the hell is wrong with you? So Riley left. You knew it was going to happen sooner or later, and I hate to tell you this, girl, but you denying him sex wouldn't have made him stick around. He would have left even earlier – found a woman who was good in bed and didn't say no. Stop being such a damn baby, and be happy you had him for as long as you did.

But he hadn't even said goodbye.

We'd had a quick round of morning sex before I showered and left for work. Nothing about him seemed different or off. If I'd known I would never see him again, I would have held him a little longer. I would have memorized the sound of his voice saying my name and the look on his face when he was deep inside of me. I would have –

Maddie! Stop it! You're acting like he's dead, for fuck's sake.

The tears leaked down my face, and I wiped them away. Okay, Riley was gone. I needed to accept it and –

The front door opened. I hurried out of the living room and into the hallway, relief flooding through me when I saw Riley.

"Hey, Mads. How was your… Mads? What's wrong?" he asked.

"I didn't know where you were!" I blurted out. "I thought you had… never mind. How was your day?"

He pulled me into his arms, and I sagged against him, burying my face in his neck as he patted my ass. "Tell me what's wrong."

"Nothing," I said. "There's nothing wrong. It was just, um, weird to come home, and you weren't here."

I gave him a kiss that was almost a bit desperate. He returned my kiss as I reached between our bodies and rubbed at his cock. My relief that he hadn't left had turned into a fiery hunger for him, and I tugged frantically at his belt.

"Maddie, wait."

"What's wrong?" I asked.

"Nothing. I just – I have something to tell you."

I stiffened against him, and he rubbed my hip through my skirt. "It's nothing bad, Maddie."

"What is it?"

"I got a job."

"You got a job?" I echoed.

"Yeah. I went to see my old boss at the construction company, and as luck would have it, he had a guy quit on him yesterday. He hired me, and I start Monday."

He gave me an oddly vulnerable look. "It doesn't pay much, but it's something."

"Riley! Congratulations! That's fantastic!" I kissed him enthusiastically before hugging him. Some of the tension eased from his body, and I kissed him again. "Are you sure you're healed enough to do construction?"

He nodded. "Yeah."

"Maybe you should double-check with Roman. You're going to his place tomorrow to teach him some exercise stuff, right?"

"Yes, but I'll be fine."

"Promise me you'll mention it to him," I said. "Just to be on the safe side."

He rolled his eyes, and I pinched his ass. "Promise me, Riley."

"Fine, I promise."

I gasped when his hand slipped under my skirt and cupped my pussy through my damp panties. "My kitten's nice and wet again. You been thinking all day about getting your pussy eaten?"

I ignored the slow beat of arousal coursing through me. "Maybe. But we need to celebrate."

He grinned at me. "Tasting your sweet little pussy is celebrating."

"I'm taking you out for dinner."

His hand, which had started to creep under my panties, paused. He gave me an odd look. "You want to go out in public with me?"

"Yes. Why wouldn't I?"

"In case you haven't noticed, we're not exactly at the same

187

class level. What if you run into someone you know? You really want to be seen with me?"

I pushed away from him and poked him in the stomach. "You don't honestly think I give a shit what other people think or say, do you?"

He just shrugged, and I poked him again. "You're just as good, if not better, than me or anyone else I know, Riley Walker. If I hear you talking shit about yourself again, I'll beat the crap out of you."

A grin crept across his face, and I glared at him. "I'm tougher than I look."

"Yeah, I know, Mads." He pulled me against his hard body and kissed me, sweeping his tongue into my mouth until I was panting and rubbing my pelvis against his growing erection.

"You sure you want to go out? Because I was thinking a good way to celebrate would be you riding my dick all night."

I moaned as he sucked on my earlobe. "We can do both."

"I guess," he said before squeezing my breast.

I wiggled out of his grip. "I just need to change, and then we'll go. I know the perfect place to celebrate."

He looked down at his T-shirt and jeans. "Is this place fancy? I don't do fancy."

"It's not fancy. Don't worry, you'll like it."

I started down the hallway before pausing. "Can we take your bike?"

"You want to ride the bike?"

"Yes, if you don't mind."

"I don't. But," he grinned wickedly, "you might want to reconsider having your pussy eaten first. The vibrations might be too much to handle when you're as horny as you are, Kitten."

I stuck my tongue out at him. "I think I'll manage."

"I guess we'll find out."

CHAPTER 12

Riley

I shut off the bike and waited patiently as Maddie climbed off a bit clumsily. Her face was flushed, and I grinned at her as I dropped the kickstand and slid off my bike.

"That is so awesome! I mean, I was pretty sure I would still like it, but it was even better this time."

"I'm glad you liked it," I said.

"I loved it!"

She had a child-like look of glee, and I laughed. "Maybe I'll teach you how to drive it one day."

Her eyes widened, and she shook her head. "Nope, I'll stay strictly a passenger, thanks. Now, c'mon, I'm starving."

I stared at the restaurant in front of us. "What is this place?"

"It's a sushi restaurant. The best in the city."

"No way. I'm not eating raw fish."

"Have you tried sushi before?"

"No, and I'm not going to."

"How old are you?" she asked.

"Thirty-one, why?"

"No one can go thirty-one years without at least trying sushi. If you don't like it, we'll leave and go somewhere else. Okay?"

"I already know I'm not going to like it."

She laughed. "You don't. C'mon, Riley. Be brave and try something new."

"Fine," I grumbled. "But when I spit the sushi all over the table, don't say I didn't warn you."

* * *

"Well, what do you think?" Maddie asked.

"It's not half bad," I admitted. "I don't like that one, though." I pointed to the raw tuna sitting on the small block of rice.

"It's an acquired taste," she said cheerfully before popping one into her mouth.

I watched as she used the chopsticks. She had taught me how to use them, giggling a little at my awkward attempts, but her gentle teasing hadn't bothered me.

Abandoning my fumbling with the chopsticks, I picked up a larger roll with my fingers and dipped it gingerly into the soy sauce before eating it.

"Hey, this one is pretty good."

"That's a dynamite roll," she said. "Here, try this one."

I picked up the small roll and ate it gingerly. "It's okay."

"That's the smoked salmon. It's one of my favourites."

We ate in silence for a few moments before Maddie smiled at me. "Thanks for trying the sushi."

"You're welcome. How was your day?"

"It was pretty good," she said. "I have a new client who -"

"Maddie?"

My back stiffened, and I stared at Maddie's co-worker, who had stopped at our table.

"Hi, Tim." Maddie glanced at me.

"I didn't know you ate here," he said. "It's great, isn't it?"

"It's my favourite. You remember Riley."

Anger surged through me at the blank look in Tim's eyes.

"Uh," a flicker of recognition crossed his face. "Right, right – the roommate. How are you?"

"Fine," I grunted before looking back at my plate.

"If I had known this was your favourite restaurant, I would have invited you out tonight," Tim told Maddie. "I'm here with a few other people from the office."

He pointed across the restaurant to a table of people. Maddie waved at them before smiling at Tim. "I guess you'll know for the next time."

"I will." Tim's gaze dropped briefly to her cleavage, and fresh anger burned in my belly.

"Say, why don't you join us? We have more than enough room at our table," Tim said.

"No, thank you. Riley and I are having a private cele-bration."

"What are you celebrating?" Tim asked.

"None of your damn business," I said. "Get lost, Tim."

He stared at me in surprise. Maddie frowned at me before saying, "Thanks for the invitation, but we'll pass."

"Right." Tim still stared at me, and I returned his look with undisguised contempt until he flushed and looked away.

"Are you attending the client appreciation dinner next month?" he asked.

I sighed irritably as Maddie said, "Yes."

"Good, good. I am, too. Maybe we should go together."

"Oh, um, that's nice of you but -"

"Say yes, Maddie," Tim wheedled. "We can be each other's plus one."

"Actually," Maddie said, "I'm bringing Riley as my plus one."

I hid the look of surprise on my face as Tim looked at me. He studied the tattoos on my arms and neck before turning to Maddie. "You're taking him?"

"Yes, I am."

Tim hesitated. "Maddie, are you sure that's a good -"

"Goodnight, Tim," Maddie said. "It was nice to see you. I'll talk to you on Monday at the office."

"Right. Have a good weekend." With one final glance at me, he returned to his table. Maddie released her breath in a loud sigh and smiled at me.

"That guy's a dick," I said.

She shushed me hurriedly. "He'll hear you, Riley."

"Like I give a fuck." I sounded like a grouchy toddler. "He wants in your fucking pants, Maddie."

"No, he wants me to have a smaller pant size."

"What?" I scowled at her.

"Never mind. I'm not interested in Tim, okay?"

My good mood had vanished, and I stared sullenly at her. "I don't care if you are. We're just roommates, remember?"

"Riley -"

"Forget it, Maddie. Just eat your damn sushi so we can get out of here."

* * *

Maddie

I STORMED INTO THE HOUSE AND DROPPED MY PURSE ON THE hallway table before kicking off my shoes. I had spent the entire ride home angry and confused. Riley was sullen and quiet for the rest of the meal. I had no idea what his problem was, but I was pissed.

Riley slammed the door shut and tugged his boots off with a grunt before hanging his leather jacket on the hook. Ignoring him, I walked into the kitchen and poured myself a glass of water. Riley followed me, and I glared at him as he leaned against the wall.

"What's your problem, Riley?"

"I don't have a problem."

"Bullshit. Tell me why you're being such a dick."

He shrugged. "This is just who I am, Kitten. You don't like it, I can leave."

"And go where?" I asked. "You need me, Riley."

"I don't need anyone," he growled. "Never have and never will."

"Of course you don't. Big tough Riley is perfectly fine on his own."

"That's right."

"It isn't a weakness to need someone, Riley. Or to allow someone to care about you."

"Care about me?" he said with a bitter laugh.

"Yes, I care about you and want what's best for you."

"No, what you want from me is my dick in your pussy," he said crudely. "I give you something you never got from your dickhead fiancé and -"

"You asshole!" I shouted. "Do you honestly think that's why I let you stay here? Because of your dick?"

"Isn't it?" he asked.

"No! It isn't!" I shouted again.

"Of course, it isn't."

Anger and shame made my entire body tremble. Riley thought I was a whore.

Are you so certain you're not? You like what Riley does to you and how he makes you feel. You like knowing someone like him – a

*man who could have any woman he wanted – wants you. Fat
Maddie who turned her fiancé gay. You have nothing else in
common other than sex. If he weren't fucking you every night,
you'd ask him to leave.*

My stomach dropped, and I blinked back the hot tears.
Yes, I liked the sex, loved it, in fact, and there was no point in
denying that knowing Riley wanted me made me feel
powerful and desirable for the first time in my life. But that
wasn't the only reason I wanted him to stay. Was it?

"Maybe you should sleep in the guest room tonight," I
said dully.

"Maybe I should."

I slipped past him, trying not to cry and mostly succeed-
ing. "Good night, Riley."

* * *

HIS CRIES FROM THE GUEST ROOM WOKE ME. I STARED SILENTLY
at the ceiling. It was just after three, and I had fallen into a
restless sleep less than an hour ago. I sat up and threw back
the covers as Riley's moans grew louder. I was angry with
him but couldn't lie in the dark and listen to him suffer.

I walked to the guest room and stood by the side of the
bed. Riley had thrown off the covers, and his naked body was
covered in a sheen of sweat. His entire body shuddered
before he lifted his hand.

"Andrea? Oh please, no, Andrea," he moaned.

Goosebumps broke out on my body. I sat down on the
side of the bed before shaking him roughly. "Riley, wake up."

His eyes popped open, and he sat up, nearly knocking our
heads together. "Maddie!"

"It's okay. Just a nightmare." I patted his bare shoulder.
"It's okay."

I gasped when he threw his arms around my waist and

pulled me down onto the bed. I sprawled across him, feeling the rapid beat of his heart against my breast as he panted into my neck and shuddered wildly.

I squirmed off of him, and he immediately rolled to his side, burrowing his body against mine. I patted his back gingerly before returning my hands to my sides. "You're okay, Riley."

When his shaking had stopped, and his breathing had returned to normal, I touched his hip briefly. "Better?"

He nodded, and I tried to push away from him. "I'm going back to -"

His arms tightened around me. "No, don't leave me."

"Riley, I shouldn't -"

"I'm sorry," he whispered against my throat. "I'm sorry, Mads. Please stay with me."

I sighed before nodding. I didn't have to touch him or hold him. I could just sleep in the bed with him. For whatever reason, sleeping in the bed with me seemed to keep Riley's nightmares away. I couldn't deny him that small comfort.

When he cupped my breast and kissed my neck, I pushed at his chest. "Riley, no."

"I need you."

"No, we can't."

"Why not? You want me."

He stared at my breasts, my arousal evident by my hard nipples, before leaning down and kissing one hard bud. "Let me make you feel good."

"You think I'm a whore."

He jerked against me, his hand tightening around my breast. "I don't."

"You do," I whispered. "You think I'm only using you for your dick, and if I fuck you now, it will just prove you're right."

"I'm sorry." He brushed his lips against mine in a tender caress. "I shouldn't have said that. I didn't mean it."

He kissed my mouth again. "I didn't mean it, Mads. I swear. I know that's not why you're letting me stay with you. I've just never had anyone care about me other than Ma. It's hard for me to believe that someone like you would care about someone like me."

"What's that supposed to mean?" I asked.

He sighed. "You saw the way that guy Tim looked at me. Like I was a piece of dog shit smeared on his shoe. We come from two different worlds, and I will never fit into yours."

"You shouldn't care what other people think. I don't."

"Maybe you should care. If your boss found out who I was, what I did for a living – you think he wouldn't fire your ass?"

"You're not that person anymore, Riley."

"I am."

"You're not," I insisted. "People change all the time. You're smarter than you give yourself credit for. You can be or do whatever you want. The only thing that stopped you before was bad circumstances."

He laughed bitterly. "Yeah, that's all it was."

"I do care about you. Whether you want to believe that or not is up to you, but it isn't just about your dick for me."

"I know it isn't," he said. He kissed me a third time before smiling. "But you do still really like my dick, right, Mads? Because it really likes you."

I smiled a little. "Yes, I still like it."

"Will you let me show you how much it likes you?" he asked before trailing a path of kisses down my throat.

He pushed his thigh between mine, slipped his hand under my nightshirt and cupped my bare pussy.

I moaned quietly. "You make it very hard to resist you, Riley Walker."

"Good." He rubbed my clit. "I like knowing you want me as much as I want you."

He helped me out of my nightshirt before moving between my thighs. I pressed my legs against his hips, pushing my pelvis against his in a gentle rhythm as he rubbed his cock over my pussy and bent his head to my breasts. He sucked and licked at my nipples until I moaned his name and dug my nails into his back. His cock probed at my opening, and we both gasped when he pushed just the head in.

"Riley," I moaned.

We stared at each other in silence for a moment. He knew I was on the pill - hell, he watched me take it every night - but we had always used condoms.

"Maddie," he whispered, "I've never once gone bareback."

"Never?" I said.

He shook his head before kissing me. "No. I get tested regularly, and they're negative."

"You get tested?"

He smiled at my surprise. "Yes. Personal health is very important."

A small grin crossed my face, and he kissed the tip of my nose. "I'll show you my medical records."

"I was tested after I found out Jordan was cheating on me," I said. "They were negative."

"I want to be in you without a damn rubber," he confessed hoarsely, "but I'll stop right now and get one if that's what you want."

I lifted my pelvis in response, sliding his cock in deeper, and he groaned before thrusting hard and seating himself entirely within me.

"Oh!"

"Fuck, I'm sorry. Did I hurt you?"

"No, just a bit unexpected." The sudden invasion had my

muscles clenching around him. I forced myself to relax as he waited patiently.

"Holy shit," he muttered. "You have no fucking idea how good this feels, Kitten. So warm and wet."

He thrust hard back and forth. I wrapped my legs around his waist and cupped his face. "No, go slowly."

"I can't," he groaned.

"You can. Slowly, Riley. Nice and slow."

He muttered a curse under his breath but propped himself on his hands above me and moved with slow, easy glides that sent shivers of pleasure through my body.

"That's right," I whispered. "Just like that."

I eased my hand between our bodies and traced the hard muscles of his abdomen before rubbing at my clit. Warmth bloomed in my belly, and I made small moans of pleasure as I pressed on my clit before cupping my breast. Riley watched, lust flickering across his face as I tugged and pinched my swollen nipple.

"You have no fucking idea how hot you are, Kitten," he said.

"Suck," I said.

He bent his head, still moving in that slow, gentle rhythm and sucked hard on my nipple. I continued to rub at my clit, my breath coming in harsh gasps as my climax approached. I forced my hand still as Riley lifted his head.

"Don't stop, Kitten. I want to feel you coming all over my cock," he pleaded.

I bit my lip and rubbed at my clit again. Riley was moving faster now, with deeper and harder strokes that made me tremble and shudder. I closed my eyes as we moved together in an easy rhythm.

"No," Riley said. "Look at me, Mads."

I stared unblinkingly at him as my fingers stroked and caressed, and Riley's cock pushed and retreated.

"Riley, I'm going to – I can't wait," I whimpered.

"Yes," he groaned. "Yes, honey."

The unexpected endearment sent me over the edge, and still holding Riley's dark gaze, my orgasm swept through me. My pussy clenched and unclenched around his thick cock, and Riley made a hoarse shout of pleasure as he thrust a final time. Warmth flooded through me as he came deep inside of me. I clung tightly to him as we rode out the pleasure of our orgasms together.

"Holy shit, Mads." Riley rolled off of me with a soft groan and gathered me against his chest. "Please don't ever ask me to wear a rubber again. I can't go back after that."

I laughed. "I think that can be arranged."

He snuggled into me and pulled up the covers. "Do you want to go back to your bed?"

"No, this is good."

"Good night, Mads." He kissed me, and I rubbed his back.

"Night, Riley."

* * *

Riley

"Shit," Roman groaned as he slid onto the barstool next to me. "I can barely take a piss without everything hurting."

I snorted laughter and sipped at my beer. "It's only been three weeks. Your body needs time to adjust to the new exercise routine."

"Or maybe," Roman groaned again before taking his own drink of beer, "you could take it a little easier on me."

"I didn't expect you to be such a pussy." I grinned at him.

"I'd tell you to go fuck yourself, but since I'm already seeing results, I'll keep my insults to myself."

I shrugged and patted my abdomen. "Hey, you want to look like this – you need to work for it, buddy."

"I could work out four hours a day, and I still wouldn't look like you," he said. "But I'll settle for a somewhat visible six pack and an ass you can bounce quarters off of."

He held his beer bottle up, and I clinked mine against it before we both drank again.

"How's the new job going?" Roman asked.

"Fine. Busy right now. The company picked up another contract, so I'll have work for at least another six months."

"That's good. How are things going with Maddie?"

"Fine," I repeated. "Why?"

"Just wondered. You two have been living together for nearly two months now. You officially a couple or what?"

"None of your damn business, Roman."

He laughed. "Fair enough."

I stared moodily at my beer bottle. Things were going great with Maddie, but I had started looking for apartments. Although part of me believed that Maddie cared about me, a bigger part was waiting for her to ask me when I would move on. We had no future together, and just because neither of us brought it up, it didn't make it untrue. I needed to leave before it got to the point where I didn't want to go.

You're already there, asshole.

I ignored my inner voice grimly. I wasn't getting attached to Maddie, and I certainly wasn't falling in love with her. Men like me didn't fall in love with women like Maddie. And even if I did – she would never love me. I had nothing to offer her other than great sex, and sooner or later, that wouldn't be enough.

"Maddie wants to know if you're still coming over tomorrow," I said. "She's making lasagna."

"I'll be there. I have a shift at the hospital until three, but I'll come by after. If I can fucking walk, that is," Roman said.

"I never thought I'd spend my Saturday night lifting weights until I begged for mercy."

"We're drinking beer, not lifting weights."

"Good point," Roman replied. "Truthfully, I was surprised you agreed to have a beer with me after the workout. You and Mads are attached at the hip, it seems."

"Whatever, Roman."

We sat silently for a moment before I said, "I need a favour."

"What's that?" Roman perused the bar menu. "I wonder how many calories are in this spinach dip."

"Too many. I need you to help me buy a suit."

"Sweet baby Jesus." Roman grabbed his chest. "Are you – are you asking me to go clothes shopping with you? Fuck, I might have just gotten a stiffy."

"Keep it in your pants. Mads has some client dinner thing on Thursday night, and she wants me to go with her. I need a suit for it."

"Well, we don't have time to get one custom made," Roman said. "That's a shame."

"I don't need no custom-made suit," I said grouchily. "Can't you just take me to a damn department store or something?"

He stared at me in horror. "No department store suit. But I know a guy downtown who sells great suits for reasonable prices. We should be able to find you a decent one. I'm not working on Tuesday. I'll text you the address, and we can meet there on Tuesday night when you finish work. Sound good?"

"Yeah. Thanks, Roman."

"Don't mention it. I'm doing it for purely selfish reasons. I can't wait to see you in a suit. You'll light up the room, pussy cat."

"Jesus," I muttered. "You really need to -"

"Roman?"

Roman grinned and slid off his barstool before shaking the dark-haired man's hand. "Mark! Good to see you, man."

"You too."

"How was work?"

"Good. I had a keyhole craniotomy. It went well," Mark replied.

Roman clapped Riley on the back. "Riley, this is Mark. He's a neurosurgeon at the hospital. Mark, this is Riley."

"So, you're Roman's new trainer?" Mark shook my hand and sat down on the barstool beside me. "I have to say I'm pretty impressed. Roman's looking damn good after only three weeks."

"Stop it, you're making me blush," Roman said. "Seriously though, Riley's a beast. I'm lifting weights I never thought I could do."

"Are you taking on more clients?" Mark asked. "I could use some help."

I stared blankly at him. "Oh, uh, I'm not really -"

"He is," Roman broke in smoothly. "He's got other clients during the day, but he's available evenings and weekends. Isn't that right, Riley?"

"Uh, I guess so," I said.

"Great. What's your rate?" Mark asked.

"Uh..."

"Eighty an hour," Roman said. "It's a steal of a deal considering how fucking good he is. He'll get his NASM certificate in the next few months, and his rate will increase. You should get in now with him while he's offering lower prices."

"Sounds good to me," Mark said. "How about Saturday morning around eight? I have a personal gym, or we can meet at your gym, whichever is more convenient."

"Your gym is fine," I said. "It's better to work out on equipment you're used to."

"Makes sense," Mark replied. "Give me your number, and I'll text you my address. I'm going out of town for a couple of weeks, so could we start on Saturday after next?"

"Sure."

I gave him my cell number, and he typed it into his phone before smiling at Roman. "Thanks, Roman."

"Anytime, man. Have fun in Hawaii."

"I will. Talk to you later. Riley, it was nice to meet you. I look forward to training with you."

He left, and Roman leaned back and studied Mark's retreating ass. "God, that man has the best fucking ass I've ever seen. When he's back from Hawaii, I'm biting the bullet and asking him out."

"Roman, what the fuck did you just do?" I said when Mark was out of earshot.

"What?"

"I'm not a goddamn personal trainer. I don't have experience, and that guy is going to pay me fucking eighty bucks an hour. I'm not worth eighty bucks an hour."

"Sure, you are. Besides, Mark is a neurosurgeon and a highly successful one at that. He's got plenty of money to burn, trust me."

"That's not the point," I said. "You can't be pimping me out as a personal trainer – I don't have the qualifications for it."

"So you get your NASM certificate," he said blithely.

"I don't even know what the fuck that is."

He laughed. "It's the National Academy of Sports Medicine personal trainer certification program. I researched, and all you need is your high school diploma and CPR and AED certificates."

"I don't have a high school diploma or CPR and AED certificates."

"So you get your GED and take the certification courses. No biggie."

"This shit costs money, Roman."

"I can loan you the money," he said. "Honestly, it's not that expensive and would be well worth it. I have lots of connections with rich doctors who want to pretend they're bad boys with hard bodies. You're good at training even without the damn certification. You could make a killing, Riley."

He clapped me on the back. "There isn't anything wrong with working construction, but you love the training thing. Don't try to deny it. Why not make a living from it?"

"Because I can't, I don't…"

He grinned at me. "Exactly. You have no reason not to. Listen, I'll text you the websites for the information. Just look into it, okay? I think you should at least consider it."

I studied my beer as Roman tapped me on the shoulder. "Promise me, Riley."

"Yes," I said irritably. "I'll look into it, Roman."

"Good. Now, what do you say we try that spinach dip?"

CHAPTER 13

Maddie

I'd just poured myself a cup of tea when there was a knock on the door. Riley was out with Roman, and he must have forgotten his key. I walked down the hall and opened the door.

"Hey, did you forget your..."

I stared blankly at my former fiancé. "Jordan? What are you doing here?"

"Hey, Madeleine. Can I come in?"

I studied him. He had lost weight, he had dark circles under his eyes, and his thin hair was uncombed.

"You look like shit," I said.

"Yeah, I know. Can I come in?"

"Why?"

"I really need to talk. Please, Madeleine. I need to talk to you," he pleaded.

I sighed and stepped back. "Come in."

"Thank you."

He followed me down the hall and into the kitchen. "Do you want some tea?"

"Sure, that would be great."

I poured him a cup of tea and sat at the far end of the table. "What do you want, Jordan?"

He rubbed at the back of his neck and took a sip of the steaming liquid. "My parents discovered I'm – about Kurt and me."

I didn't reply, and he smiled faintly. "They cut off my trust fund nearly two months ago."

"Tough luck."

"Yeah," he sighed. "I lost my place, and I've, uh, I've been living with Kurt for the last month."

"Oh?"

"Yeah. It's been kind of challenging, I guess you'd say. Kurt wants me to get a job, says I need to stand on my own two feet because my parents aren't going to get over this, you know?"

I shrugged, and he picked at the top of the table. "Kurt's kind of difficult to live with."

"Is he? Or are you difficult to live with?" I asked.

"You know I'm not." He gave me a hurt look.

"We never lived together, Jordan. You always had an excuse for why we couldn't. Remember? Of course, I didn't realize the real reason was that you wanted to keep crossing swords with Kurt, but hey, my bad, right?"

He scowled at me. "I said I was sorry, Madeleine."

"Yeah. Why are you here?"

He picked nervously at the handle of his mug. "Okay, this will sound strange, but just hear me out. I want us to get back together."

My jaw dropped. Jordan's face turned bright red when I burst into loud laughter. I held my stomach and laughed until tears leaked down my face, and I could barely breathe.

"This isn't fucking funny, Madeleine."

I laughed harder, gasping for air and rubbing my stomach as Jordan glared at me. "Are you finished?"

I held up one finger. "One…minute," I gasped between giggles.

Slowly, I gained control and wiped my cheeks again before staring at Jordan. "Jordan, pudding, you're gay."

"I know that! But listen – my parents fucking love you. They were devastated when you broke off the engagement. If you and I get back together, it'll convince them that I'm not gay, and they'll give me back my trust fund. I need that money, Madeleine. I can't get a job, okay?"

I stared at him in silent amazement. "This is a joke, right?"

"No, it's not a joke," Jordan said. "We got along fine before, didn't we? We can go back to the way we were. Obviously, it won't be exactly the same. I'm gay, and I - I want to continue my relationship with Kurt, but I'd be willing to, you know, have sex with you once or twice a month in return for your help with my parents. We were pretty good in bed together despite…"

"You liking dick?" I asked.

"There's no need to be rude," Jordan said. "I can't help who I am."

He glanced around my small kitchen before leaning forward. "I know you're lonely, Madeleine. I know you miss me, and a part of me misses you too."

"You have no fucking idea who I am, do you?" I stood and dumped my cup of tea down the drain. "You honestly think I'm that desperate, that pathetic, that I would take you back?"

"I'm the best you're going to get, Madeleine. You know that." Jordan stood and walked toward me, grasping my wrist tightly. "Do you want to spend the rest of your life alone? I'd be willing to give you a kid or two. I know you want kids."

I shook my wrist free of his grip. "You're not the best I'm

going to get, and for the record – you suck in bed. You made me think it was me, but I now know it wasn't. I want you to leave, Jordan, and God help you if you ever come back."

He frowned at me. "You haven't even considered it. Just take a day or two to -"

"She asked you to leave, dickhead."

Jordan stared in surprise at Riley standing in the kitchen doorway. "Who the hell are you?"

"The roommate," Riley said. "Get the fuck out of here."

"You have no right to talk to me like that, buddy," Jordan said.

Riley took a step into the room, and Jordan backed away nervously. I burst into laughter again. Jordan glared at me as a small grin crossed Riley's face.

"He can't speak to me like that, Madeleine," Jordan said.

I shrugged. "He lives here. You don't."

"You're living with this guy?" Jordan stared at me in horror.

I nodded. "And fucking him, sucking his dick – am I forgetting anything, Riley?"

He grinned at me. "I particularly enjoy eating your pussy every day."

"Definitely can't forget about that," I said cheerfully.

Jordan was still staring at me with horror on his face. "What the hell happened to you, Madeleine?"

"I realized I could do better - *much* better - than you," I said. "Now leave, Jordan, and don't come back. Ever."

"Madeleine -"

"Get out now," Riley growled, taking another step toward him.

Jordan stalked from the kitchen. I waited until I heard the front door slam shut before smiling faintly at Riley.

"Sorry."

"For what?"

"I was being pretty crass – not exactly an attractive quality for a woman, I know - but Jordan made me see red. Thinking that I'd take him back and that I was sitting around and pining for him."

Riley stalked forward and grabbed me around the waist. "Kitten, I have never found you more fucking attractive."

I laughed. "I'll remember that the next time I worry about being too crude. How was your beer with Roman?"

"It was good." Riley unbuttoned my jeans and stuck his hand into my pants. He pressed me against the counter and wedged his thigh between mine until my legs were spread. I gasped when I felt his cold fingers touching my pussy.

"Cold hands," I complained.

"They'll warm up soon." He caressed my clit. "Roman has a friend named Mark."

"Mark the neurosurgeon?" I moaned as he tugged on my clit.

"You know him?"

I nodded. "Well, I know of him. Roman's had a crush on him forever."

"Roman set me up with him to do some personal training for eighty bucks an hour."

"That's great." I wrapped my hand around his wrist and forced his hand still.

He shrugged. "I'm not really a personal trainer, though."

"I guess not," I said. "But you could be. Roman says you're fantastic at it."

"He thinks I should get my NASM certificate," Riley said.

"I have no idea what that is, but I agree."

He took my hand and kissed the palm of it before stroking my clit again. "It's a personal trainer certificate."

I rubbed against him. "Are you going to do it?"

"I'll think about it."

"Riley -"

He kissed me. "Can we talk about this later, Mads? After watching you verbally destroy your ex-fiancé, I'm so fucking hot for you I can barely think straight."

I grinned at him and rubbed his cock through his jeans. "Well, when you put it that way – take me to the bedroom, handsome."

* * *

Maddie

"Riley? Are you almost ready?" I stuck my head into the bedroom. "We need to leave soon."

He turned around, and my breath caught in my throat. He wore a charcoal grey suit with a white shirt, and he looked so damn hot my knees started shaking.

"Oh my God," I breathed.

He flushed with embarrassment. "I look stupid."

"You do not look stupid. Trust me, Riley, you'll have every woman in the room drooling over you."

I had to touch him.

I nearly tripped over my own feet as I stumbled forward and smoothed my hands across his broad shoulders. "You look so good."

My voice was faint, and Riley frowned. "Mads? Are you okay?"

"Fine," I breathed. "Just really horny."

He grinned. "Maybe we should skip the dinner."

"You have no idea how much I want to say yes, but I need to be there. My boss will give me hell if I don't show up."

He ran his hand over his jaw. "Should I have shaved?"

"No. I like the stubble."

"You can still see my tattoos." He tugged at the collar of his shirt where his neck tattoos were visible.

"You can see mine too." I turned so he could see the daisy tattoo peeking out from under the strap of my dress.

He leaned down and pushed the strap to the side before kissing the tattoo. "Not the same thing, Mads."

"Sure, it is. Besides," I turned to face him, "it doesn't matter. Your tattoos are part of who you are, and I like them."

"I couldn't get the tie to work." He picked up the scarlet-coloured tie from the top of the dresser. "I haven't worn one since I was a little kid, and Ma dragged me to church every Sunday."

"Lucky for you, I am an expert with ties." I smiled at him before lifting his collar and sliding the tie around his neck. "Hold still."

He stood patiently as I worked. When it was perfect, I folded his collar, smoothed my hands across his shoulders again, and turned him to the mirror.

"What do you think? Is it too tight?"

"No, it feels good."

"Great, let's go." I started toward the door, and Riley tugged me to a stop. He pulled me into his embrace.

"You look really pretty, Maddie."

"Thank you, Riley."

I had put my hair up in a twist, and he caressed the exposed skin on the back of my neck. I shivered a little, and he cupped my neck and kissed me until I was breathless.

"You have lip gloss all over your mouth now," I scolded.

"Worth it," he said before licking his lips. "Why does it taste sweet?"

I laughed. "It's flavoured."

"Weird." He wiped his mouth with the back of his hand. He studied my body in the dark green dress, his eyes lingering on my exposed cleavage. "Sure you don't want to just stay home, Kitten?"

He dipped one rough finger between my breasts. I shivered all over before stepping away. "I would love to stay home, but I can't. C'mon, we'll be late if we don't leave now."

* * *

"Don't be nervous." I smiled reassuringly at Riley as we stood outside the hotel banquet room.

"I'm not."

"You'll be fine," I said. "Just be yourself."

"That's the last thing I should be."

Before I could disagree with him, the doors opened, and my boss, Justin, stepped into the hallway.

"Maddie, good to see you." He pressed a polite kiss against my cheek.

"Hi, Justin. Sorry, we're a little late."

"Nonsense. They haven't even started serving appetizers yet and half the clients are still missing in action. If they don't show up soon, we'll be paying for a hell of an amount of food to go straight to the garbage."

I turned to Riley. "Justin, I'd like to introduce you to my good friend, Riley Walker. Riley, this is the head partner of my firm, Justin Turner."

"Nice to meet you." Justin held his hand out, and Riley shook it.

Justin's gaze lingered on the visible tattoos on Riley's neck before he said, "Head on in and start mingling. I'd advise you to give Mr. Triden a wide berth. He's already had too much to drink, and Loretta says his wandering hands are out in full force."

He rolled his eyes, and I laughed. "Thanks for the tip."

I tucked my hand into the crook of Riley's arm. "Mr. Triden is one of our biggest clients."

"Which is the only reason I invite him to these dinners," Justin said with a long-suffering sigh. "I can't tell you how many of our female employees he's groped at these events once he gets a few drinks into him. If it gets any worse, I'm firing him as a client."

He leaned closer to me and grinned conspiratorially. "Just between you and me – I hate these damn dinners. They're so damn dull."

I laughed as he grinned and patted me on the arm. He headed down the hallway, and I squeezed Riley's arm. "Ready?"

He nodded. His tanned face was a bit pale, and he rubbed compulsively at his jaw as I led him into the room.

"Everything will be fine," I murmured. "Don't worry."

I TOOK A SIP OF WINE AND SMILED HAPPILY. THE DINNER HAD gone well, much better than even I had expected. Despite my reassurances to Riley, I'd been feeling nervous and uncertain, but everything went smoothly. Riley was anxious. I knew him well enough now to see the tell-tale signs, but no one else had picked up on it. He was polite to everyone I introduced him to if not a little quiet. More than once, I had to suppress a giggle at the looks on my female coworkers ' faces when they met him. Riley was sexy in jeans and a T-shirt. In a suit, he was downright deadly.

The guy really had no idea just how hot he was, I mused. Pride tingled through me. Riley wanted me, and I knew I wasn't imagining the envious looks my coworkers and some of the clients were giving me.

That's right, ladies. He's all mine, I thought with glee.

Is he, though?

I ignored my inner voice and took another sip of wine as I watched Riley and Justin talk animatedly in the corner of the room. To my surprise, the two of them were getting along extremely well. I had no idea, but Justin was a motor-cycle enthusiast. When he discovered that Riley rode one, he'd immediately engaged him in a loud and enthusiastic conversation about different types of bikes that went completely over my head.

I'd wandered away after fifteen minutes, Riley hadn't even noticed, and chatted with a few of our clients. I glanced at my watch. We'd been here long enough, and I figured it was safe to say our goodbyes.

Watching Riley in that suit, feeling his hard thigh pressed against mine as we sat at the dinner table, and knowing that a good three-quarters of the women in the room were lusting after him, had notched my lust to an almost unbear-able level. I wanted to get him home, strip away that suit, and spend the next few hours kissing and touching that deli-ciously hard body.

My pelvis throbbed, and I shifted, pressing my thighs together as I spotted Mr. Triden weaving his way toward me.

Shit. I walked toward the large French doors to my left and stepped onto the patio. I glanced behind me, sighing with relief when I saw Mr. Triden stumble to a stop as Bethany, one of our legal assistants, crossed in front of him. He grabbed her arm and smiled at her as she nodded politely and stepped back.

Sorry, Bethany, I thought before smiling at the couple standing at the far end of the stone patio. Holding hands, they crossed the patio and stepped inside the room. The doors closed behind them, muting the chatter of voices. I took a deep breath of the cool night air. It was chilly, and I wrapped my arms around my torso. I would finish my wine, take Riley home, and ride him like a pony. I grinned to myself. God, I was insatiable when it came to sex with Riley. We'd hit the ninety-seventh sex mark by next month if we kept up our current pace.

Next month? Who says Riley will even be in your life next month? He has a job now, and if you don't think he's looking for his own place, you're fooling yourself. What's happening between you isn't going to last forever. Sooner or later, he'll tire of you.

I grimaced as the doors opened, and a blast of warm air rushed by me.

"You've been avoiding me, Maddie."

I smiled stiffly at Tim. "I haven't been. Just visiting with clients. It's a client appreciation dinner, remember?"

"I remember," Tim said.

I suppressed my groan when he stood next to me, and the scent of whiskey washed over me.

"How much have you had to drink tonight?" I shuffled a step sideways, frowning when Tim followed me.

He shrugged. "Probably too much."

"Maybe you should stop then. Whiskey probably isn't the healthiest for your body." I tried to keep my voice light. For some reason, I felt nervous and unsettled. Tim's usual cheerful smile was gone, and he stared gravely at me.

"Are you and your roommate a thing?"

"Why are you asking?" I said.

"You know why." Tim ran his fingers down my arm.

"No, I'm afraid I don't," I said. "My personal life isn't any of your business."

"I like you, Maddie," he said. "I want to get to know you on a more personal level."

"No, thank you. I'm not interested in dating someone who thinks my ass is too big."

He laughed. "I don't think it's too big. I just think you could learn to eat a little healthier and maximize your potential. You've got a great body underneath the chub, and I think you'd be much happier if you let me help you discover it."

"Are you kidding me?" I scoffed. "Tim, if this is you trying to compliment me, you need to work on your game."

He sighed and drained the rest of his whiskey before setting the glass on the table next to us. "What's wrong with wanting to help you live up to your potential?"

"Live up to my potential or mold me into what you want?" I said with a raised eyebrow. "I appreciate your," I paused, "determination to make me think I'm lacking, but I don't need that type of negativity in my life."

He gave me a look of surprise. "Negativity? Maddie, you're reading me all wrong."

"No, I don't think I am. Excuse me, Tim."

He grabbed my arm and pulled me against him. "Don't leave yet. Let me show you what I can do for you, how I can make you feel, okay?"

He bent his head, and I jerked mine back. "Stop it. You're drunk and making a fool of yourself. Go home and sleep it off."

He shook his head. His eyes were bloodshot and slightly out of focus. "I'm fine. Kiss me, Maddie."

"Not a chance." I saw some of our clients glancing at us through the glass doors, and I smiled politely for their benefit. "Let go before you embarrass the both of us in front of our clients."

He pulled me closer in response. I was getting ready to knee him in the groin, clients be damned, when the doors flew open, and Riley appeared on the patio. The look of rage on his face scared me badly, and I held my hand toward him. "Riley, wait -"

Ignoring me, he grabbed the back of Tim's suit and tore him away. I stumbled back as Riley fisted his hands in Tim's shirt and dragged him forward. "Stay the fuck away from her, or I'll break your arm, you fucking shithead."

"Get your hands off of me!" Tim shouted.

"Riley, let him go," I said as clients and coworkers, drawn by Tim's shout, gathered around the doors.

Riley released Tim. His nostrils flared, and his eyes flashed with anger. "I mean it. Keep your fucking hands away from her."

"You think I'm afraid of you?" Tim sneered. He weaved a little and straightened his suit before glaring at Riley. "I know guys like you. You think you're tough, think that everyone's afraid of you, but you're just scared little boys who fall apart the minute a real man challenges you."

I actually laughed out loud. I was terrified and sick to my stomach over what was happening, but the laughter came braying out of me anyway.

"You have no idea how dangerous I am," Riley said. "But touch Maddie again, and you'll find out."

"Riley, let's go." I swallowed down my laughter and tugged on his arm. "He's drunk, okay? It's time to leave."

He stared at me, and I felt a tingle of nervousness and - God help me - lust. The Riley from the club, the one who had claimed me in front of a roomful of men and forever changed me, was back.

Did you think he'd ever left? Riley is dangerous, and playing house with you for two months doesn't change that.

No, I suppose it didn't. But what did it say about me that knowing he was dangerous only made me want him more?

"Riley?" I touched his face. "Take me home."

I breathed a sigh of relief when he took my hand, and we started toward the doors.

"That's right," Tim sneered behind us. "Run away like the scared little boy you are. Doesn't matter – I don't want her fat ass anyway."

Riley roared angrily, and I made a sharp cry of dismay when he dropped my hand, turned, and punched Tim in the face.

"You fucking cocksucker!" he shouted as Tim flew backward and landed on the stone patio with a hard thud. "I'm going to break your fucking arm!"

"Riley!" I lunged forward and stood between him and Tim's sprawled form. "Stop!"

He grabbed me around the waist, but before he could lift me out of the way, I cupped his face and squeezed tightly. "No! Please don't."

He stared over my shoulder at Tim, and I forced his gaze back to mine. "I don't care what he says. Do you hear me? We need to walk away."

"I'm not letting him insult you like that," Riley said.

"It doesn't matter. Walk away, honey. Please."

When he didn't move, I stood on my tiptoes and pressed a kiss against his mouth. "Please, honey. For me."

He stared silently at me for a moment. I released my breath in a trembling rush when he nodded. He took my hand again, and we turned around to see all of my coworkers and most of our clients staring at us.

"What are you looking at?" Riley growled.

I squeezed his hand and pulled him through the crowd of people. I had to get Riley out of there before anyone said anything else. We were nearly to the conference room door when Justin called my name.

I froze, closing my eyes, as Riley cursed again under his breath.

"Maddie," Justin said, "I need to talk to you."

"Justin, I'm sorry. I didn't mean for this to happen. We need to go – can I talk to you tomorrow?"

"What did Tim do?" Justin asked.

I hesitated, and Riley said, "He was hitting on her. Touching her after she told him not to."

Justin scrubbed at his forehead before glancing behind him. Tim was being helped inside by a few of our other coworkers, and I winced when I saw the blood pouring from his mouth.

"Fuck," Justin said. "Well, I guess this is one client dinner that won't go down as boring as hell."

"I'm sorry, Justin." My stomach churned with nausea. "But it's better if we go. If Tim wants to file charges, just -"

"He won't be," Justin said. I stared at him in confusion as he gave Tim an angry look. "Go, Maddie. I'll call you later."

CHAPTER 14

Maddie

My cell phone rang just as we walked into the house. I pulled it from my bag as Riley stomped to the bedroom. I took a deep breath and hit the answer button.

"Hello, Justin."

"Hi, Maddie. You get home okay?"

"Yes." I waited until I was sure that Riley was in the bedroom. "I'll hand in my resignation first thing tomorrow. I enjoyed working for you, Justin, and I wanted to thank you for everything. I've learned so much, and I won't -"

"I'm not accepting your resignation, Maddie."

My mouth dropped open. "You have to. Justin, my date punched your employee in the face during a client appreciation dinner. I have to quit. I've embarrassed the firm, I've embarrassed you, and I've -"

"I just finished firing Tim. If you leave, I'll have no one to work on the Simpson file," Justin said.

"You fired Tim?"

"Yes. You're not the first coworker he's sexually harassed,

Maddie. He's done this at least three times before, that I know of, and he's been formally reprimanded twice for it. Third strike, and you're out."

"I can't believe this," I said. "Justin, I'm not sure if it was sexual harassment. Tim was drunk, and all he did was grab my arm."

"Obviously, it was more than that, or Riley wouldn't have felt the need to punch him in the face." Justin laughed. "He knocked out one of Tim's front teeth."

"Oh shit," I said.

Justin laughed again. "Don't worry about it, he deserved it. And don't worry about Tim filing charges against your guy. He won't be. I had a talk with him about the severity of office sexual harassment and what it would do to his career if someone from our office formally charged him with harassment. After that, he was remarkably less enthusiastic about filing charges against Riley."

"Justin, I don't know what to say. Thank you."

"You're welcome. Don't worry about the clients, okay? Surprisingly, many of our clients like a little 'fight club' with their dinner."

I groaned in dismay, and Justin chuckled. "I mean it. I think this might bring in more clients when they find out we're not the stuffy old law firm they think we are."

"Thank you, Justin," I said again. "Truly."

"Don't mention it. I'll see you tomorrow."

I set my phone on the side table and headed toward the bedroom. My job was safe – the career I had worked so hard for was intact - so why did I feel like the hardest battle was yet to come?

When I entered the bedroom, Riley was stuffing his clothes into a bag.

"What are you doing?"

"Leaving."

"Why?"

He barked harsh laughter. "Why? I ruined your fucking life, Maddie. Have you forgotten that?"

"You haven't. That was Justin on the phone. He was calling to tell me he fired Tim."

Riley paused. "He what?"

"He fired Tim. Apparently, this isn't the first time Tim's been handsy with his coworkers. Justin fired him and convinced him not to file charges against you."

Riley stared at me before returning to stuffing his clothes into the bag.

"Riley, stop. You aren't leaving."

"I am."

I stared at him, my heart breaking at his look of shame and confusion. I hated seeing the man I loved looking so worried and ashamed and –

Love?

Holy fuck. I loved Riley Walker. The truth hit me like a damn freight train, and I staggered back a little with the force of it. I did love him.

"This was a mistake," he said. "I should never have come here. I shouldn't have stayed and dragged you into my fucked-up life."

"You haven't," I said. "Riley, you're good for me. I know you don't want to believe that, but you are."

"I'm not! You think you know me, Maddie, but you don't. I'm not a good guy."

"Yes, you are. You're the best man I know."

"Don't say that!" he shouted. "I told you – you don't know the real me!"

"Then show me the real you. Tell me who Riley Walker really is."

"You don't know what you're asking," he said.

"I do. Tell me, Riley."

"Why? What's the point?"

"I want to know."

My calmness seemed to make him angrier, and he threw the bag on the bed before slamming his hand against the wall. "Just let me go, Maddie. Please!"

"No," I said. "I won't. Tell me who you are, Riley."

"Why?" he shouted again. "Why the fuck do you even care who I am?"

"Because I love you."

Riley

MY MOUTH DROPPED OPEN, AND I STARED LIKE A GODDAMN idiot at Maddie.

"What?" I said hoarsely.

"I love you," she repeated calmly.

"No, you don't."

She laughed. "Yes, I do."

"You – you can't love me. Women like you don't fall in love with guys like me."

"Why not?'

"Because we're too different."

"Opposites attract," she said.

"This isn't just a case of opposites attract, Maddie. We come from two different worlds and -"

"Yeah, you keep saying that and, frankly, I'm a little tired of hearing it," she said.

"It's the truth! Have you forgotten what happened tonight?"

She cocked her head. "No, I don't think so. I had some guy try to sexually harass me, and you came to my defense by knocking his teeth out. Does that sound about right?"

"This isn't a joke."

She sighed. "I know it isn't, but you're blowing what happened out of proportion."

"I almost got you fucking fired."

"Did you not hear what I said earlier?" Now, there was an edge of anger in her voice. "My job is safe. Tim was fired. Not me."

"And what happens the next time I lose my temper and try to beat the shit out of some guy who looks at you the wrong way?" I asked.

She shrugged. "Luckily, I don't have that many guys hitting on me, so I don't think we need to worry about it."

I ran my hands through my hair. "Maddie, this – this is madness. You don't love me."

"I do, and you know what?" She smiled at me. "I think you love me too."

Fucking right we do!

Not helping! I snarled at my inner voice.

"I'm not a good guy." Even I could hear the desperation in my voice. "I'm really not."

"You are."

"I'm not!"

"Tell me why you're not."

"It doesn't matter!" I shouted. "Why can't you just trust me on this?"

"Because you haven't done anything to prove you're not a good guy," she said. "So, unless you tell me why you're not, I am never, ever going to believe that you aren't. Never, Riley. I mean that. So, you'd better start talking or -"

"I killed my own sister!" I shouted. "Does that sound like something a good guy would fucking do, Maddie? Does it?"

Her eyes widened, and her face paled. I immediately regretted my outburst. I hadn't wanted to believe that Maddie loved me, but now, knowing that I was about to watch that love die made me want to fucking cry and puke all at the same time.

I turned away and stared out the window into the darkness. Maddie would ask me to leave now. Hell, I'd be lucky if she let me finish packing my shit. She'd kick me out, and I'd never see her again. Despair washed over me. How the fuck could I live without her?

I jumped like a fucking girl when her arms wrapped around my waist and she pressed her warm body against my back.

"I love you," she said. "Tell me about Andrea."

I opened my mouth to tell her I was leaving and instead said, "She was three years younger than me. Ma said I was super jealous of her when she was born. I used to take her bottle and hide it behind the couch when Ma wasn't looking. When we got older though, I looked out for her, you know? She was a pretty girl, and I kept the assholes away from her and made sure she didn't hang out with the wrong type of people."

I sighed. "She was always so serious, so sad, even as a little kid. Ma always said she overthought things. She used to hate it when Dad and Ma fought. When we were kids and they were screaming at each other, she would sneak into my room. I'd build us a blanket fort and tell her stories to distract her from the screaming."

Maddie kissed my back. "You sound like a great big brother."

"I wasn't," I said. "After Dad left us, I thought things would get better. They did for Ma and me, at least, but not Andrea. She just seemed even more, I don't know, withdrawn. She did okay at school, but she didn't have many friends. She spent most of her time in her room, but we just thought she was - I can't remember the word for it."

"An introvert?" Maddie said.

"Yeah," I grunted, "that's it. Anyway, I had dropped out of school and started working in construction, but Ma made sure that Andrea graduated. She was so proud of her. Ma had never made it past grade ten, and she was determined that at least one of her kids would graduate high school. She even talked about sending Andrea to college. She had saved up a little bit of money, and she figured Andrea could apply for student loans, but Andrea refused. She didn't want to go to college. She said it was a waste of money."

I tried to shift away from Maddie, but she refused to let me go, hugging me more tightly and rubbing my abdomen with her warm hands.

"I moved out when I was twenty," I said dully. "I was tired of taking care of Ma and Andrea. Tired of listening to her worry about shit that was never going to change. I moved in with friends of mine and spent the next eight years drinking and partying and– and fucking any woman who would open her legs for me."

I swallowed thickly and forced myself to go on. "I knew Andrea was struggling. Ma would call and tell me how worried she was about her, but I didn't want to hear it. I pretended that everything was fine, that Andrea just needed to be left alone, and she would be happy, but deep down, I knew it wasn't true. She never moved out of Ma's house, had a boyfriend, or did things that girls her age did. She worked as a cashier at a convenience store but spent most of the time in her room when she wasn't working. Ma would sometimes force her to go out with her, shopping and shit like that, but even that was getting more and more difficult."

I reached for Maddie's hand, feeling some comfort when she linked our fingers. "When I was twenty-eight, Andrea tried to commit suicide."

"Oh, honey." Maddie kissed my back again and hugged me.

"She slit her wrists. Ma called me from the hospital. She had found Andrea in the bathtub and called 9-1-1. She – she nearly died from blood loss, but they did a bunch of transfusions at the hospital, and it saved her life. When she woke up, the doctors had a shrink visit her, and he said she was severely depressed. Had been for most of her life, he said. He recommended we – we put her in a mental hospital. He said she would try to kill herself again if we took her home. Andrea didn't want to go, but Ma and me - we convinced her to go. It was fucking expensive, but Ma used the money she had saved up for Andrea for college. It wasn't enough. The doctor said she needed treatment for at least three months, and the money only covered the first month. That's when I quit my job at the construction company and started dealing drugs with Frank and the others."

I closed my eyes, saw Andrea's bloated face with the noose around her neck, and opened them in a hurry. "At that time, the club was doing pretty good. Frank and the others were making money hand-over-fist, and I made enough dealing drugs to keep Andrea in treatment for the three months. I didn't want to do it, Maddie. I didn't even do drugs, but I had no choice, you know?"

"I do, honey," she said.

"Andrea did real well at the hospital. She took her meds, and she went to daily therapy. Her doctor was proud of her and said Andrea was making a good effort. Ma and I visited her every Sunday, and she looked happy for the first time in her life. The doctor said she was well enough to leave when the three months were finished. She promised Ma and me that she was doing better and that she would keep taking her meds and going to therapy. Only," I paused and blinked back the hot tears threatening to fall, "she was fooling us all. She was always so smart. Way smarter than me. She said and did exactly what she knew she needed to in order to leave the hospital."

"What happened, Riley?" Maddie whispered.

"Two weeks after she left the hospital, she hung herself in her bedroom. Ma didn't even know she was home. She came home from work and thought Andrea was at therapy. She heard creaking noises upstairs and thought it was rats in the walls again. She called me and practically begged me to come over. I didn't want to. I was tired, but Ma started to cry, so I went over. I went upstairs and could hear the noise coming from Andrea's bedroom, so I…"

My voice stuttered to a stop, and Maddie hugged me again. "It's okay, honey. It's okay."

"I opened the door and Andrea was hanging there. She had gotten a rope from the garage and used a kitchen stool to stand on. She'd been dead for a few hours. Her – her face was swollen and starting to turn black, and her tongue stuck out. It was windy that day, and her window was open. She was swaying back and forth, and the rope was creaking, and I couldn't – I couldn't…"

I cleared my throat roughly. "Ma was coming up the stairs, and I screamed at her to go back downstairs. I wanted to go to Andrea, wanted to – to lift her down, but when I touched her, she was so cold, and I couldn't do it. I closed the door, went downstairs, and told Ma that Andrea was dead. She started screaming and tried to go upstairs. I had to pin her down on the couch until she stopped struggling. She punched and screamed, but she was going through chemotherapy, and she was pretty weak. It didn't take long for her to stop fighting me. Then I called 9-1-1. We buried Andrea two days later, and a month after that, Ma died from the cancer, and I was alone."

I told myself to shut up, that Maddie had heard enough, but I needed to tell her about the nightmares, about how she kept them away. Maybe it would make her feel sorry enough for me that she wouldn't kick me out.

"I – I've had nightmares every night for the last three years. I would live it over and over again – hearing the noise, seeing Andrea's body swaying and her – her face. But then I met you, and you keep them away. I need you, Maddie."

Maddie pushed away from me, and terror knifed through me. Now, she would tell me to leave. Now that she knew what I had done, she would never want to see me again. I would spend the rest of my life alone. I deserved it. After what I had done, I didn't deserve Maddie's love.

"Riley, look at me."

My entire body shaking, I turned around and stared at the floor. I couldn't look her in the face. I didn't think I could stand to see the disgust in her eyes, but Maddie placed her hand under my chin and forced my gaze up.

"Honey, it wasn't your fault."

She wiped away the moisture on my face as I stared at her. Her eyes showed no disgust, just kindness, compassion, and love. I couldn't fucking believe it.

"Yes, it was," I rasped. "If I hadn't been so fucking selfish, if I hadn't been so wrapped up in my own life, I would have seen how badly she was hurting. I could have helped her sooner, but I wanted to get away. I wanted to live my own life without worrying about her or Ma, and my selfishness killed her."

She shook her head. "No, honey. Her mental illness, her depression, killed her. Not you. Even if you had done every-thing right, even if you had realized what was wrong years earlier, that isn't a guarantee that she wouldn't have killed herself. People who are severely depressed aren't thinking straight. They *can't* think straight. Blaming yourself for your sister's disease is pointless."

She cupped my face and stared at me. "You need to stop

listening to that voice in your head and listen to me. I love you, and your sister's death wasn't your fault."

"You believe that, don't you?" I said as a huge weight lifted from my shoulders.

"Yes, and I promise you'll believe it someday, too."

"You're not going to leave me." There was soft wonderment in my voice.

"Never."

"I love you, Mads," I whispered.

She smiled her sweet smile and stroked my cheekbones with her thumbs. "I love you too."

I picked her up and buried my face in her throat, hugging her tightly before carrying her to the bed. I curled up against her, cupping her breast and feeling the steady beat of her heart beneath my hand.

"I love you," I repeated.

"Of course you do," she said teasingly.

I kissed her on the mouth, and she rubbed my back.

"You really had nightmares every night for three years?" she asked.

"Until I started sleeping with you," I said.

She touched my face, and I kissed the palm of her hand. "You saved me, Maddie."

"You saved me." She touched my face again. "But that doesn't mean I won't insist you go to therapy."

I squeezed her breast. "I don't need therapy. I have you."

"That's sweet, but you're still going."

"Will you always be this bossy?" I asked.

"Yep, so get used to it. Seriously though, will you try therapy? It will help, I promise you."

"Yeah, I'll do whatever you want me to, Mads."

Another small grin crossed her face. "I like the sound of that."

I rubbed my thumb across her nipple, smiling when it

hardened immediately. "You know, if we work really hard at it – I think we can make the magic ninety-seven number by the end of the month."

"Impossible," she said primly. "But I'm willing to give it a try. For science."

I laughed and nuzzled her neck. "I love you, Mads."

"I love you, Riley."

EPILOGUE

Riley shut the front door and dropped his gym bag on the floor.

"I'm home!" he shouted.

Tiny feet thundered down the stairs. He grinned and kneeled as the little dark-haired girl appeared in the hallway and ran straight at him.

"Hi, Daddy!"

"Hello, Princess. How was your day?" He stood and set her in the crook of his arm before kissing her smooth cheek.

"Good. I look just like you now." She pointed to the princess tattoos plastered across her neck.

"Does your mama know you did that?" He laughed.

"Yep. She helped me put them on."

"Did she now? And how will you find a job with those tattoos?" he said.

She giggled. "I'm only four. I can't have a job."

"Someone has to pay for those tattoos." He tickled her round belly.

"They're not real, Daddy!"

"Oh." He kissed her cheek again. "Where's your mama?"

"She's feeding Ty again. He's always hungry."

"Babies eat a lot, Princess."

"And poop a lot." She made a face, and he laughed before carrying her up the stairs.

"Uncle Roman and Uncle Mark are coming for dinner tonight," the little girl said. "I helped Mama peel the potatoes."

"Did you? That was nice of you to help your mama."

She rested her head against his broad shoulder. "I'm going to put tattoos on Uncle Roman's neck, too. Mama said I couldn't, but Uncle Roman will say its okay."

"I'm sure he will," Riley laughed. "You have him wrapped around your little finger."

He opened the door to the nursery and smiled at Maddie. She was sitting in the rocking chair, humming quietly as Ty suckled noisily at her breast.

"Hello, Kitten." He leaned over and kissed her before kissing the top of Ty's head. "How was your day?"

"Hi, honey. Fine. Justin asked me to review a file this morning, and then I plastered your daughter with temporary princess tattoos. Oh, and your son is going through a growth spurt." Maddie laughed. "I swear the kid eats more than you do."

He grinned at her as Maddie smiled at their daughter. "Andrea, can you help Mommy and get the diaper cream from the bathroom? Ty will need his diaper changed when he's finished eating."

"Sure," Andrea said. "Daddy likes my tattoos."

"I knew he would." Maddie grinned at Riley as he set Andrea on the floor. She skipped out of the room, and he brushed his hand against Ty's warm cheek. The baby turned his head and smiled toothlessly at him before latching on to Maddie's nipple again.

"Did you have a good day?" Maddie asked.

"Yes. I picked up another new client."

"Again?" Maddie gave him an admiring look. "You'll need to open your own gym soon."

He laughed. "I don't think we're quite there yet."

"You will be soon."

He squatted next to her and stroked her thigh as he watched Ty feed noisily. "Hey, Mads?"

"Hmm?"

She was stroking Ty's thick, dark hair, and he squeezed her knee until she glanced at him.

"I love you."

She smiled happily. "I know, and I love you too."

* * *

Keep reading for an excerpt of "Broken."

BROKEN EXCERPT

His face was one that only a mother could love. An odd mixture of harsh corners and ridges and awkward, oversized features. In truth, his mother didn't love him. She was perplexed and a little horrified by the child she had birthed. To have this red-faced, oddly silent creature come sliding out of her after the perfection that was her firstborn made her more than a little uneasy.

Later, long after her husband had returned to their home and the nurses had left her room, she held her baby in her arms and studied each feature silently. He was ugly. She couldn't - hadn't wanted to - deny it. The looks on the nurses' faces, the grimace from her husband when he had first surveyed his new son, had filled her with an odd kind of shame as if she and she alone were to blame for the monstrosity she had given birth to.

As he grew into a man and his body filled out to become an impressive and unforgiving block of sinewy muscle and harsh strength, her unease turned to fear. It didn't matter that he was gentle and quiet or that her dislike and fear obviously crushed him. He had the face and body of a man who would use his fists instead of his words to solve his problems, and she cringed away from his fumbled attempts to win her love.

Eventually, he gave up. He retreated into his own world and bore his family's repulsion toward him with a stoic solemnity. His weekly visits turned to monthly, and neither she nor his father and siblings could hide their relief.

He found solace in books, in art, and with the few friends he made. Friends who didn't care that nature had played so cruelly with his looks or that he was so quiet one would almost believe he was mute. His life was good, if not a bit lonely, and he was content.

Until he met her.

* * *

Stella Johnson pressed the lobby button and rubbed at her back as the doors slid shut and the elevator carried her smoothly and efficiently down thirty-seven floors. The doors opened with a soft ding, and she walked briskly toward the atrium to the left of the front doors, holding her lunch bag in her hand.

Her stomach growled softly, and she patted her round tummy before smoothing her dress. It was one of her favourites. A chocolate brown maxi dress that clung to her full breasts but flared out around her stomach and wide hips. It fell to the middle of her calves as most of her dresses did. She liked to hide the depressing way her thighs touched, and she preferred to dress conservatively anyway.

Her shoes click-clacked on the tile floor of the lobby. Bright red and with a heel too high for the office, she loved them with the same passion she imagined a mother might feel for her child. Ridiculous, of course, but her love for shoes came by her naturally. Her mother had close to two hundred pairs of shoes, and Stella was certain not a single one of them had a heel less than two inches high.

"Stelll-lllaaa!"

She grinned at the short, blond man sitting behind the security desk. "Hello, Jimmy. How are you?"

"Can't complain. Well, I could, but no one would listen." He stood and stretched. "You're running late today."

"Amy had an appointment," she said.

"Enjoy your lunch."

"I will." She hid her small grin as his face suddenly lit up, and he hurried around the desk. She didn't need to look behind her to know that Jasmine, the owner of the small flower shop in the lobby, was walking behind her. The woman was a gorgeous piece of art. Slim and tanned with bright pink hair that should have looked ridiculous on someone her age but didn't.

A month ago, Stella had coaxed Jasmine into sitting for her. She'd snapped photo after photo of the pink-haired beauty and was delighted with the results. Jasmine was a natural with the camera, and Stella hoped she could convince her to sit for her again.

The entire security team in the building constantly vied for Jasmine's attention. As Jimmy said hello to Jasmine in a tone entirely different from the one he used with her, Stella smoothed back her own hair.

She knew it was her best feature. Dark red, it was a thick, curly mass that flowed down her back to her waist. Men and women alike complimented her on it daily. Although truthfully, she didn't always understand the appeal. She longed for smooth, straight, dark hair. She'd almost cut it short last year, but her boyfriend at the time was horrified by the idea.

"Your hair is beautiful, Stella," he'd said earnestly as they lay in bed. "If you cut it off, the only thing people will notice about you is the extra weight you carry around. Do you want people to comment on the size of your ass instead of your hair?"

He hadn't understood her indignation. He honestly thought he was complimenting her. The relationship limped along for a few more weeks until she finally ended it. Although she was self-confident and mostly happy with her looks, her weight had always been a sore spot.

She'd made an appointment at the hair salon to cut her hair but chickened out. She told herself it was because her hair had never been shorter than mid-back, and it would be too strange to see it otherwise. But her ex-boyfriend's words were always in the back of her mind.

She headed into the atrium, her gait slowing when she saw how full it was. She regularly took a late lunch, covering Amy's lunch break at reception before taking her own. She didn't mind. She liked the quietness of the atrium with the lunch crowd long gone.

Although it was never completely empty, there were always a few people milling about and Ford, one of the security guards, took his lunch at the same time. She suspected he also enjoyed the solitude, so she never spoke to him. Not that he even acknowledged her existence. He ate his lunch and then sat with a pencil and sketchpad in his hand. She was often tempted to sneak up behind him for a quick glance, but she didn't have the nerve despite her curiosity. He might wield a pencil instead of a camera, but he was an artist like her, and she would have liked to talk to him about his work.

Today, all the small tables were full, and the loud chatter of people echoed in the atrium. She thought briefly of taking her lunch outside to the small park across the street, but the storm that was threatening when she arrived at work now lashed rain against the windows of the atrium.

Her gaze landed on Ford. He sat at his usual table, hunched over his sketchpad, ignoring the curious glances of the people sitting at the closest table. She had a feeling that he learned at an early age to ignore the looks and the whispers.

There was an empty chair at his table. Stella wasn't surprised. She doubted anyone would have the courage to approach him and ask to sit at his table. If the sheer size of his body and the obvious hard line of his muscles didn't deter them, his unconventional looks definitely did.

Gathering her courage, she weaved between the small tables scattered across the atrium until she stood before him. Engrossed in his sketch, he didn't look up. She cleared her throat and tugged nervously at her hair. "Hello, Ford."

She strained to see what he was drawing. It looked like a portrait, a woman with large eyes and high cheekbones and –

He put his arm over the drawing, blocking it neatly with his large forearm. He gave her a quick, fleeting glance. "Hello, Stella."

"Would you mind if I shared your table? The atrium is busy today."

He made a small backward twitch as if he were simply going to stand up and walk away before nodding. "Go ahead."

She sat down as he slid his sketchpad into the large fabric bag that served as his lunch bag. He pulled out an apple, a banana, an orange, a block of cheese as thick as her wrist, a plastic container filled to the brim with roast beef, two hard boiled eggs, and a large muffin.

She opened her lunch bag and brought out her lunch. A small garden salad with an even tinier container of raw almonds that she sprinkled over the salad. Ford opened his container, and the smell of roast beef drifted across the table to her. Her stomach growled, and he gave her another one of those quick glances as she blushed.

"Sorry, apparently I'm hungry today."

She nibbled at her salad, forcing herself to chew slowly as Ford ate his lunch. They sat silently as she finished her salad and put away her container. Normally, she would pull out her book and spend the rest of her lunch hour reading, but it seemed rude when she was sharing a table, even if Ford hadn't said a word to her.

She looked up as two women she'd never seen before stopped a few feet from their table. They stared at Ford with curiosity and undisguised pity, and she glared frostily at them until they moved on.

If Ford noticed their stares it didn't seem to affect him. Stella stared at her neatly painted fingernails. She'd worked in the building for nearly six months, and this was the first time she'd really gotten a good look at his face. Well, as good as she could with him staring grimly at the table.

She wondered if he would be surprised to know how much she wanted to photograph him. She was fascinated by the shapes and contours of his face. While others called him ugly, she thought his face was unique – almost beautiful in its ugliness.

Her stomach growled again, and Ford finally raised his gaze to her. She studied his face - the harsh angles, the bulbous nose, the heavy brow, and the black stubble that grew on his cheeks.

"You don't eat enough."

"I'm sorry?" She blinked at him.

"Every day, you eat a salad that wouldn't be enough to fill up a rabbit. You need more protein."

"I put raw almonds in it," she said.

He snorted. "A few almonds aren't a sufficient amount of protein. Protein fuels the body and the muscles."

She grinned at him. "I haven't got any muscles."

"Everyone has muscles."

"All right, fine. My muscles aren't as well-defined as yours, and probably don't need half a roast beef to make them happy. How often do you work out, anyway?" She eyed how his shirt hugged his broad chest and pulled at his shoulders and arms.

"Every day," he grunted.

"Shocking." She glanced around the atrium. "It's busy in here today."

"The law office on the seventeenth floor is having some kind of conference."

"Oh." She cast about for something else to say. She was a talker, always had been, and Ford's silence unnerved her a bit. "You like to draw, huh?"

He gave her a cautious look before nodding and biting into his apple.

"I'm a photographer. Well, amateur, but I love it. I mostly take portraits. I convinced Jasmine to sit for me a few weeks ago."

He glanced over to where Jimmy and Jasmine were still conversing in the lobby.

"Someone's got a crush." Stella grinned.

He grunted and stuffed his empty lunch containers and trash into the fabric bag.

"So, have you been drawing since you were a kid?"

He pushed back his chair and stood. "Lunch break's over. Bye."

"Bye, Ford."

He didn't return her smile. She watched him walk away as people naturally moved out of the way of his large body. She took her book out of her lunch bag and wondered what it must be like to be that intimidating. To never have to throw a thought toward personal safety. She was tall and weighed more than she would have liked, but she was also as weak as a kitten. She was being honest when she told Ford she didn't have muscles. He opened the door behind the security desk and disappeared into the office. With a soft sigh, she opened her book and blocked out the sounds of the chatting and laughter around her.

* * *

Ford crammed his massive body behind the tiny desk in the office and stared at his hands. He wasn't surprised to see them shaking. She had talked to him. He had an actual conversation with her. Well, if you called telling her she didn't eat enough, a conversation.

He didn't think she would show up at the atrium today. She was late, and he'd already resigned himself to the fact that his brief glimpse of her this morning would be it for the day unless he happened to see her as she was leaving.

A small thrill went through him when she'd finally shown up with her lunch bag in hand and wearing his favourite dress. When she had actually approached him, tugging on a strand of that amazing, flame-coloured hair, and asked to join him, he'd nearly run like a startled deer.

Staring at her from a distance was a completely different experience from having her sitting across the table. Ford hoped she didn't get a good look at his sketch. He was certain that women didn't like the idea of a man drawing secret pictures of them.

He was ridiculously pleased that she shared information with him. He knew she liked to take photos. He'd heard Jasmine telling Jimmy about it at the security desk and caught a glimpse of the pictures Jasmine showed Jimmy. Stella was good, and Ford admired her ability.

He took a deep breath. Christ, she smelled good, like a

combination of vanilla and some type of flower. He was struck by how she'd looked at him as if she noticed the ugliness of his features but wasn't horrified by it like so many other people were. He rubbed his forehead. Thinking that she didn't mind his looks was a bad idea. Women were disgusted by him, even someone as sweet as Stella.

Ford's stomach tightened painfully, and he stood up and returned to the front desk. Stella sat with him today because she had no choice, and that was it. His pointless crush on her needed to end.

ABOUT THE AUTHOR

Elizabeth Kelly was born and raised in Ontario, Canada. She moved west as a teenager and now lives in Alberta with her husband and a menagerie of pets. She firmly believes that a person can survive solely on sushi and coffee, and only her husband's mad cooking skills prevents her from proving that theory.

For more information about Elizabeth, check out her website at

www.elizabethkelly.ca

f facebook.com/EKellyBooks

⊙ instagram.com/elizabethkelly_author

ⓐ amazon.com/Elizabeth-Kelly/e/B00EOHZ0MS

BB bookbub.com/authors/elizabeth-kelly

ALSO BY ELIZABETH KELLY

Tempted Series

Tempted

Twice Tempted

Forever Tempted

Breathless

Tempted Trilogy (Books 1-3)

Red Moon Series

Red Moon

Red Moon Rising

Dark Moon

Alpha Moon

Pale Moon

The Recruit Series

The Recruit (Book One)

The Recruit (Book Two)

The Recruit (Book Three)

The Recruit (Book Four)

The Recruit (Book Five)

The Recruit (Book Six)

The Shifters Series

Willow and the Wolf (Book One)

Ava and the Bear (Book Two)

Katarina and the Bird (Book Three)

Porter's Mate (Book Four)

Bria and the Tiger (Book Five)

Rosalie Undone (Book Six)

The Dragon's Mate (Book Seven)

Rise of the Jaguar (Book Eight)

The Assassin and the Bear (Book Nine)

Elora and the Crow (Book Ten)

The Draax Series

Reign (Book One)

Rule (Book Two)

Rebel (Book Three)

Surrender (Book Four)

Survive (Book Five)

Salvation (Book Six)

Harmony Falls Series

Sweet Harmony (Book One)

Perfect Harmony (Book Two)

Forbidden Harmony (Book Three)

Redeeming Harmony (Book Four)

Absolute Harmony (Novella)

Beautiful Harmony (Book Five)

Reckless Harmony (Book Six)

Seasoned Romance Series

Bet Your Heart on Me (Book One)

Take a Chance on Me (Book Two)

Place Your Trust in Me (Book Three)

Individual Books

The Necessary Engagement

Amelia's Touch

The Rancher's Daughter

Healing Gabriel

The Contract

A Home for Lily

Saving Charlotte

Shameless

The Fairy Tales Collection

Broken

An Unlikely Seduction

Holiday Romance

The Christmas Wife

The Christmas Rescue

The Christmas Nanny

The Christmas Boss

Sordid Games